Mel Bay Presents

EXPLORING THE FOLK HARP

By Janna McCall Geller & Mallory Geller

- ♪ Choosing a harp
- ♪ How to play and sing with your harp
- ♪ Developing your personal style and technique
- ♪ Improvisation, chord reading and ear playing
- ♪ Accompaniment, arranging and playing with a group

- ♪ Harmony, scales and the modes
- ♪ Renaissance songs, traditional ballads, folk songs and classics with lyrics and chord symbols

and much more...

Plus:

Tim McCurdy on Harp Construction

Jon Lackey on Renaissance Music

Dinah LeHoven on the Wire Celtic Harp

Veronica Diamond on Singing Properly

Acknowledgements and Thanks

Fools may well rush in where angels fear to tread—even angels carrying folk harps. This book could only have been undertaken by two such: passionately foolish about a singular instrument which has bewitched us, enchanted us and transported us on a fantastic voyage of exploration—part of which is recorded on these pages. This volume is our personal music journal; others have chosen different routes and so well may you. Our hope is that *Exploring the Folk Harp* can be an atlas to get you oriented.

The folk harp movement is vital and growing. The resources are astounding; our task with this book was not where to find material but, with such a wealth from which to draw, what to read, study and utilize. Fortunately, there is the International Society of Folk Harpers and Craftsmen and the wonderful *Folk Harp Journal*, ably and tirelessly edited by Nadine Bunn. This quarterly, and many other publications, some of which are listed in the Bibliography, give us the harpers' world in print.

But it is the harpers, harpmakers and their music that make it all come alive. Sylvia Woods has been especially instrumental in making the folk harp movement thrive by directly and indirectly helping thousands to learn to play through her writings, teaching and playing. Thanks must also go to all the harpers and harpists who took time at concerts and fairs to explain their instruments to us when we hardly knew a folk harp from a blues harp. By letting us touch and even play their wonders, they baited their sweet trap! Steve Kundrat, who sold us our first instrument, set the hook. The good folks at Triplett Harps reeled us in.

Although we have drawn from diverse sources and many have helped us in myriad ways, final responsibility for *Exploring the Folk Harp*, its opinions, and especially any omissions or errors inadvertently included, is solely our own.

Special thank-yous to Jon Lackey, Dinah LeHoven, Tim McCurdy and Veronica Diamond who took their valuable time to write about their specialties. Thanks also to the late Robbie Robinson, co-founder of the I.S.F.H.C., for his help in understanding both the Latin harps and folk harps in general. Ron Archibald, Lowri Sprung, Michele Woodward, Laurie Riley, Antoine and Anne Skelton, Howard Posner, Rod Basler, Allegra Hardulfi, Steven Ernst, Cathy Chance, Debbie "V.B.C." Triplett, Paul and Marcia Secord, Ileana Medrano and Victor Salvi all helped, knowingly or not.

And, most important, our sincere and grateful thanks to the good people at Mel Bay who suggested this book and then graciously hung in there with this pair of too zealous writers!

Exploring the Folk Harp is fondly dedicated to Steve Triplett and Tim McCurdy.

A Forest of Harps.
Harps in the harpmaker's shop waiting for new owners.
Photo by Mallory Geller at Triplett Harps in San Luis Obispo.

Harper Sean Hunt takes to the water in a Celtic boat.
Photo by Jon Lackey.

About the Authors

Mallory Geller and Janna McCall Geller, "Mallory & McCall," have been featured together as entertainers (and husband and wife) since 1973. Although they currently devote much of their performing to folk harp and vocals, they have explored many aspects of music, writing and theater. For 14 years they wrote, produced and acted *The Janus Company Radio Theatre,* broadcast live weekly in Los Angeles. A sharp eye might discover them in the guise of various historical and fictional characters, including Mr and Mrs Dickens and Queen Victoria and her equerry, or in Renaissance garb playing and singing and giving "Phree harpe lessons" to all takers at fairs and musical events. They can also be found in and around the Southern California area playing and singing in a wide range of styles: folk to Irish to Broadway, with a lot in between. In addition, they are free lance writers with experience in just about everything from newspaper reporting to poetry.

Janna's background is in music and performing. She majored in music composition and arranging at Los Angeles Valley College and UCLA. She went on to become an entertainer in clubs, musical theater, and comedy. She has written music for broadcast, stage and even King Henry VIII (now ruling in Fresno, California).

Mallory is an authentic ex-Greenwich Village poet whose current specialty is singing everything from Gilbert & Sullivan to Simon and Garfunkel. He has appeared off Broadway, worked in television production and is a Craftsman member of the Piano Technician's Guild.

Their **Janus Music** offers harps and harp-related materials as well as Celtic, Renaissance and folk instruments, sheet music and accessories. They can be contacted at P.O. Box 191084, Los Angeles, California 90019.

Mallory & McCall performing
"O, are you going to Scarb'ro Fair?"
Photo by Jon Lackey.

Table of Contents

The Purpose of This Book

Exploring the Folk Harp is your companion in discovering the many, diverse aspects of the harp. It gives special emphasis to the wealth of creative options that you, as a player, have, literally at your fingertips. It is not a primer, as such, but an informal exploration of what we, and others, have learned about playing this beguiling instrument.

Here we deal with the harp as a folk instrument—which we define as one learned and taught in an informal manner—but we also include material for those with more structured goals. In our opinion, there are no wrong ways to play, as long as you get (and, if it is your wish, give) satisfaction. The only exception to this "rule" is playing in a position or style that hurts you physically.

The harp can be approached in several different ways: A good **teacher** can pass on to you proven approaches and techniques, and can spot problems of which you may not be aware. A teacher can motivate you and show you things that a book would be hard-pressed to explain. A good **primer**, taking learning step by step, will lead you through your studies in a proven, orderly way. A good **guidebook** can direct an eager explorer toward some alternative approaches that can help you expand your musical horizons and make your harping your own. All are valuable; here we aspire to the latter, with a very friendly nod toward any and all other methods.

Exploring the Folk Harp supplements other harp books with information not usually included in books designed with the beginner in mind. Through our own experience teaching ourselves, we discovered that there is much more to learning the instrument than scales and studying by rote. We wanted to break away from rigid structure and soar right from the start; the harp is that kind of instrument.

As so many harp players either sing with their instruments or play for other singers, we have made a special effort to include lyrics and instruction in accompaniment, plus an article on how to improve your singing when you play. Many harp books are frustratingly lacking in this information; in this book we have made a start toward remedying those omissions. We have also included chord symbols to encourage improvisation and to allow the music to be played by other instruments.

We have covered quite a bit of material, some of which may not attract every reader. Consider it a useful reference source. Experienced musicians will find some of the general material elementary; beginners may at first find some of the more specialized material a bit daunting. But there is something of interest for everyone. You should not be disappointed.

Introduction

THE MAGIC OF THE HARP

There is something about a harp that brings a light to people's eyes, even when it is silent. As we've traveled about, it never ceases to delight us when we see that glow, that enchantment which so many people radiate when they are around a harp. Perhaps it is something out of childhood: a fairytale instrument that accompanies magical wonders and spellbinding dreams. Harps are the music-makers of choice for elves and bards, mystics and angels.

Perhaps it is only natural. One of the earliest known musical instruments, its very rightness, its simplicity of form and function strike recognition and approval. Standing alone, it is like a sculpture of exquisite proportions.

And then, there is the music. Sit down at a harp—even if you've never played any instrument in your life—and stroke the strings. It will respond with a wondrous sound vibrating into your body. It becomes an extension of you, and you, it. You stroke it and play it like a lover and it responds as only a lover can.

We have introduced hundreds of people to the harp for the first time, giving free harp lessons at Renaissance, music and Celtic fairs. From the smallest child to the biggest, brawniest biker, we've come to know just how compelling an experience it can be. We got hooked on harps in a similar way and we understand.

THE EASE OF LEARNING THE HARP

Many people have the misconception that the harp is a very difficult instrument. It can be, if you want to play concert harp in a symphony or if you aspire to master level performance. But for the rest of us, it is one of the easiest possible instruments on which to make pleasing music rather quickly. Many with musical background, especially keyboard, can play something presentably in minutes, although a few hours or days is more usual. **Everyone** who stops at our harps and gives us a very few minutes of their attention learns at least to play *Twinkle, Twinkle Little Star*. Previous musical experience is not requisite. The only real problem we face is getting the harp away from one new harp player so another can try.

Of course to get from *Twinkle* to, say, a nimble fingered jig— melody and all—is a big leap. But there's a lot of good music in between. And maybe you'll never want to play intricate pieces. You don't have to. One of the beauties of the harp is that even very simple music sounds wonderful and is easy to produce once you understand how the instrument, and its music, work.

WHAT, EXACTLY, IS A FOLK HARP?

"Folk Harp," a catch-all term for harps other than the pedal or "concert" harp, is a label coined by Robbie Robinson, a major figure in the current revival of the non-pedal harp. It was chosen as a term of convenience for, historically, the harp was not a common but a courtly instrument. Players of harps were among the musical elite. King David played the harp. Images of harpers can be found in the tombs of Pharaohs, on the vases of the Greeks, on elegant tapestries and frescos of the middle ages and the Renaissance. European gentlemen and ladies were taught to play as part of their education. Harpers were highly skilled and prized; it was a status symbol for a fine household to have a harper in residence.

Then, with the coming of chromatic music, the harp fell out of favor—in large part because of the limitations imposed by its diatonic nature. The line was nearly broken. Only the Latin harps claim an uninterrupted lineage from Spain to the new world. In the old world, inventors looked for ways to make the harp more accessible to chromatic music. They tried to access the **accidentals**[1] by adding extra strings in a variety of different arrangements, but these proved awkward for most players. They also tried adding sharping levers, but it was necessary to remove one's hands from the strings in order to operate them. The pedal harp was the solution of choice and was welcomed into the pantheon of 19th Century musical instruments.

For thousands of years various kinds of non-pedal harps flourished, but by the dawning of the 20th Century, they had become rare and exotic. Now when people said "harp," they meant the big gold concert harps and few knew anything or thought much at all about what happened to the non-pedal harps, except for those made by the harp companies as student instruments. Some may have heard of Irish harps, but these were a novelty, even—and in some ways, especially—in Ireland. We'd never even seen a Celtic harp until we bought our first.

But when builders started once again remaking and reinventing non-pedal harps as serious musical instruments, a growing movement of enthusiasts emerged: scholars searched out historic music; modern musicians developed whole new sounds. While it still retains its courtly roots and is played by serious virtuosos, the folk harp has finally become a true folk instrument as well. Folk music is especially comfortable on the folk harp because of its diatonic nature. So while Robbie Robinson and the others may have been looking for a convenient label to call their instruments, "folk harping" is indeed an excellent name for the techniques and music found in this book.

[1] Accidentals, despite their name, are not notes played by mistake. Rather, they are sharps, flats and naturals not in the key signature in which the harp is tuned.

How to Use This Book...

There is material in *Exploring the Folk Harp* for the seasoned musician as well as the complete beginner. How you use this book depends on what you want to do with your harp. Therefore, you do not have to read every word or take the songs in order. You can learn best by being creative; this book will get you started.

There are just about as many approaches to the folk harp as there are harpers (that is, players of most of the non-pedal harps—pedal harp and Latin harp players are called harpists). It is a very personal instrument; you will develop your own style, your unique approach to your harp.

...IF THIS IS YOUR FIRST MUSICAL INSTRUMENT

If you have never played an instrument before, you are about to experience something truly exciting: the thrill of having music emerge from your fingers. The folk harp is an especially good choice as it is easy to make lovely sounds on it literally minutes after you pick it up. Pay special attention to the chapter on tuning; if the harp is not in tune, it will sound wrong and may well end up unplayed and unloved. Try out some of the glissandi and free-form improvisations to get the feel of your instrument. Try to pick out melodies or make up your own. Check out the chapters on harmony and chords; once you understand how music works you will find it is not nearly as mysterious as you may have thought. But don't wait—start in playing right away.

You will need to know a bit about reading music in order to play the songs in the book. If you don't read, consult the Appendix for an overview to get you started. Consult a music—especially, but not necessarily, a harp—primer. Learn the note names of the strings. It is perfectly all right to write these note names in pencil above the melody notes of the songs or to circle the *C's* on the staff with red and the *F's* with blue to correspond to the colored strings. This is your book for you to use in any way that works!

...IF YOU HAVE SOME BACKGROUND—ANY BACKGROUND—IN MUSIC

Even if you only took a few music lessons when you were a kid you have an advantage: you already know about note names and scales and the like. Take some time to review MUSIC READING BASICS in the Appendix to remind you of anything you may have forgotten. The musical knowledge necessary to play the folk harp is quite rudimentary and will come back quickly.

More advanced musicians will find the harp easy to comprehend. You may find yourself a bit frustrated at first with a sharpless-flatless diatonic instrument, but what initially seems a limitation often provides a fascinating challenge. No, you will probably never be able to play *Flight of the Bumblebee*; but you may discover unexplored beauty in the ancient modes, or create transcendent new-age sounds. If you have sharping levers, you will learn to flip them during a song for occasional accidentals. And in an ensemble, the lack of accidentals becomes much less of a problem as the other instruments can fill in the missing notes. Harpers jam on Elizabethan dance music, Irish jigs and even the blues. The only constraint is your imagination.

...IF YOU ARE COMING TO THE HARP FROM THE KEYBOARD

Pianists and other keyboard musicians have a fairly easy time transferring their skills to the harp. Since the harp is diatonic, you can think of its strings (when tuned in *C*) as the white keys of the piano. There is usually a period of adjustment for your hands and eyes to realign with the vertical plane of the harp strings, but most people find that the worst is over very quickly.

Note also that the right hand fingering goes in the opposite direction. On the piano, you finger up the scale starting with the thumb on the lowest tone. On the harp, the thumb plays the highest tone. Harp players do not use their little fingers, so you only have to worry about eight fingers instead of ten.

...IF YOU ARE COMING TO THE HARP FROM THE GUITAR

Folk and classical guitar players bring a special style to the harp that many of us envy: the ability to pick out lovely patterns on the strings with their right hands. If you sing with your harp, you will find this especially useful. The down side is that your left hand will be in uncharted territory; many guitarists complain that they do not know what to do with it. The answer is simple, although perhaps not what you were hoping to hear: practice more with your left hand. In the meantime, concentrate on simple bass lines; let your pickin' hand do most of the work.

Classical guitarists who have cultivated their right hand fingernails may be distressed to learn that the nylon harp is usually played with the pad of the finger. Purists will encourage you to cut your nails. However, this should be your personal decision. We have seen and heard wonderful harpers who play with a combination of their nails and their finger pads. After all, this is a folk instrument and you can play it any way that works for you. Paraguayan nylon harps are supposed to be played with fingernails.

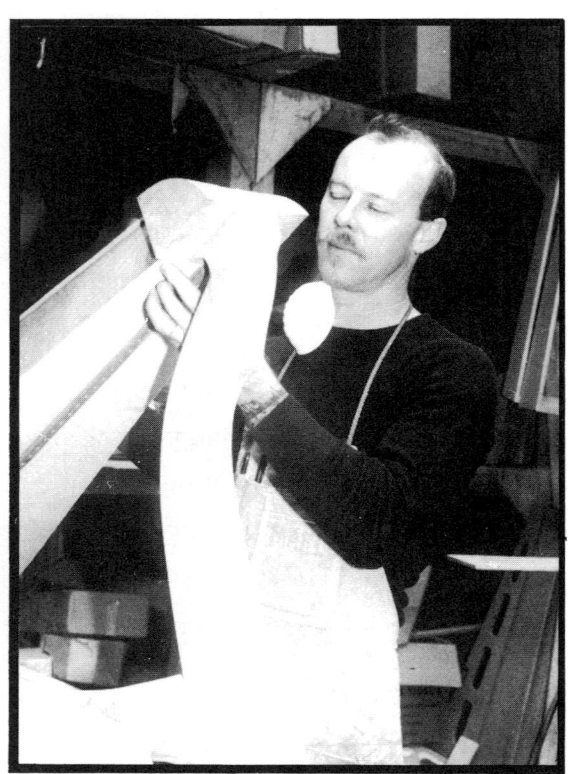

Steve Triplett examines a harp under construction.
Photo by Janna McCall Geller.

Part One: Harp Basics

OVERVIEW OF HARP HISTORY AND CONSTRUCTION

by Tim McCurdy

Let's now take a closer look. We have asked harpmaker Tim McCurdy of Triplett Harps—Tim and his partner Steve Triplett have made more than three thousand quality instruments—to begin with an overview of the folk harp, its history and construction.

Tim McCurdy in the Triplett workshop.
Photo by Janna.

This article is intended to help you become more familiar with the construction of the folk harp. Harps are one of the most ancient stringed instruments known to mankind. The earliest harps were bow harps. These were developed from the hunting bow and the simplest bow harps were just a single string fastened to each end of a flexible stick. Later developments were additional strings and resonators.

The angle harp came to Egypt from Asia in about 1500 B.C. The angle harp was comprised of a hollow soundbox and a straight string arm. The angle harps were played in classical Greece and later in Rome and are still popular in Africa. The angle harp was also the precursor to the next development in the evolution of the harp, the frame harp.

The frame harp differed from the angle harp in that it had a pillar to support the string arm. The pillar made the instrument rigid enough to allow higher string tension than on previous harps. There are many references to the biblical King David and his harp, making him, quite probably, the first famous harp player. It is not certain whether King David played a frame harp or some earlier variation.

The Romans are thought to have been responsible for bringing the harp to Ireland and the British Isles around 50 B.C. The Irish had developed a frame harp by 400 A.D. that would be the predecessor to our modern harps. The most famous of these early Irish harps were the Brian Boru (sometimes called the Trinity College) and the Queen Mary, which date from the 15th century or even before and are among the oldest surviving Celtic harps. These ancient Irish harps were wire strung instruments and the soundboxes were carved from a single piece of wood.

There were both wire and gut strung harps being used in the British Isles by the 1500s. The first double and cross strung harps were being built in Europe about this same time. These harps enabled the musician to play a chromatic scale, but they were difficult to play. The first really functional chromatic harp was the pedal harp, which was developed by Sebastian Erard in 1811. Prominent American pedal harp manufacturers included Lyon and Healy, and WurliTzer. (See Appendix Two: THE PEDAL HARP)

In recent years there has been a resurgence of interest in the Celtic harp both here in the United States and abroad. There are now many makers of these non-pedal harps and many sizes and styles from which to choose. I am going to briefly discuss the basic construction of the modern Celtic harp or Neo-Celtic harp as it is sometimes known.

It will be helpful to have a basic understanding of the parts of the instrument and what their roles are in producing music. Reduced to its fundamentals, the harp is a hollow wooden box which has strings running at an oblique angle from the soundbox to the instrument's neck. When the strings are plucked they produce complex vibrations which are transmitted through the string supports to the soundbox. The surfaces of the soundbox oscillate and then produce vibrations in the air that are audible as sound.

The diagram on page 16 shows the main components of a typical harp. I will discuss the various techniques employed by different makers to produce their instruments and let the reader decide which type of harp is best suited to his or her needs.

The single most important part of any stringed instrument is the soundboard and the harp is no exception. A soundboard that is poorly made or constructed of inferior materials will result in a poor sounding harp and may even part company with the rest of the instrument.

Nylon strung harps typically have either a solid spruce soundboard or one made of laminate or ply construction. Wire strung harps usually have a solid hardwood soundboard, although softwoods such as spruce and fir or laminates can be used if the harp is designed properly.

Solid soundboards and ply soundboards each have their respective merits and disadvantages. The prime advantage of a solid spruce soundboard is that it will appreciate tonetically, or sound better, with time. Just as an old guitar or violin will have better tone and volume than a new instrument, a harp with a high quality spruce soundboard will sound better and better the longer that you own and play it. A laminate soundboard will improve slightly with time and use but not as dramatically as a solid soundboard. A high quality spruce soundboard should be straight, fairly close grained and vertically cut (quarter sawn).

The greatest advantage of a laminate soundboard is durability. Extreme cold or sudden changes in weather, heat and humidity can cause a solid soundboard to shrink or shift and result in cracks along grain lines or glue joints. The cross grain lamination of ply construction results in a soundboard that is much more resistant to damage caused by weather changes.

The materials used for the sides and back of the soundboard are somewhat less critical, but good joinery is essential to insure that the soundboard will not separate from the body because of the considerable tension of the strings. Proper thicknessing of body parts is important. Ideally, a harp should be built heavily enough to be sturdy, but excess thickness results in a dead sounding instrument and one which is difficult to carry. A harp that is well built can be durable and still not be excessively heavy.

The neck (or harmonic curve) extends from the body of the harp and, with the pillar, completes the frame. The neck holds the tuning pins and the pillar supports the neck. Most harpmakers use solid hardwoods for the neck and pillar, although laminate hardwoods and even plywood are sometimes used. These pieces need to be of adequate size and strength to support the strings. On larger harps there is usually a crosspiece or forepillar attached to the pillar. This helps keep the pillar from twisting to one side as a result of the offset string tension. The joinery of neck to pillar, and neck and pillar to the body, should be secure and well fitted. There should never be any visible glue or fasteners (nails, screws, etc.).

Modern harpmakers use a wide variety of finish materials. Nitrocellulose lacquer traditionally has been the finish of choice for fine musical instruments, but modern production techniques and environmental concerns have led manufacturers to try a number of other finish products. Many makers use some type of polyurethane to finish their harps. These finishes are desirable for their good looks and extreme durability. Current technological developments have some harpmakers looking at new waterborne finishes because they are environmentally friendly and easy to work around (no toxic fumes). The best of the new waterborne finishes yield results almost as nice as those of the more traditional finishes. A good finish should be smooth and free from drips and bubbles. Finishes are available in either gloss (shiny) or satin (matte). Most harp makers use a satin finish to achieve a more natural look.

The hardware on a harp should be well machined and free from sharp edges that can damage strings. Steel parts should be plated to prevent rust. The tuning pins must rotate smoothly and without sticking. Sharping levers should move easily and should not rattle or buzz. There should always be eyelets or string shoes where the strings leave the soundboard.

Larger harps or floor harps need some kind of feet or stand. Harps are, by the nature of their shape, intrinsically top-heavy, and feet or stands help to balance the harp and provide stability. Many harps feature removable legs or feet which gives the owner another option.

A well made harp usually comes with a warranty. The warranty protects the buyer from defects in materials and workmanship. Beware of harps sold without a good warranty and look for a maker who has a reputation for standing behind his or her product.

The resurgence of interest in harps and harp music has led to a revitalization of harp building as well. There are currently a number of qualified harpmakers producing high quality instruments. There are also some harps on the market which are not of very good quality. It is a good idea for a first time buyer to buy a harp from a well respected maker and to ask a more experienced player or teacher for advice before making a purchase. I hope that the information in this article will be of assistance in making that decision.

Harp Anatomy

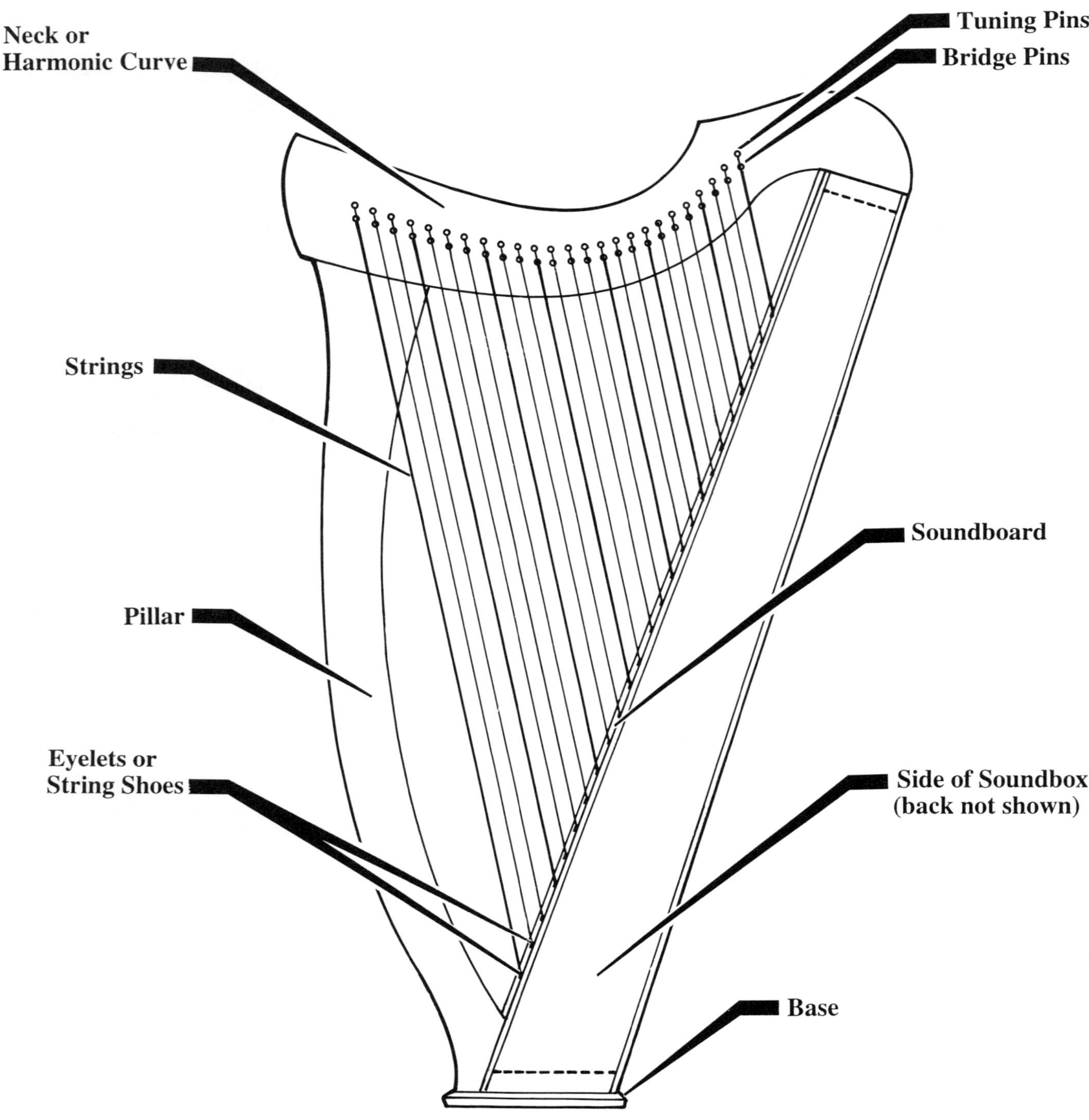

MORE HARP BASICS

As Tim mentioned, the folk harp is among the most basic of musical instruments. There is no mechanism between the player and the music—no hammers or bows or keys. The harper plucks the strings; the harper directly makes the sound.

When you pluck a string, you cause it to vibrate, sounding a musical tone, sending its reverberation humming into the air and, at the same time, through your body, helping to make the harper and the music one. If you pluck harder, the sound is louder. That's about all there is to it, although many generations of harpers and harp makers have labored long and hard on improvements to make our harping more pleasurable and the tone more beautiful.

The strings of a harp are knotted on the underside of the soundboard. They exit through holes in the board which are reinforced with metal eyelets, or string shoes, set in a wooden strip. This strip may be on the outside or the underside of the board, or both.

When the strings reach the neck of many folk harps, they take a turn around a set of bridge pins. These pins give the speaking length of each string a positive terminus while keeping the plane of all the strings in a straight line. Your harp may not have bridge pins but you will notice that the strings are wrapped around tuning pins. These pins usually go all the way through the neck so the harp is tuned by turning the pins from the opposite side. There are a few kit harps and other variants which use zither pins that do not go all the way through the neck. These are tuned on the same side as the string coil. In any case, tuning pins are turned with a tuning lever. The tighter the string the higher the pitch. You can tune by ear, to another instrument or use an electronic device (see TUNING YOUR HARP and Appendix Six: TUNING BY EAR).

The strings are arranged from low (the longest) to high. The high strings are thinner, the low strings thicker and sometimes wrapped to increase their diameter without losing flexibility. Harps are tuned diatonically—that is: *do, re, me, fa, sol, la, ti* and then *do* again—just like in the song from *The Sound of Music*. In the most usual "*C*" tuning, the strings are like the white keys of the piano; there are no strings for the sharps and the flats. (But some of these notes are available. Read on.)

To continue for a moment our comparison to a piano keyboard, consider that if there were no black keys on a piano for reference, it would be almost impossible to tell the white ones apart. Likewise with harp strings. Someone had to invent a system—some kind of code—and portraits from at least as far back as the Eighteenth Century reveal that some clever harpers hit upon a grand and beautifully simple solution: color-code the strings. The current system for most harps (the Paraguayans are one exception) is to color all the *C* strings red and the *F* strings blue or black.

So, when your harp is tuned in *C* you know that the red strings are the first note of the *C* major scale and the blue strings the fourth *(F)*. It is easy to find your way around. For example, if you want to play a *G*, look for the blue *F*. The *G* is one note closer to you (higher than, or shorter than) the blue string, an *A* is two notes closer to you than the blue string and two farther away than the red *C* string. You will very quickly pick up the relationships of all the notes to the colored strings.

Keyboard Relationship to Harp Strings

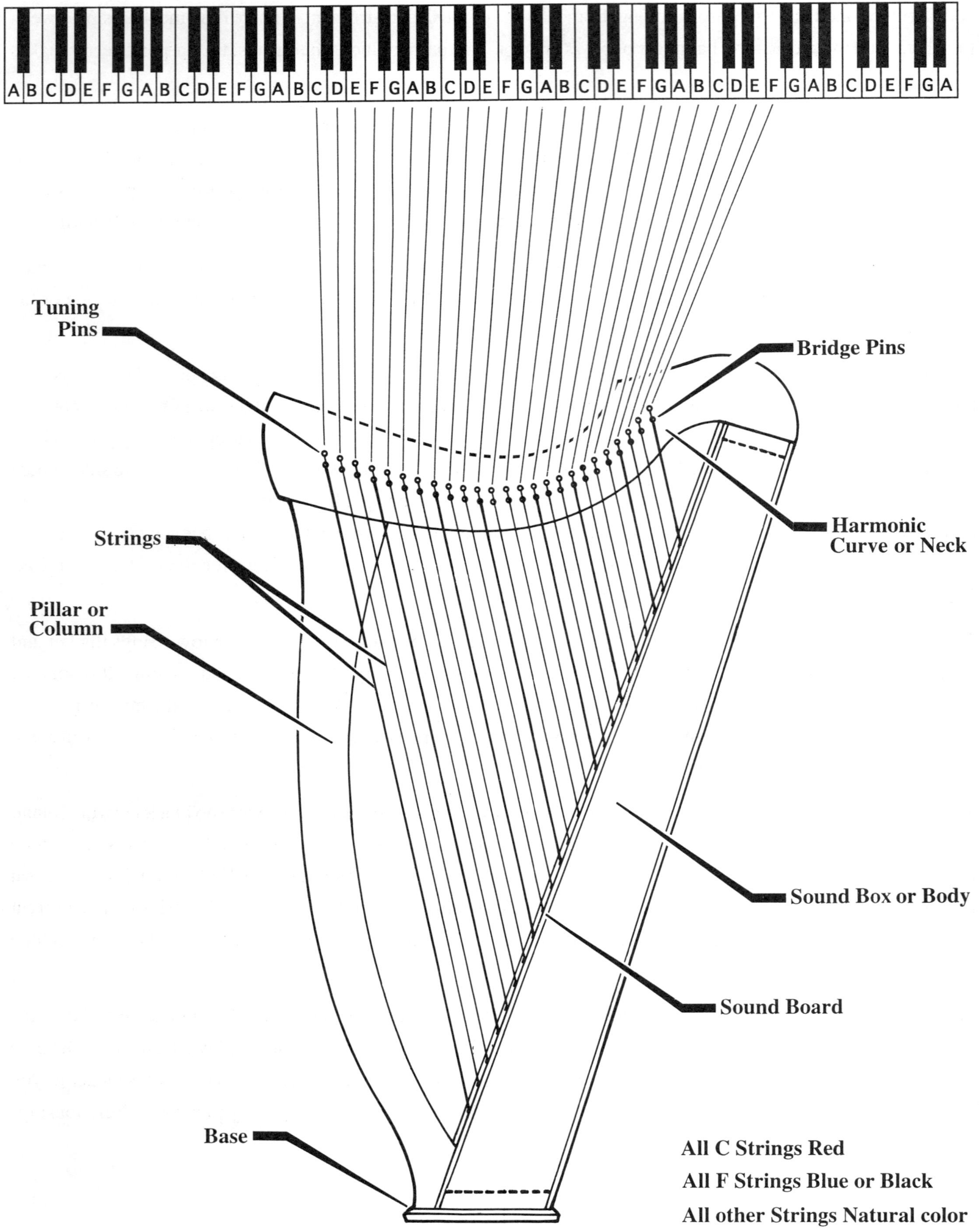

Tuning Pins
Bridge Pins
Strings
Harmonic Curve or Neck
Pillar or Column
Sound Box or Body
Sound Board
Base
All C Strings Red
All F Strings Blue or Black
All other Strings Natural color

On harps so equipped, sharping levers give us access to accidentals and allow the harper to play in several different keys (which ones depend on the particular tuning). Levers are a relatively new invention, only predating the first pedal harps by a hundred years or so. To some purists, they are new-fangled gizmos which are to be used sparingly, if at all. But the rest of us find them mighty handy—especially when accompanying singing and playing with other instruments. We recommend that any nylon harp be fitted with levers on at least the *C* and *F* strings, which gives the harper access to two additional major and minor keys.

Levers are designed to shorten the speaking length of a given string, thus sharping the tone by one half step (ie, *F* becomes *F♯*). The earliest style is a hook of metal rather like a shepherd's crook with the longer side set into the wood of the neck. It works to intersect a string by being rotated in the same plane as the strings until it pushes against the appropriate location. Unfortunately, as it presses against the string it often causes an alteration of the spacing of that string in relation to the others. Another, more reliable system—and a very good one tonally—is the blade lever. It, too, turns in the same plane to shorten the string but with minimal dislocation (the best ones have a stop which locks the pitch in exactly) and it gives a solid, clear tone.

Flip levers act by stopping the string on the other axis, perpendicular to the plane of the strings. The simplest of this kind is a protruding tab that, when the harper flips it up, pivots to push up from under the string, creating a new terminus (but sometimes causing the string to buzz). The better ones grab the string in two places, holding it tightly and keeping it in line with the other strings.

There are many different types and qualities of levers by diverse makers. Generally, the flip type is easier to change while you are playing; the blade kind often sounds truer. It's really a matter of taste—and how and what you intend to play. There are no "flatting" levers. If your music calls for a *B♭*, you can tune a *B* string flat, play the enharmonic note, *A♯*, or omit it altogether (see ALTERNATE TUNINGS). Sorry about that, but this is a folk instrument and working with the limitations is part of the fun. Be creative!

WHAT KIND OF HARP IS FOR YOU?

If you do not already own a folk harp, you may be surprised at the diverse selection available, from inexpensive Celtic style instruments imported from Pakistan, to artist quality harps made to order by skilled craftspersons. Folk harps can range from two octave miniatures to floor harps with five octaves or more.

Here is a short summary of the types of harps available:

THE NEO-CELTIC HARP is the most common folk harp in the United States, Ireland and Britain today. It can be of just about any size. The "neo" in the name refers to the nylon strings found on these harps (the ancient Celtic harps used wire, see below). Most people find these harps the easiest on which to learn and are delighted by the warm, rich sound they produce. They range in style from very plain to hand carved ornate beauties. They can be purchased with or without sharping levers (See THE LEVER HARP). There are many makers of quality harps, from the individual working in a small shop to the well-organized, established instrument crafters like Triplett and Dusty Strings.

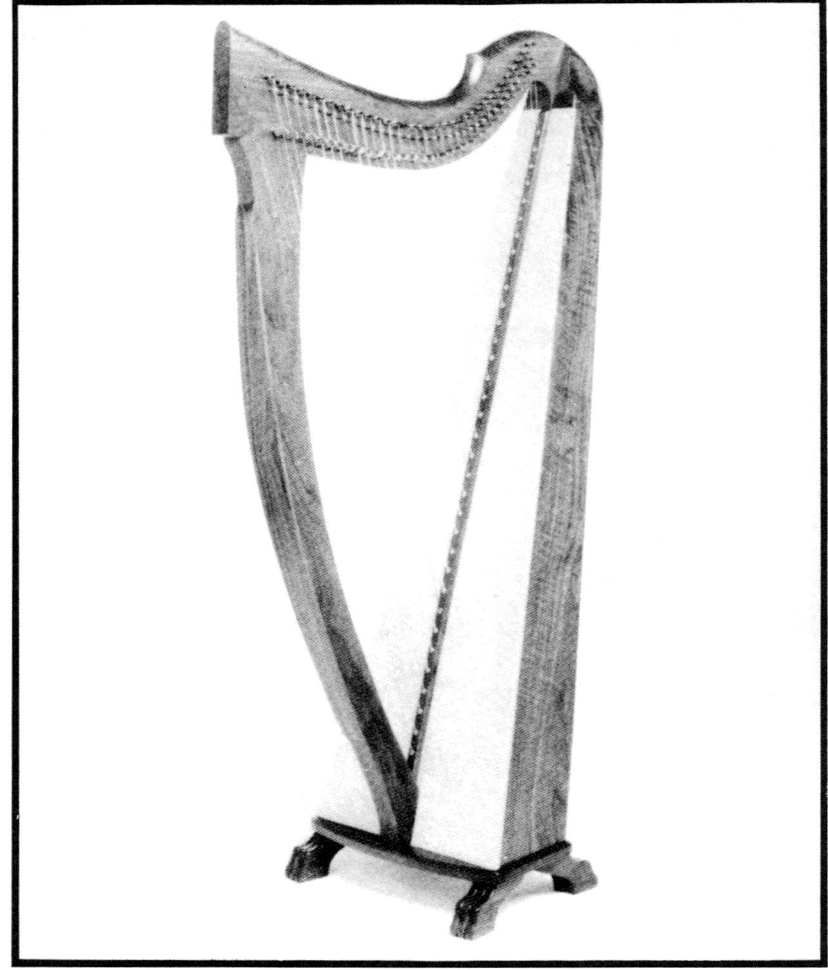

THE WIRE CELTIC HARP is very like the harp that was so much a part of the Irish musical tradition until it faded out in the late 18th century. There is a significant revival that is bringing more players to this fascinating instrument. Patrick Ball is perhaps the best known wire harper and his recordings are big sellers. Also, the trend toward authenticity at the Renaissance fairs has encouraged its study. The wire harp is usually played with the fingernails, which needn't be long but must be well cultivated. As the wire harp produces a clear ringing sound which sustains for a long time, it is easy to sound good as you do not have to play as many notes as with its nylon Celtic cousin. However, special damping techniques may be desirable for more complex music to keep the sound from blurring. It is considered by some to be more challenging as the colored string markings can be difficult to see in some lighting situations. Wire harps are usually strung in phosphor bronze, brass or, sometimes, steel. They come in a wide range of sizes. Some have blade levers.

The wire harp is such an important part of the current folk harp movement that we have asked Dinah LeHoven, editor of "Ringing Strings," the wire harp section of the *Folk Harp Journal*, to write a more extensive article for *Exploring the Folk Harp.* You will find it in the Appendix.

A new treatment of an old design: The Triplett Ancient Irish 25 String Wire harp.
Photo by Mallory.

THE LEVER HARP is a special term used to describe a style of playing a nylon strung instrument equipped with a full set of sharping levers. These are used to deftly change keys and add accidentals. (See also BASIC AND ALTERNATE TUNINGS.) To use a folk harp as a "lever harp," you must have quality levers that do not change the pureness of the sound.

PRE-PEDAL HARPS FOR CONCERT HARP STUDENTS, although they can serve quite well as folk instruments, are primarily designed for those who plan to move on to the pedal harp. The most famous of these are the Lyon & Healy *Troubadour* models. Salvi has recently introduced the *Ana*, which looks like a concert harp without pedals, and other pedal harp makers offer similar instruments. These are made with concert harp spacing and tension to make the transition easier (although a quality nylon folk harp, with its special bright and vibrant sound, will serve most students well). All these harps come standard with full sets of flip-up sharping levers.

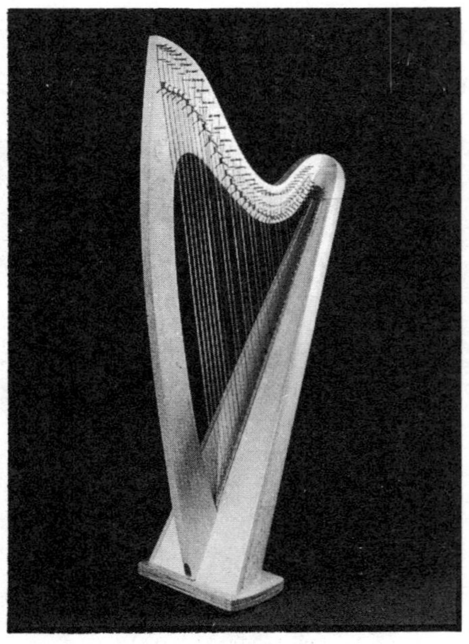

THE LYRE, the favored instrument of classical Greece and Rome, is beginning to reappear. Beautiful examples are being made in Israel in honor of the biblical King David. Inexpensive but pretty ones are imported from Pakistan and are suitable for singers who just want to chord. We've seen them in metal and nylon and, more authentically, they may be strung with gut. They are played with one hand only and have a limited number of strings, but they are perfect for a strolling bard or minstrel at a costumed event. Unfortunately, because of their shortcomings, they are not very effective solo instruments.

HISTORICAL RECREATIONS of ancient harps are becoming more popular and can be heard, increasingly, in concert and recordings. Many are meticulously researched from old manuscripts and paintings and can be quite expensive. Scholarly studies of the playing and construction of ancient instruments can make fascinating reading.

THE LATIN HARPS consist of a number of varieties which have developed in the Americas. All are descended from the Spanish harps brought to the new world by the influx of conquerors and colonists in the 16th and 17th centuries. The varieties are often named after the country or town in which they developed. The most commonly seen in the United States come from Paraguay, Mexico, Venezuela and Peru. Each is different from the others although they do share some characteristics. All have a large soundbox, a thin, straight column and a slender neck. The majority are nylon strung. They tend to be of lighter construction than comparably sized Neo-Celtic instruments, weighing perhaps half as much as their counterparts. They are nimble and lively instruments to play. In Paraguay, harp playing has evolved into a highly sophisticated art form. Harp makers there have developed a unique harmonic curve, centrally strung, and are producing exquisite musical instruments. Latin harps are plucked with the fingernails and with their own specialized vigorous and vivacious technique.

Left to right: Mexican harp maker unknown; Paraguayan harp builder Maestro Miguel A. Mendoza; John Westling, U.S.A. The next two harps by Maestro Vedois Rojas, Paraguay; the last two harps by Maestro Timuteo Rojas, Paraguay. Photo property of harpist Allegra Hardulfi, U.S.A.

WHAT TO LOOK FOR WHEN BUYING A HARP

Your first harp should be one that best fulfills your immediate goals. If you know some harpers, ask about their instruments and, if they'll let you, try them out. Here are some specifics to consider (unless otherwise noted, we are talking about nylon strung harps):

SIZE AND RANGE. Harps come in a variety of sizes. Consider portability if you want to carry yours around. Small lap harps are great on the go but sometimes lack the notes and volume needed for soloing. Lap harps, lyres and the like, however, do well for singers who wish to accompany themselves. They are also at home in an ensemble. They are much more authentic for Renaissance and medieval music and look good with period costumes at fairs and similar events. If you're a Celt in your Middle Ages garb, you'll want to consider a wire harp.

Floor harps with at least 30 strings are excellent all-around instruments. Mallory's 30 string Triplett *Axline*, for example, is his basic gig harp. It's relatively easy to carry around and the low wound *G* in the bass gives it a nice bottom end. Larger floor harps have more sound and more notes. They are also bulky and harder to transport. The biggest ones won't fit in some cars. But they make such impressive music that most owners gladly put up with the problems. (You might be amazed how much one or two extra strings will cost on a quality harp. Be aware that you are not only buying more notes, but a larger sound box and more robust structure as well.)

The range on a folk harp is not standard. It differs from maker to maker and from harp to harp. Smaller harps usually play the top end of the scale, thus they sound at a higher pitch. You may have to put some arrangements up an octave. The larger harps with wound bass strings have ringing low notes and a richer sound. Part of this richness is sheer size, of course, with more instrument to vibrate, but there is also another important factor. Strings that are not plucked are not totally silent. Rather, they resonate in harmonic reinforcement of the strings being played and, in a properly scaled instrument, make an appreciable contribution to tone color and vibrance.

STRING SPACING AND TENSION are also important. Pedal harps have what is called "concert spacing" and are pretty consistent from harp to harp. A few folk harps have narrower spacing. There is a good case for both the wider and the narrower spacing. If you plan to play pedal harp, consider a folk harp near concert spacing. Closer spacing allows for a wider reach; someone who can barely span an octave on the piano can stretch at least a 10th on any harp. We switch from harp to harp with all kinds of spacings and find that while we have our favorites we can play the others without too much difficulty.

Latin harps and some folk harps have graduated spacing: narrow at the high end and wider at the bottom. This is often because these harps have a slacker scale; the strings are not at as high a tension so the bass strings need room to vibrate. Severely graduated spacing on some instruments could present problems if you plan to double on more than one harp. (However, when we tried out a Paraguayan harp we found its graduated spacing surprisingly easy to adapt to—it all depends on the harp and the harper.)

String tension also affects the sound of a harp. Everything else being equal, the tighter the strings, the brighter the tone. Slacker strings usually have a more mellow sound. They are also easier for very small children to pluck.

Tight stringing calls for high quality construction. Fine instruments are made to withstand the pull on the structure and the soundboard. Therefore, they not only sound better but they are sturdier and will last longer.

THE LOOK OF A HARP is at first its most compelling factor. Some are ornately carved and/or painted, others lovely in their simplicity. Remember, however, that you are buying a musical instrument. A quality instrument builder's work shows not only in the sound of the harp but in the workmanship as well. Do all the joints fit well? Is it well finished?

And while you're asking questions, find out about the makers. Do they have an established, longstanding reputation? If you are making a custom order, can they deliver when they say they will? Do they guarantee their product? (You should get at least a year's warranty on less expensive harps and five years on a quality instrument.) Is the price fair for what you are getting? Consider the people who are selling the harp. Do they seem knowledgeable? Do they take the time to answer your questions?

FINALLY, check out your gut feelings. Time and again we have seen a person have a visceral response to a particular harp, and this type of bonding is often quite appropriate. But sometimes our emotions can carry us away. So, keep your wits about you, and if you need to take a walk around the block to get some space and view this wonder rationally, do so. We did just that before we bought our first harp (and still decided that it would be hard living without it).

If you have more than one vision of yourself as a harper, you'll probably end up owning more than one harp. Harps are addictive. We own small, medium and large neo-Celtic and wire Celtic models, lyres in both nylon and wire, and even an old pedal harp. Each has its own unique feel and personality. Each is special.

CAN I TEACH MYSELF TO PLAY OR DO I NEED A TEACHER?

Folk music is the music of, by and for the people. Songs are passed along through generations, from one musician to another, each adding his or her touch. There are no hard and fast rules. People make music because it is part of their lives.

The instruments of folk music (and we mean that in the widest sense, from Renaissance country dances through the balladeers of today) are often learned by listening to and observing other players, experimenting with styles or following old traditions. Some require years of study with, or of, a master player, a sort of apprenticeship. On other instruments, proficiency can be achieved with a little good sense and a willingness to be open.

Depending on your approach and your personal goals and aptitudes, the harp can fall into either category. A large number of folk harpers, however, are completely or partially self-taught.

Probably the most famous modern harp player is Harpo Marx. There have been many stories about him, some of them approaching legend, but there is no doubt that he was self-taught. Chico had his piano, Groucho his guitar and Harpo wanted to contribute to the vaudeville act, so he found an old harp (as the story goes, without working pedals) and soon was playing it on stage. At the height of his career he practiced four hours a day, and it showed. Take a look at the early films before he was miming to a pre-recorded track. His inventiveness was delightful. Who cares if his technique wasn't exactly kosher? The music was.

And if Harpo did it, so can we! In fact, thanks to pioneers in the current resurgence of folk harping like Sylvia Woods, hundreds, maybe thousands, have taught themselves to play. It's really not that difficult to begin. It is our opinion that you shouldn't wait for a teacher to start exploring your harp; tune her up and get going. Usually, "bad" habits picked up in the beginning can be corrected and the more you know your harp, the better.

It is your decision, of course, whether or not to go it alone. Some people need the discipline of a teacher to make progress. Others want to take a few lessons every so often to be sure that they are making the most of what they do. If you yearn to play intricate, fast tunes, your fingering and hand position will be especially important. A teacher can help to you to get it right. Some of us have specific physical needs, especially when playing and practicing several hours a day. The wrong body, arm or hand positions (which differ from person to person) can cause chronic discomfort; a good teacher's advice can be invaluable.

As we have said, "folk harp" is used as a generic term. Much more than folk music can be played on non-pedal harps. This book stresses the freer folk styles, but you may want a more classical approach. By all means, then, get a concert-oriented instructor who will help you achieve those goals.

If you decide you want a teacher, first ask any harpers or harpists you may know for a referral. Check with the people who sold you your harp. Contact the International Society of Folk Harpers and Craftsmen or the American [Pedal] Harp Society (see RESOURCES) for a list of names.

There is another way to learn to play, one that we have found works very well. That is to get two or more novices together and form a harp circle. You will find that you will be teaching each other. Invite more advanced players to attend and exchange ideas. Start playing in ensemble at parties, in the park or for children. Keep the arrangements simple and, most important, keep the harps in tune with each other.

Janna with a lap harp.
This inexpensive harp made in Pakistan evokes an earlier time.
Photo by Mallory.

Part Two: Getting Started

TUNING YOUR HARP

Perhaps the saddest sight for a harper is a harp standing in a corner unplayed and forlorn. This is, alas, the fate of many a harp, all too frequently because the owner didn't keep it in tune. Just about anything sounds magical on a tuned harp. And just about anything sounds absolutely wretched on an out-of-tune instrument. Taking a few minutes before you play to tune may make the difference between having a rewarding experience learning to play or giving up altogether. Even if you don't play every day, take a few minutes to be sure your harp is at least roughly in tune. Once you let it get way out, it becomes a chore to tune it and you may decide to clean out the garage instead. This is serious! **Keep your harp in tune.**

THE MECHANICS

Learning to tune your harp is the first and most important skill that you'll need in order to make music. Don't be daunted by the idea of tuning all those strings; it soon becomes second nature, especially if you have a little help.

Unless you are a trained instrument tuner or have a fabulous ear, we recommend you invest in a chromatic electronic tuner. Even the most inexpensive model will make your job much easier. It will hear the note (that is, the plucked string) you play and, either with a meter or a system of moving lights, show you if the pitch is sharp, flat or right on. The machine does the listening; you don't have to (although you'll want to in order to develop your ear).

Electronic tuners come with various features. Many have a light which indicates the name of the note being played. Some allow you to adjust the tuner to other than standard pitch if, say, you are playing with a piano that is flat. There are tuners which can be made to sound a reference tone as well as hear pitch. Most come with a built-in microphone, but for best results it is a good idea to buy some kind of external mic or pickup that will plug into the tuner. This allows the tuner to hear better and more selectively, especially in a noisy room or outdoors. If you have a pickup built into your harp (see Appendix Four: AMPLIFYING YOUR HARP) you can plug right into its cord (and even keep the tuner in-line with the amp if you wish). If your harp is strictly acoustic, you can choose from several mics and tuner pickups available, some with suction cups for the soundboard or clips which attach to a tuning pin. Ask your music dealer for the best kind for your instrument and tuner.

The price of the tuner usually determines how high or how low a tone it will successfully hear. Most of them claim a range wide enough for harps, but in reality the less expensive models don't do as well on the very low and very high strings, especially on a larger harp. You can tune the middle of the harp electronically and then tune the bass and the treble by ear. Match the untuned strings with the tuned strings by octaves (see Appendix Six: TUNING BY EAR). It's easier than it sounds. Really.

If you don't want to buy a tuner, you'll need some kind of pitch source—if only a tuning fork or pitch pipe—to get you in tune with other instruments. One way to tune is by matching the harp strings with the corresponding note of another instrument, like a keyboard, but this can be a bit awkward, especially if you have to do it alone. If you have an excellent pitch sense, you can tune a scale by ear in the middle of the instrument and then match up the rest of the strings by octaves.

As we mentioned in Part One, you'll do the actual tuning by placing a tuning handle (or **T**) on the tuning pin for the string you want to adjust. Tightening the string makes the pitch go higher; slackening the string lowers the sound. Most harps are strung so that turning the handle clockwise raises the pitch. If a harp is flat and you'll be adding tension, tune from the bottom up.

A new harp takes time to settle. Until the strings stretch out and the wood becomes more stable, frequent tunings are required. This will speed both settling and the maturation of tone. Always tune a new harp from the bottom up.

Note that not all harpmakers use the same size tuning pins. They range from small zither pins which don't go all the way through the neck up to large pins almost as big as those used on pianos. Be sure your handle fits neatly on the end of your pins, without sloppiness or binding.

<u>**WARNING!!!**</u> Be sure you are on the correct tuning pin. Many a string has been broken by tightening one string while playing ("tuning") another. If you have any doubt, before pulling up a string lower the tension slightly, listen for the pitch to go down and watch for the pin to turn on the string side. If nothing happens to the string you are plucking, you are on the wrong pin. Don't be embarrassed—we still do it. And fume a lot.

Sometimes changes in humidity will cause the wood to expand or shrink, causing one or more pins to be tight or loose. Tight is good—but a bit harder to tune. A loose pin will not hold pitch; you'll need to push it in.

To push in a loose tuning pin, put your tuning handle on the pin, let the tension down a bit and, supporting the neck of the harp from the other side with your left hand, use the handle to push the pin farther into the wood. The pins are tapered from smaller on the end on which the string is coiled to larger on the end on which the handle fits. Push until the pin feels snug, then bring the string up to the desired pitch.

If you are new to tuning a musical instrument, learning to tune will take time and patience. Sometimes the pitch will jump past where you want it and, if you are like most people, you'll feel some frustration. It is a skill which improves with practice, however, so keep at it. Remember: it's important to keep your harp in tune, for your sake and the harp's.

Tuning Handle

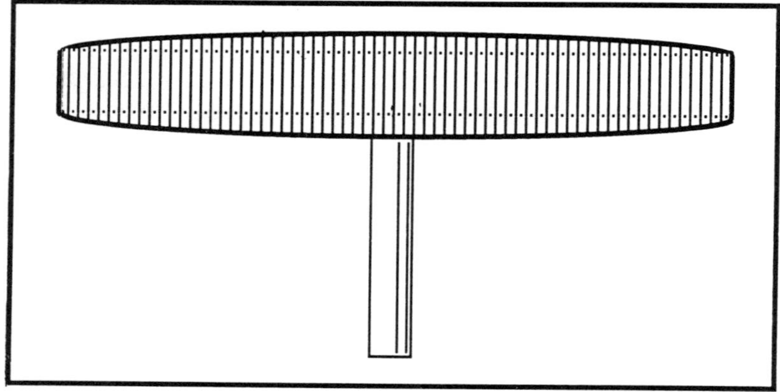

BASIC AND ALTERNATE TUNINGS

So far, we have referred to the basic *C* tuning. The red strings are tuned to *C* and the blue or black strings are tuned to *F*. The rest of the strings fall in line: red *C*, uncolored *D* and *E*, blue *F*, uncolored *G*, *A* and *B*, and back to red *C* again. This is the scale of the key of *C*, which has no accidentals (sharps or flats) and falls on the white notes of the piano. With this tuning you can play songs in the key of *C* major as well as the related minor (*A* minor) and the corresponding modes (see THE HARMONY OF HARP MUSIC) without flipping any levers.

> **NOTE FOR BEGINNERS TO MUSIC:** If we lose you somewhere along the way in the following discussion, don't worry. Skip this part for now. It is necessary information to the full understanding of harp music, but you can come back to it later. Just tune your harp to the basic notes and start playing in the key of *C*.

If you have a full set of levers and your harp is in the basic *C* tuning, you can also play in the sharp keys: *G, D, A, E,* etc., with their relative minors and modes. But, unless you have excellent levers, you may find that the notes sharped are not as clear as the open strings and/or that the sharping levers move the string out of line. For this reason, and the fact that many harps do not have levers, we have put the songs in this book in keys that require either no sharps or only one, a simple retuning, sharping all the *F* strings.

Right about now some of you with musical background may be asking, somewhat plaintively, "But what about the flat keys?" Unfortunately, you cannot play in the flat keys with this basic tuning. For most people who play solo, or from music designed for the folk harp, this does not present a serious problem. But it might if you sing with your harp or play with other instruments. Then you must retune. And changing keys by retuning several notes in each octave is only really workable in a recording session or if you have loads of time and patience. Few of us do.

The solution advocated by many harpers and harpists is to tune a lever harp in *E♭*. This means that you flat *B, E* and *A*. You have really lost nothing as *B* natural sharps to *C*, *E* natural sharps to *F* and *A♯* is the **enharmonic** (that is, sounds the same pitch as) *B♭*, which you now have available. This gives you the keys of: *E♭, B♭, F, C, G, D, A* and *E*, assuming that your levers give you satisfactory sound. This is the method often taught to students of harp who are planning to go on to the pedal harp.

There can be a problem with this tuning, however. If you play a lot in *C* or *G* and you want to add accidentals while you play (and you eventually will), you may find it confusing "on the fly" to visually sort through the sea of already flipped levers to engage (or worse, restore) the right one. It takes some getting used to. Some of us have opted for a compromise: tune the *B*'s to *B♭* and leave the rest of the strings natural. This allows you to play in *F*, a very common key, with no levers up. By flipping the *B* lever, you can play in *C*, and by flipping the other appropriate levers you can play in the sharp keys.

Each harper has his or her special needs. If you can only sing sweetly in four flats, by all means tune your harp to accommodate your voice. The important thing is to know what can and cannot be done so that you have the greatest freedom of choice.

CARING FOR YOUR HARP

Your harp is a fine musical instrument made with skill and meticulous attention to detail. Glance back for a moment to the section on Harp Basics. You will notice that many stresses on the structure are created by the pull of the strings. This interrelated system of stresses is what makes your instrument sound wonderful. However, these same stresses can cause problems if the harp is not properly cared for or if there are flaws in the workmanship or the structural design. While there is not much you can do about the latter except, in the event of difficulty, exercise your warranty, there is a great deal you can do to keep a well-built instrument healthy.

HUMIDITY, HEAT AND OTHER DANGERS

Your harp is made mostly of wood, probably two or three different kinds. Wood is a natural material which responds to a variety of natural phenomena. Changes in humidity can be quite damaging. The single most significant protection you can give your harp is to control the amount of humidity to which it is exposed. Control is the key. A stable environment is the goal.

It is important to note that too little moisture is a worse problem than too much. Wood swells in dampness and shrinks in dryness. Imagine what happens when a wooden instrument is allowed to dry out after being in a moist environment. Joints fail, tuning pins loosen and the structure is jeopardized, often warping at the neck. Sometimes the soundboard will become detached.

You may think that you would never let that happen, but all you need do is to put your instrument in a heated winter room (especially near a heating vent) for a period of time after it has been exposed to even normal humidity. Dry heating can lower the relative humidity in a closed room to five or six per cent. Therefore, be aware and take precautions.

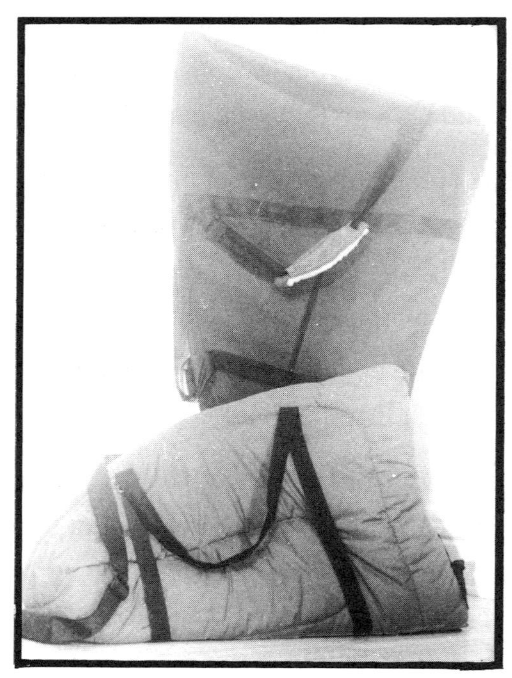

A custom VBC case for a large harp, and one home-made from a child's sleeping bag and some straps from a surplus store.
Photo by Janna.

Respected harpist and harp technician Carl Swanson has made it a point to insist that placing a humidifier in the room where you keep your instrument is immensely important. But not the kind that makes a visible mist; they don't really do much and can even cause harm. He recommends the belt type that dispenses an even vapor into the air. As he puts it, an extra hundred dollars or so is a worthwhile expenditure if it protects your investment. This is especially needed in dry climates.

On a smaller scale, many makers recommend a *Damp-It* (a musical instrument humidifier available at most music stores) or a damp rag or sock inside a vented baggie placed in the harp case. This can provide a humidity source for a bit of extra protection against drying out when transporting the harp. The device can then be placed inside the harp soundbox while playing. But be careful to keep any liquid from getting directly on the harp.

A similar situation can occur in closed cars. The temperature in a closed car on a sunny summer day can often exceed 130 degrees! That kind of baking can be murder on your harp—literally. It gets hot enough in a parked car to melt the glue on some harps, not to mention what it can do to the wood. If your car can't be kept cool, don't leave your harp in the car. And one way to further protect your instrument is to cover it with a space blanket over its case, shiny side out. This thin, reflective blanket developed for the astronauts can keep the immediate environment around the harp somewhat more stable than otherwise.

But even normal environmental fluctuations can cause lesser problems. So keep your harp covered. The best way to do this is to keep it in a padded case (your harp dealer or maker can order it for you if you do not have one). We've found, however, that we seldom put our harps away on a daily basis, even though we know we should. If you're like us, you can compromise and drape the case over the instrument or make a cover from quilted material that is easily removed for playing. If you are on a budget, you can make one from an inexpensive mover's blanket or a sleeping bag (be sure to measure—a child's bag may work for a small harp). Our 1930s pedal harp came with a lovely quilted velvet cover that was obviously hand made. Cases and covers are also necessary when you transport your harp, so whether you make it or buy it, get yourself something.

If you are playing outside, try to keep in the shade. The direct sun will wreak all kinds of havoc, merrily breaking strings even when the instrument is not being touched. We performed at a Renaissance fair in the sun, by a lake. We spent the entire time changing broken strings. Be sure to talk with whomever is in charge when you are playing outside and arrange for a suitable location. Harps are usually sturdy beasts but they can take only so much. And harpers suffer as well. Be warned!

BASIC HARP MAINTENANCE

Triplett Harps recommends cleaning the wood on your harp with Martin Guitar Polish, which works quite well. It is made for musical instruments and will not harm them in any way. We do not favor oiling the instrument with furniture oil.

Occasionally metal flip levers will squeak or be stiff (especially after an afternoon playing in the sun by a lake!). One very tiny drop of sewing machine oil can be put on the moving parts. **Never put any kind of oil near the tuning pins.**

Part of harp maintenance is keeping the instrument in tune, even when it is not being played. A fine harp will improve with age and keeping it at the proper pitch will aid in this process. Also, replace broken strings as soon as possible; missing strings will alter the stress on adjoining strings, often causing them to break as well. Harpmakers Lyon & Healy point out that this occurs because of unequal tension across the soundboard.

If you discover a structural difficulty, contact the builder immediately. If it is in any way effected by the pull of the strings—and most are—you should let the string tension down until repairs can be made. Also, if you are shipping your harp, it is often a good idea to let the strings slightly down, but not so far as they are slack and the coils around the pins are in danger of coming undone. When you pull the harp back up to pitch, you will have to do so more than once. Treat it like a new harp, tuning from the bottom up.

Replacing Strings

Harp strings break; it's a reality of harping. Usually the string is simply old or faulty. But notice where it broke. If you have a particular note that breaks frequently in the same place you should look for the cause. Check for rough metal or friction points at the soundboard eyelet, the bridge pin, sharping lever and the tuning pin. It is also possible, though less likely, that the harp's scale design—the precise length and thickness of the strings to provide correctly pitched notes at appropriate tension—is faulty. Try a string of a slightly lighter gauge, and/or consult with the maker.

The sooner you learn to replace strings, the more quickly you'll be back up and playing. Don't shy from the task. Some strings are awkward to get at, and it is a skill, but the more you do it the easier it will be. Here's how:

   1. Remove the old string, pulling it out from the inside of the soundbox. Take off any coil left on the tuning pin. Save the string if it is of usable length for a higher note of the same gauge.

   2. Select a replacement string of the proper size. Ideally, you'll have one that is marked by string number and pitch (see more about that below). If it is a colored string and you do not have one of the proper color, you can replace it with a clear string and color it with a permanent marker (not great, but O.K. in a pinch). In an emergency, you can also use regular monofilament fishing line—stiffer is better—although most brands don't sound quite as good as the strings sold by the suppliers and makers. An additional negative is that you have to buy an entire spool of a particular size. Weed whacker line likewise can be used for the lower strings. Be sure you measure the diameter of the old string to get a match. This can be done with a micrometer, which you should take with you when you are shopping for monofilament line. But remember—this is for emergencies; you're far better off with the right string from the harpmaker or a good supplier.

   3. If the string is already prepared with a backing knot for the soundboard end, thread it through the hole from the back of the soundboard. If you need help, look at the other strings. Strings of small diameter usually carry a short thick piece of string or metal in the knot to secure it. Sometimes round pieces of leather with a hole for the string to pass through or other such devices are used to better anchor the string.

If you have to make a knot do so as follows: Make a loop in the end of the string by passing the short end clockwise in front of the long end and hold between thumb and forefinger. Make a second loop to the left of the first loop by passing the short end clockwise again in front. Hold this second loop between the other thumb and forefinger. Now put loop two inside loop one from behind and pull the long end of the string tight. That's all there is to it. If you need to insert a piece of thick string into the knot, do so just before drawing the knot tight.

Tying and Installing String

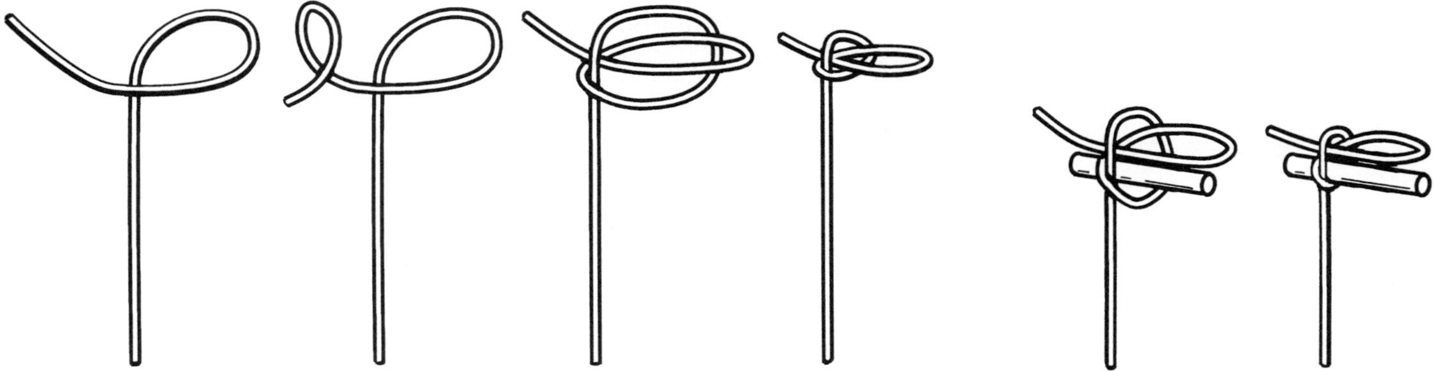

If replacing a high string with difficult clearance on the inside of the soundboard, thread the string from the outside of the soundboard, through the eyelet (string shoe) and pull it partially out the back. Then make your knot and pull from the front. It will make life a lot easier.

Be sure your knot is big enough so that it will not pull through, which is very frustrating. That's the purpose of the thick piece of string in the knot. You'll know that's what's happening when you tighten and tighten a string and it slips down in pitch over and over and cannot be made to hold. Eventually, the knot will pop out of the hole.

4. Cut the string about two inches beyond the tuning pin so that it will wrap around at least three times. If it is too long, there will be too much string to fit on the tuning pin, or at least so much that there may be pressure to push the tuning pin back into the neck. You'll have to let it down and pull the excess through the hole in the tuning pin and trim it off. Bring the string up through the sharping lever, past the bridge pin, and thread it through the becket hole in the tuning pin. Take a look at the other strings to confirm you are doing it correctly.

5. Pull the string carefully up to pitch by turning the pin with your tuning handle. Remember, clockwise sharpens the pitch. It's a good idea to take the first turn on the opposite side of the becket hole from where the rest of the coil will be wound. This helps to secure the coil and aids in tuning stability. You will find that the string, especially an unwound string, will stretch for some time and you'll have to retune it frequently. That's part of playing the harp. Always have your handle nearby. You shouldn't need an electronic tuner; tune by ear from neighboring octaves.

NOTE: For the sake of replacement, the strings are numbered from the top down, the highest usually being #1. This can get confusing as folk harps come in so many different sizes. One harp may have an *A* for the #1 string and another a *C*. When you are ordering replacements it is a good idea also to give the note name, ie. String #17, *A*, and say if it is nylon wound, metal wound or non-wound. If you are ordering from a supplier who is not the maker you should know the speaking length (the distance from the eyelet to the bridge pin, if so equipped, or the tuning pin), gauge and, if it is a wrapped string, the gauge and composition of both the core and the wrap.

FURTHER NOTE: Pedal harps, and therefore many folk harps made by concert harp makers, use a different system. Strings are designated by the octave number starting at the top of the large concert harp. This does not include the top two strings, *G* and *F*, which are called "extra." Thus, the highest octave, high *E* down to *F*, is the "1st Octave." The highest string on the Lyon & Healy *Troubadour III*, a 36 string lever harp, is 1st Octave *C*. The lowest string is 6th Octave *C*. To confuse matters more, while harp people refer to notes and octaves from the top down, piano people, singers and other musicians start from the bottom and number up. (One haven of consistency: middle *C* is always *C*4, that is, *C* in the 4th octave. From there things go in different directions.) Don't lose sleep over all this, but be aware that there are different systems and know how your harp is set up.

HOLDING YOUR HARP

How you hold your harp depends somewhat on the size and kind of instrument you have. Most harps are held (or pulled) to the right shoulder and should balance there comfortably without your having to support the instrument with your hands or arms. The strings should be perpendicular to the floor. Usually the right hand plays the higher strings and the left hand the lower strings (and flips the levers during playing as needed).

Position yourself so that the background you view through your strings creates the least possible distraction; avoid having to look at lines parallel to the strings or a disturbing light pattern. Some harpers carry a cloth to spread over jumbled backgrounds. An electric light shining on the strings—but not in your or your audience's eyes— can help, especially with a wire strung harp.

THE FLOOR HARP is usually played in a position where you can comfortably pull it onto your shoulder, between your legs. Experiment with various chair heights so that you can easily reach all the strings without twisting your body. It is important that you and your harp can move freely without the feeling that it might fall. If the floor is slick, you may need to have something to anchor the feet of the harp (we often carry a small rug to a gig to go under the chair and the harp).

Harp duo Laurie Riley and Michael MacBean in their booklet *Preventing and Correcting Chronic Harp-Related Injury* make a strong case for modifying the classic positions. They stress keeping the back straight, and the harp in a more upright position, not bearing weight on the shoulder. Be sure that your body is aligned; don't tip your head or twist your spine. Position the harp to accommodate you, not the other way around.

Another approach is offered by Nancy Calthorpe, a harp teacher in Ireland. In her book, *Begin the Harp*, she suggests that the harp may be played sidesaddle, that is with both legs on the left side of the instrument. This can be more graceful for women in short skirts and does allow easier viewing of the strings, but posture and the potential for stress on the body must be carefully considered. Each of us has different needs. It comes down to this: if it hurts, change what you are doing. Consult a professional.

You may also play the harp standing up by placing the harp on a box or platform. This position makes it easier to sing properly. It can also be useful to not have to sit in a group situation, especially when everyone else is standing.

Janna holding a floor harp. (A Nova by Triplett)
Photo by Mallory.

THE LAP HARP is a small harp supported by your legs, thus the name. The ancient Celtic style has a projection below the sound box that helps to stabilize it between the knees. Larger lap harps can be a real handful for small or short-waisted harpers. One way to solve this is by placing such harps on a stool or box and treating them like floor harps. Some in-between models even come with detachable long legs.

Mallory holding a lap harp (wire strung).
This harp is held in a position suitable for nylon also.
Photo by Janna.

Laurie and Michael pass along a fine suggestion for playing lap harp, especially if the harp is a bit large to hold. Place a board on the seat of the chair and straddle it, with the harp resting on the projecting board. This puts the harp right in front of you and makes the upper strings easier to reach.

LYRES can be held in several ways; there is some debate as to what is the correct way to play one. A look at old paintings, friezes, vases and the like can be helpful, but remember artists are not always musicians and so they give the impression of what something looks like to them which may or may not be right. We've experimented and find that the easiest way for us to play is with the high strings against the right shoulder. The left hand grasps the side of the lyre away from the body. The instrument is then played one handed, looking through the strings, with the right hand. You may find a better position with your lyre; there is no rigid rule. We do suggest, however, that you orient it so that the highest strings are closest to your body.

Mallory in medieval garb with lyre made in Pakistan.
He plays lyre as shown here, but historic art depicts several other positions.
Photo by Janna.

Some scholars suggest that lyres were strummed with one hand while the other hand damped the unwanted strings, rather like the bars of an autoharp, only from the back side. Sounds difficult.

THE WIRE CELTIC HARP is now-a-days most usually held the same way as the other folk harps, but there are a growing number of harpers who play with the harp on the left shoulder, in the true, historic style. The old Irish harpers also played with the hands reversed: the left hand played the high strings and the right the low ones. If you plan to play only wire harp and specialize in the Celtic literature, you may want to consider learning in this position. You will want to do some research and, perhaps, consult with other wire harpers. If, however, you want to play both wire and nylon harps, you'll find it easier to play with your harp on the right shoulder.

FASHION NOTE: Women or men who wear robes as part of their historical garb, will want to be sure that their skirts are harp friendly. That is, they are full enough to allow the harp to reside gracefully between the knees while sitting down. If in doubt, sit down in front of a full length mirror with your legs in playing position. Also, avoid jewelry, armor, chain mail, etc. which might scratch the wood on your harp. While you are playing, the harp is an extension of you. Consider that when you choose your performing clothing.

Janna and Mallory at a Renaissance Fair. Janna plays her 38-string Triplett Premiere. Photo by Jon Lackey.

Part Three: Making Music

BASIC PLAYING TECHNIQUES

Perhaps the most discussed and debated subject in folk harp playing is hand position. Some of us are self-taught and have found our own ways of playing; others, with excellent effect, study the various methods used by concert harp players. In this book, we'll call these latter methods the "classical style." It is important that you know what is considered the classical hand position and stroke. If you choose to play in a different manner, you should do so by choice, not ignorance.

The classical playing position for a nylon strung folk harp is with the thumbs up and the fingers curved inward. The ring finger extends down to the low notes.

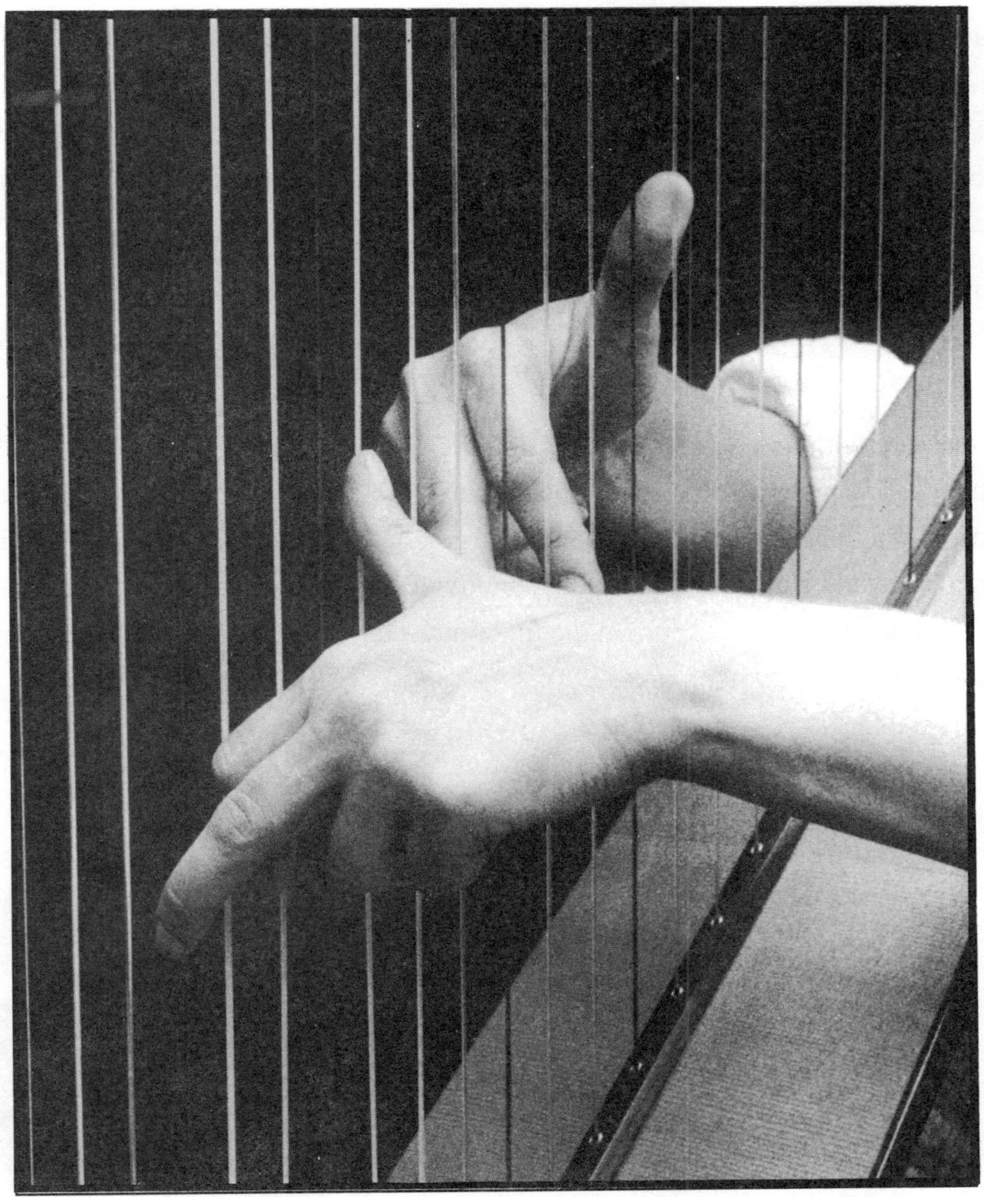

The hands of traditionally trained harper Cathy Chance.
Photo by Jon Lackey.

If you go by the rules, you'll play your nylon harp resting lightly on your right shoulder, play with the pads of your fingers only and "place" the fingers on the note or group of notes before you play them. You'll use three fingers and the thumb of each hand (harpers do not use the little finger) and you'll probably work out the fingering of each number before you play it. You'll play with a firm finger action, closing your hand as you pluck the notes. You should have a full, clean sound and develop dexterity and strength as you learn. Your elbows should float naturally, not rest on the soundboard of the harp. You'll want to experiment with the height of your chair or of your harp to get the most comfortable position. Arrange you and your harp so that you sit up, shoulders level, spine straight. Fingernails should be short so that they will not contact the strings. (See also THE WIRE HARP in Appendix.)

Since each of us has unique needs, instruction from a teacher might be useful to get you started—classic hand position is difficult to learn from a book. And it must be noted that a few harpers may be faced with hand and arm problems which can be helped by a change in style suggested by a qualified teacher. If any technique hurts, it is wrong for you.

That said, it is also important to reiterate that there are almost as many playing styles are there are folk harpers. We have seen and heard wonderful music from harpers breaking all the rules. Some play with the thumbs low in the style of the wire harp players (and occasionally use a bit of fingernail for accent). One problem with this hand position is that it is difficult to cross the fingers under the thumb in scale passages, which can slow you down if you want to play quickly.

Some players don't place, favoring the jab method. Again, there is some loss of control and the danger of stabbing at wrong notes. But many harpers make it work—some wonderfully. Distinctive sounds and styles can come from creatively breaking rules.

Mallory came to the harp with no previous musical training and first learned to play in the same way he types: two-fingered. From playing melodies this way—and the harp is one of the few instruments that allows you to play complete music using only one finger on each hand—he graduated to chords using all eight fingers. The two-finger method got him up and playing right away and motivated him to go further. Perhaps he might have been discouraged if he'd felt the need to learn it right the first time. Only you can decide your proper approach. And you can always make changes as you progress.

THE HARMONY OF HARP MUSIC

This is a hands-on section; have your harp tuned and ready! For the sake of this exploration, tune your harp in the key of C (check out the tuning section if you are not sure how).

INTRODUCTION TO SCALES AND CHORDS

There are 12 different tones in the **chromatic** scale—the white and black keys on the piano. There are many scales based on the use of some, but not all, of these tones. For example, try playing only the non-colored strings of your harp. This is a pentatonic scale, a five note scale used in some Asian, American Indian, Medieval, Celtic and early folk music. You can get the same effect playing only the black notes of the piano. Pentatonic scales are an easy place to start improvising. More about that in the section called FREE FORM MUSIC.

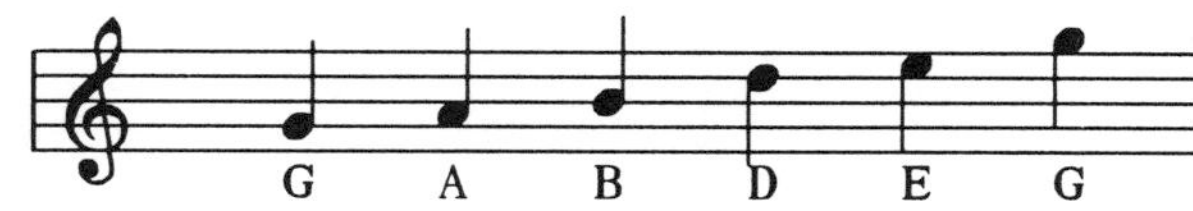

The most common scales (the **diatonic** scales), however, consist of seven different notes (an eight note scale if you count the duplicated top and bottom notes). These scales are made up of a series of whole and half steps. *C* to *D* and *G* to *A* are examples of whole steps. *E* to *F* and *B* to *C* are examples of half steps.

> **NOTE FOR THE HARMONICALLY CURIOUS:** The whole and half steps referred to above are also called **intervals,** in this case major and minor seconds. Intervals are basic to harmony and refer to the space between two notes as counted in scale steps, based on the names of the notes. The interval of *E* to *F♯* is a second, while *E* to *G♭*, which sounds the same, is a third. Thus, seconds are two scale steps apart, thirds are three scale steps, fourths are four scale steps, etc. *C* to *E* is an example of a major third, *E* to *G* is a minor third. Both are thirds because they are three scale steps apart, although they consist of four half steps and three half steps respectively. The number of half steps in the interval determines if an interval is major, minor, perfect (the fourth, the fifth and the octave) and, more rarely, augmented or diminished.

Play your strings in order and see if you can hear which intervals are the half steps and which are whole. What chromatic notes are missing?

With the addition of levers, some of those "missing" tones are available, but it is easier at first to treat your harp diatonically (the levers can come later). This somewhat limits what songs are playable, but there is a wealth of available diatonic music and musical styles; far more than you might imagine.

Let's examine some basic chords. **Chords** are defined as a group of three or more notes sounded at the same time. Later on, we will learn to use the separate notes in the chords in patterns and improvisations, but for now, think of them as blocks of notes.

As there are seven notes in the scale before it repeats, so there are seven triads (three note chords, each note a third above the other—called the root, third and fifth) available to you. These are: *C major (C), D minor (Dmin), E minor (Emin), F major (F), G major (G), A minor (Amin),* and the black sheep, *B diminished,* written *Bdim* or *B°*. Purists use the diminished chords sparingly or not at all, but they can be useful.

These chords are notated as follows:

ANOTHER NOTE FOR THE HARMONICALLY CURIOUS: Chords are made up of stacks of intervals (see above). A major chord in root position has a major third on the bottom and a minor third on the top. A minor chord has a minor third on the bottom and a major third on the top. Diminished chords are made up of two minor thirds; augmented chords are made up of two major thirds. If an extra note is added to a chord it is notated by adding the number of the interval from the root. *C6,* for example, adds an *A* to the chord, a sixth from the root. Common additions include the 7th and the 9th. (See the dominant seventh chord below and READING CHORD SYMBOLS in the Appendix.)

Play the chords, using any style that works for you. We're after the sound here, not finesse. Listen to the difference between the major and the minor chords. What do you think of the diminished chord with *B* in the root?

THE BASIC SCALES AND MODES

These chords are commonly used in six different scales or modes. A mode or scale is, in itself, nothing more than a series of notes in a certain order. But, because of its particular character, it acts as a framework upon which to build a melody. Modes of one kind or another are said to date back as far as the ancient Greeks. Medieval music was based on modes (unharmonized; that came later). Modes are a fascinating study but this is not a book for musicologists. Rather, our object here is to give you the modes as they are most commonly used today in a brief, rather simplified form. Investigate further if you are interested.

In order to determine if a scale is major, minor or modal you must examine the order of the whole and half tones or steps that make it up. In the musical examples, a half step is indicated by 1/2 and a whole step by 1.

The most common mode is the **Ionian**—what we now call the **major scale**. This is a fairly modern mode, gaining popularity around the 16th Century. In the *C* tuning it starts on *C* and proceeds up from there. It is the scale for the key of *C* major (no sharps or flats). It's three basic chords are *C* (called the tonic or I [one] chord), *G* (the dominant or V chord as it is built on the 5th note of the scale) and *F* (the sub-dominant, or IV chord). (See more about that below.)

THE C MAJOR SCALE

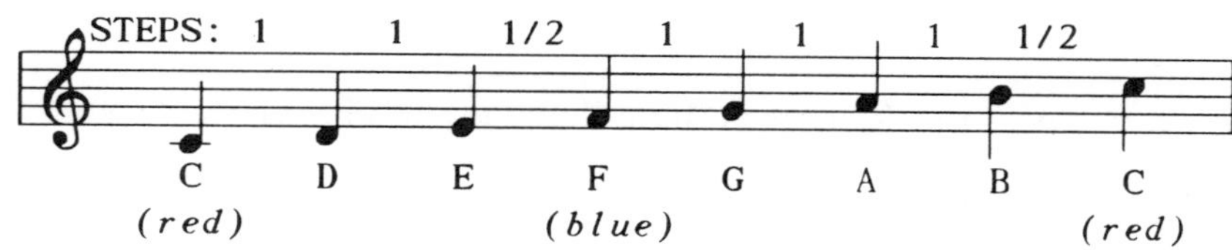

Second most common, and also relatively recent, is the **Aeolian**—a minor scale often called the **natural minor**, the minor scale most used in harp music. It is useful to know that *A* minor is the relative minor of *C* major as they share the same key signature. Aeolian starts on *A* and proceeds up from there. Its three chords are *A minor (written Amin), Emin* and *Dmin*. In this book, *Wayfaring Stranger* and *Raggle Taggle Gypsies-O* are examples of songs in Aeolian mode.

There are three types of modern minor scales. The other two, the **harmonic minor** and the **melodic minor**, are not modal and are usually harmonized with major chords built on the fifth as the dominant. (See below.)

THE A MINOR SCALES
Natural Minor (Aeolian Mode)

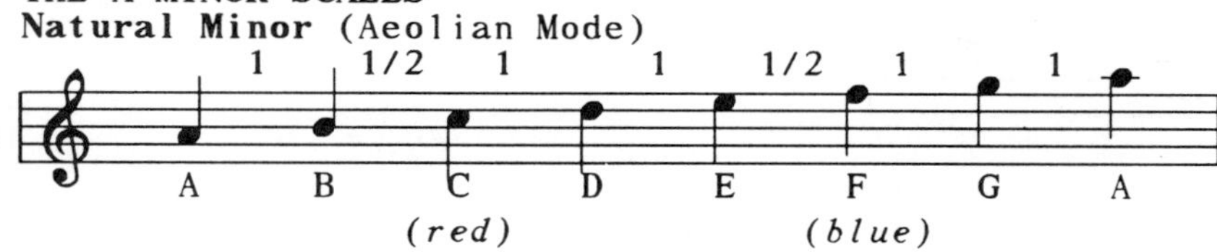

Harmonic Minor (G--ie., the leading tone of the scale-- is sharped in chords and sometimes in the melody)

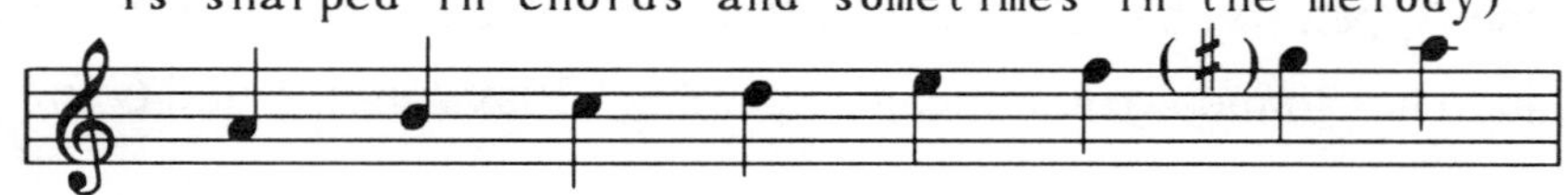

Melodic Minor (6th and 7th note sharped going up, natural going down)

A popular mode is the **Dorian**, heard in the Simon and Garfunkel version of *Scarborough Fair* as well as *What Shall We Do with a Drunken Sailor* and many other folk songs. It starts on *D* and features the chords *Dmin, G* and *C. Amin* and *F* are also common. Notice this does not follow the tonic, dominant, sub-dominant relationship mentioned above. All of the major and minor chords naturally occurring in a given scale are always available for your use. How they are used and the melody itself help define the mode. The Dorian, Mixolydian, Lydian and the Phrygian all date back to the Middle Ages, and are called "church modes" although they were common in secular music as well.

DORIAN MODE

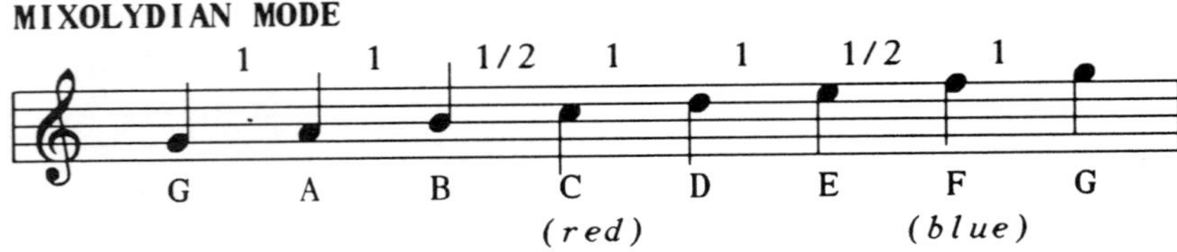

The **Mixolydian** mode sounds much like a major key except the 7th note is flatted, leaving it without the *D major* dominant chord. In the *C* tuning, its scale starts on *G*. Its principal chords are *G, F* and *C*. In this book the Scottish song *The Great Silkie* is in Mixolydian.

MIXOLYDIAN MODE

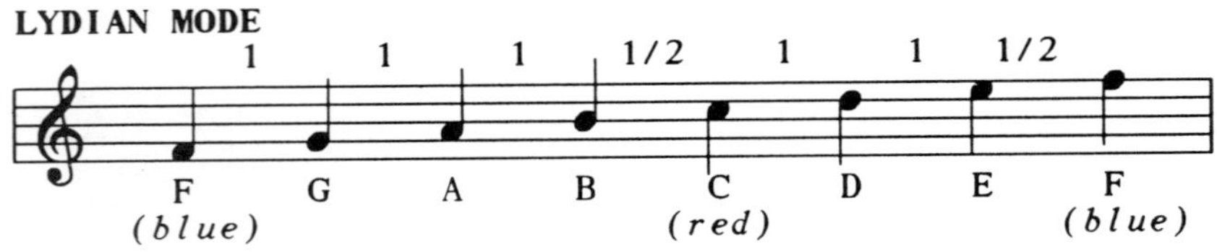

The **Lydian** begins on *F*. It is much like the *F* major scale except that the *B* is not flatted. Interesting when you play a *G major* chord in this scale, isn't it?.

LYDIAN MODE

Starting on *E* is the **Phrygian** mode. Novelist/harper Gael Kathryns' series of articles on the modes in *The Folk Harp Journal*, 1991-2, (her regular column is one of the many reasons to join the International Society of Folk Harpers and Craftsmen, see RESOURCES in the Appendix) helps to demystify these more obscure modes by suggesting ethnic sounds in the scales. Phrygian to her sounds "romantically Spanish." Play *Emin, F* and *G* for the effect and decide if you agree.

PHRYGIAN MODE

Last comes the 7th mode, the **Locrian**. Seventh mode? We said there were six. Most purists will have nothing to do with a scale that has a diminished chord for the tonic and insist that there are six basic modes. Period. It sounds wrong to them. Well, maybe it won't to you! Gael says, "...depending on your mood and your belief system [it sounds] discordant, atonal, ominous, or downright diabolical." If that doesn't peak your interest, skip this one. But if you are intrigued, start your scale on *B*.

These are the modes and scales in the *C* tuning. If you change the tuning of your harp (to *G*, for example, as many of the songs in this book are in that tuning) they will start on different notes. No matter what your tuning, the Ionian (or the major scale) always starts on the first note of the key you are tuned in (*G* if you are in one sharp, *C* in a tuning with no accidentals, etc), the Dorian starts on the second note, the Phrygian on the third, the Lydian on the fourth, the Mixolydian on the fifth, the Aeolian (natural minor) on the sixth and the dreaded Locrian on the seventh. When in doubt, identify the whole and half steps.

THE TONIC, DOMINANT AND SUB-DOMINANT CHORDS

Harmony is the study of how chords and intervals interrelate. We have already touched on the primary chords that are the backbone of our harmony, now let's examine them. The **tonic** chord is the tonal center of a given key. It is built in thirds above the first note of the scale. The other two chords, closely related to the tonic are the **dominant** (built up from the fifth note of the scale) and the **sub-dominant** (built on the fourth note of the scale). These chords in the key of *C* are *C*, *G* (or *G7* by adding a minor third on top the *G major* triad) and *F*. Find these chords on your harp. Remember, to make a chord, play every other string up (toward you) from the named (root) note.

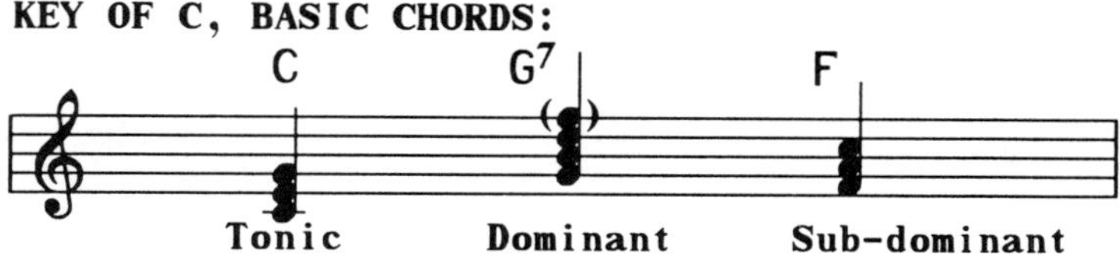

In *A* natural minor (Aeolian) these chords are *Amin, Emin* and *Dmin*, all chords available to you. Find them on your harp.

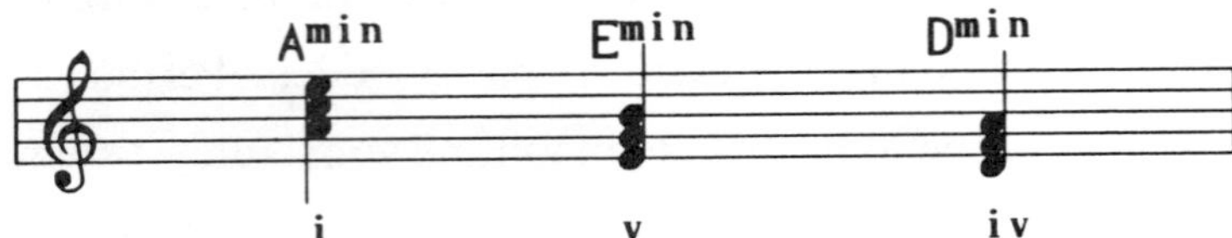

The *Emin* chord is not a proper dominant chord, however. Since it is a minor chord and has a flatted third it lacks the strong half step pull of the 7th note of the scale toward the root. Thus, in the harmony of many *A* minor pieces the *G* is sharped, making an *E major* chord. With the harp we have several options when an *E* chord is called for. The easiest is to omit the *G♯*, playing only the open interval called the fifth, in this case the notes *E* and *B*. The ear, or the other instruments or the singer, will fill in the *G♯*. Or you can reach up and flip up the *G* lever, giving you the *G♯* (remember not to play a *G* natural at the same time in another octave!). Finally, if the sharped note is in the melody you can slightly alter the melody, avoiding it or leaving it out. There are several examples of the third omitted in unavailable major chords in the songs in this book.

WORKING WITH CHORD SYMBOLS

We cannot recommend anything more highly than learning to play from chord symbols, the letters and numbers you see above the music in this book. This is a relatively easy skill to pick up on the harp and the rewards are enormous. Almost all folk and popular music is written with chord symbols. Often, you'll find all you have to work with is the melody, lyrics and chords. This is called a **lead sheet**. Knowing chords is the key that unlocks improvisation, ease of ensemble playing and facilitates transposition. And it introduces you painlessly to harmony, the basic structure of music.

As long as you know the names of your strings, you have something to play when you see a chord symbol (if it is not based on a note unavailable to you). For example, if you see a *G* chord (nothing after it means it's a major chord) you already know one note of the chord, the root, *G*.

The next step is to decide if you have rest of the chord on your harp as it is tuned. Going up (toward you) every other string from *G* gives you the *G* triad: *G-B-D*. If you're tuned in *C* you have all three notes available. Memorize all the available chords in the *C* tuning. (See THE HARMONY OF HARP MUSIC above if you are not sure what they are.)

Now, tune your harp in *G* by sharping the *F* strings. *G* is now the first note of the major scale. How are the chords different with the *F* sharped? Find the tonic, dominant and sub-dominant. If *A* minor is the relative minor of *C*, what minor key goes with *G*?

Practice the seven basic chords in these two tunings. These are, for the most part, the ones we will be using for our songs. Try moving them around, not just in the order they lie on the scale. You can go to most any song in this book and use the progressions of chords to practice changing chords in *C* and *G*. Check first to see that all the chords are available to your tuning (some of the chords indicated are for use by other instruments playing with the harp or to help indicate the harmonic structure). If there is a major chord indicated and you only have the minor chord available, practice playing the open fifth: the 1st and 5th note of the chord's scale. For the sake of this exercise, if you come across a chord with a 7 or a 9 after it, ignore that added note.

After you are comfortable with the various chords in the root position (the named note at the bottom), experiment with inverting the chords (putting the fifth or the third on the bottom) and/or playing the chords in open voicings (spread the chord out, ie: root in the bass, then the fifth and the third on top). Try to see how few notes you need to change when going from one chord to another in a progression.

INVERTED CHORDS AND OPEN VOICINGS

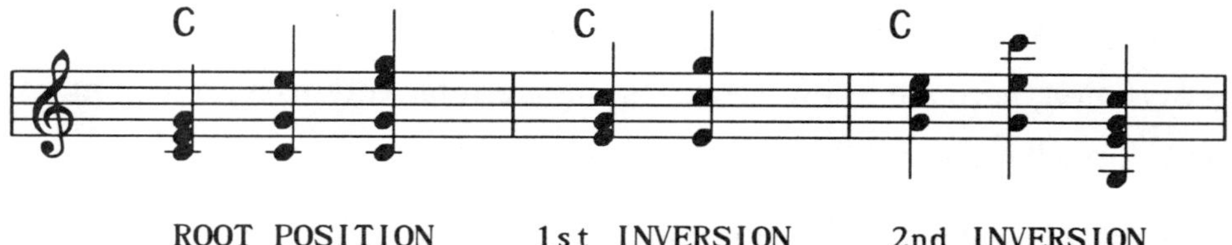

SMOOTH TRANSITIONS FROM CHORD TO CHORD (VOICE LEADING)

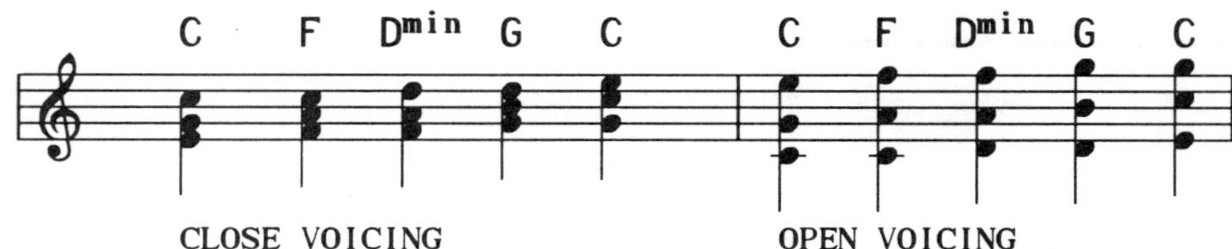

One other common chord is the **dominant seventh** chord. It is a four note chord with an added minor third on top of a major triad. It is called a seventh chord as that note is the flatted seventh of that chord's major scale (technically, a minor seventh, but the "minor" is ignored in this case so as not to confuse it with a minor chord with the seventh added. When a *7* is indicated it always means a minor seventh unless it is written *maj7*. They do that to keep us on our toes!). A *G7* chord consists of *G-B-D* and *F* natural (*F* is ordinarily sharped in the *G* scale). The dominant seventh chord is used to lead more strongly to the tonic chord (the *F,* in this case, wants to resolve the half step down to the *E,* the third of the *C* major chord, while the *B* of the *G7* chord pulls up toward the *C,* also a half step. Play the notes and you'll hear the pull).

THE DOMINANT 7TH PULL:

A Hint: The colored strings are there to help you know where you are. They are especially useful in finding chords. Obviously, the *C* chord has as its root a red string. Notice also that an *Amin* chord has the red string in the middle of its triad. How do the colored strings relate to the other chords? Using the harp, figure it out. These patterns will help you locate chords much more easily. (For those of you who are curious about more of the whys and wherefores of chords see READING CHORD SYMBOLS in the Appendix.)

FREE-FORM MUSIC

Note: This section and PLAYING BY EAR *deals with skills that are related but are by no means identical. You can start with either section, depending on your interests.*

Many fine musicians go through their lives playing everything just as it is written, never varying once they have mastered their music. Indeed, thorough study of a piece, learning it note by note, phrase by phrase until it is part of you is wonderful discipline and can make for some breathtaking music. But musicians who only replicate exactly what is on the page can be missing a further chance to be creative.

When you play something spontaneously that is not written down—whether entirely out of your head (or hands) or as a variation on a given piece, you are improvising. Improvisation is a treasured skill that has always been part of music making. Mozart was a genius at it, as are some of the greats of modern jazz and pop music.

But you don't have to be Mozart to enjoy making impromptu music. Playing notes at random on the harp can produce remarkable results. Lovely melodies often come from idle fingers plucking strings. When you are ready for some slightly more structured improvisation, here are a few ideas. Some are relatively easy, others more challenging. Do what works for you and skip what doesn't; you can try those again later.

THE GLISSANDO. Chances are you've tried this already—it's the sound many think of first when they think "harp!" Glissandi are sweeping finger strokes across the strings of the harp. The effect has been used over and over to make the "magic" happen.

Mallory playing glissandi on his floor harp (an Axline).
Photo by Janna.

Point your right index finger away from you, perpendicular to the strings. Now drag your fingertip up the strings, toward you. Do it again. Feel the vibration of the harp next to your body as the strings sing. If the sound is weak, stiffen your finger and/or press a bit harder. If it is muffled, you are pressing too hard. If you get a clicking sound, your fingernails are too long. Don't start all the way at the bottom on a big harp or the sound will be muddy. Do several glissandi until the notes sound clear and the harp rings.

Now do the same with the left hand. Keep your finger straight. Try alternating hands, overlapping slightly. Vary the length and speed of your strokes. Warning: A good percentage of people will get hooked on doing this. Mallory spent hours at it when we got our first harp.

It is a bit harder to "gliss" down; it is done with the thumb. Try coming up with the index finger and back down with your thumb, making the transition as smooth as possible.

WORKING WITH, OR AROUND, THE COLOR-CODED STRINGS. Remember the pentatonic scale made up of five notes in each octave? The easiest one to find on the harp is based on *G* and is played by ignoring the colored strings. In this scale, just about every note sounds good with every other note. Try making a melody. Avoid skips at first as the scale has some built in. Add some non-colored strings in the bass. *G* and *D* are safe.

Another non-standard scale can be created by flipping up the sharping levers on every string **above** a colored string. This exotic scale features augmented seconds, which are what give it that *1001 Nights* flavor. *C* to *D♯* is one; *F* to *G♯* is the other. They are "augmented" because they are wider than the more usual major and minor seconds (see above). Noodle around with this, lingering on the augmented seconds for effect. You can produce some very haunting music—and some very wild things, too. If you like the sound, it's easy to improvise upon.

MELODIES are easy to invent. They are simply sound patterns made up of pitch and duration. Look at written music and you'll see what we mean. Let's try some visual aids. Anything with a line of lows and highs will do: a jagged row of books, a skyline, tree branches, the top of a cloud formation, the shaggy hair on your dog's tail—most anything. Try making a melody based on what you see. When the visual reference goes up, play a higher note; when it goes down, so should your melody. When your visual reference is level, hold your pitch a bit longer or repeat the note. Keep your range under ten notes or so at first. Try playing the pattern with different starting notes or with wider skips. Play it backwards, upside down, just play around; you are improvising, after all. If you are highly visually oriented, make a drawing and play it on your harp. You can even play the graph of the Dow Jones Industrial Average.

Now close your eyes and place your fingers on the strings. Try feeling a melody. Listen to what you are feeling as you pluck. Make a tactile tune as you explore your harp strings. Be aware of the patterns your fingers are making. Now, open your eyes and see, feel and hear those melodic patterns. Music is a sensual experience. Maybe someone reading this can smell a song...or taste one.

THIRDS. Thirds sound especially nice in the higher register and are easy to play. With the thumb and index finger of your right hand, play any third (two strings a note apart like *C* and *E*, or *D* and *F*) with a pinching motion. Now move up one position, playing with the same fingers. Try a series of thirds, moving around wherever whim takes you (hint: if you play a skip of more than five notes, try coming back in the other direction by steps). Always listen to what you are doing and judge the effect. If you are tuned in *C*, you can add a low *G* bass note with the left hand.

When you are finished, end with a *C* chord. Now try an *E* in the bass, ending on *Amin*. Don't play all the thirds in the same rhythm, some should be faster, others held a bit longer.

Now try adding a beat. "Beat" doesn't mean play it fast, it just means play in a steady tempo and meter (see MUSIC READING BASICS in the Appendix if we've lost you). Tap your foot in three (<u>1</u>, 2, 3, <u>1</u>, 2, 3, etc.). Now play your thirds with that beat pattern. If you're having problems, change the speed until you are comfortable. When you're ready to change, try beating in four (<u>1</u>, 2, 3, 4, etc). Notice the different feel. Use the beat. Play with it, and around it, but keep it going.

CHORDS. If you've been going through this book in order, you have already played around with the various chords available on the harp. When you experimented with them, you were improvising. Select a simple chord progression (*C, G, C*; or the *Heart and Soul* perennial: *C, Amin, Dmin, G*; or something of your own invention). Chord progressions are the order of movement from chord to chord in a song and are often the framework on which to build an improvisation. Play the roots of the progression with your left hand in the bass over and over until you are comfortable doing it at a slow to moderate tempo. Give each root several beats, at least to start. Now add the right hand.

If that last sentence produced mild panic, relax. There's nothing to it—well, almost nothing. You already know the triads that go with those roots, right? That's a start. Triads are made up of thirds and you've played those, too. So, with a bit of practice, you can play each chord, or part of it, along with the bass note. Play the right and left hand together or stagger them, bass on the first beat, chord on the next. Take it slow and easy.

Next try breaking up the right hand chords into separate notes. Hold some notes longer than others; you don't have to play every note in the chord. Add passing notes in between: on a *C* chord you might play *C, <u>D</u>, E, G* or *G, <u>F</u>, E, C*. Now touch on the notes to each side of your chord (*C, E, G, <u>A</u>, G* or maybe *C, <u>B</u>, C, <u>D</u>, E*). After doing this a while, you'll find that you begin to create melodies that fit with the chord progression. These improvisations may well lead to original harp pieces, composed by you!

Let's make the bass a bit more interesting. Have the left hand play the root of the chord followed by the fifth. Carry this through your progression (see *Barbara Allen*). Try it in different meters: in three, hold the root or the fifth two beats; in four, each gets a beat. Now try playing the entire chord. either all together or in a broken pattern (see BEING CREATIVE WITH CHORDS in the EXERCISES for ideas if you get stuck). Practice improvising with the left hand alone. When you are comfortable with it, bring the right hand in again.

You will find that as the bass gets busier, you may want to simplify the melody. Hold some notes through more than one chord. Experiment and find out what sounds good so that next time you will have some fresh ideas to draw upon.

Go back to those visual melodies you created. Now that you have improvised with chord progressions you should be ready to start adding chords to improvised tunes. Take a look at the next section for hints on how to harmonize them.

Remember, you not only have the major and minor keys to improvise upon, but the modes as well. Try all of them at least once, even the "impossible" Locrian.

INTRODUCTION TO EAR PLAYING

As you've been experimenting with improvisation, you have probably played snatches of recognizable melodies. When you do it deliberately, you are beginning to play by ear. Some musicians—unlike their cousins mentioned above who stick to the music—never learn to read a note. We've all heard about people who hear a complicated piece once and play it—harmony and all—without mistake. If that's you, skip this chapter—maybe even skip this book! Everybody else read on.

Select a simple tune and pick it out. The key word is simple. Practically every beginning book of music starts out with *Twinkle, Twinkle Little Star*. If that doesn't interest you (Mozart liked it enough to do variations on it!) try Lewis Carroll's *Twinkle, Twinkle Little Bat.*, or *The ABC Song*. They all have the same melody. With your harp tuned in *C*, see if you can find it.

If you are having trouble here are some clues, but read them one at a time and then go back to your harp and try again.

1. Play the tonic chord *C* to get your ear in the right key.

2. Sing the tune out loud after you play the tonic chord.

3. Start on *C*, the first note of the scale and the root of the tonic chord.

4. There is only one skip used in the song (the rest is by single steps).

5. This only skip is a skip of a fifth. (Bonus clue: it is part of the *C* triad.)

By now, you've either got it or are contemplating taking up Chinese gong. Don't worry, this is a skill that can be learned. It's a bit easier for some than others, but everyone can do it with practice. (If you are really in the market for that gong, we'll talk you in: *C* [red string], *C, G, G, A, A, G* [hold]. *F* [blue string], *F, E, E, D, D, C* [hold]. Then up to *G* again and come down by steps to *D*. Repeat that part and then play the first part again.)

Chances are, you've been playing with one finger, usually the index finger. Once you've got the melody down, try using all four fingers. Just before you play the notes of the first "Twinkle," place your 4th finger on *C* and your thumb on *A*. For "How I wonder..." place you thumb on *G* and let the rest of the fingers fall in order down the scale. The rest is easy.

When you learn to place on a group of notes, you will play with more assurance and evenness. With more complex music, you will have to move the position of your hand quite a number of times. Whenever possible, work this out in advance. However, if you are truly playing by ear you don't have the luxury of advance planning. The more you practice correct placing the more it will come to you automatically.

Now pick another song. Here are a few titles that work on the harp, some easy, others harder: *Go Tell Aunt Rhodie; Freres Jacques;, Ode to Joy; Mary Had a Little Lamb; Heart and Soul; Edelweiss; Do, Re, Mi; Try to Remember; Lili Marlene; Minstrel Boy; Jingle Bells (and many other Christmas carols and songs)* or most any title in this book that you know. But don't peek. Folk songs and children's songs are good candidates as they are often diatonic. Mallory started with the Simon and Garfunkel *Scarborough Fair* (in the Dorian mode) and *Annie Laurie*.

Establish your key before starting by playing the tonic (and the dominant if you need it) and sing in your head to help find the intervals. Remember, many songs are in a minor key, so your tonic will be the relative minor (a minor third down from the key in which you are tuned).

As you try tunes on your own, you'll come across notes that you just can't seem to find. Most probably you have either picked a bad key, started on the wrong note or have encountered accidentals, those notes between the strings that can only be accessed by sharping levers. If there are only a few accidentals, you can often work around them or flip the appropriate lever. If there are many, or the song seems to go off somewhere in the stratosphere, you may have to give up on it, at least for the time being.

ADDING HARMONY

After you can play a few melodies, try adding chords. If you started with *Mary Had a Little Lamb* or *Go Tell Aunt Rhodie* you can harmonize them with only two chords. Hint: try the tonic first, unless your ear tells you otherwise; it is the most usual starting chord. The dominant (V) chord and the sub-dominant (IV) chords are common chords to harmonize simple tunes.

If you've tried these three basic chords on a given piece and they don't seem to work, examine the melody. Very often it will clearly indicate what chord to play. *On Top of Old Smokey* spells out it's first chord exactly and practically gives you the rest, with only a few non-important passing notes.

If you remember back to the section on chords, you will recall that there are seven different available triads in a given tuning. Experience and trial and error will teach you which ones to use where. Here are a few harmonic hints:

1. Every note in the scale, and therefore in your diatonic melody, is a part of three different chords. An *E*, for example, is found in the chords *Emin, C* and *Ami.* It is often a matter of your taste as to which you use.

2. Not every note is harmonized. Often you will find that one chord serves for several beats, incorporating chord notes, passing notes or added notes to create harmonic interest.

3. Chord progressions are often used in a rhythmic pattern. The blues is one example; *Heart and Soul* another. Patterns can be subtle (some Latin music) or assertive ('50s Rock and Roll). Avoid adding chords that get in the way of the rhythm.

4. As demonstrated above, the dominant chord wants to resolve to the tonic. But this gets extended much further in what is called the **Circle of Fifths**. Play the following chord progression: *Emin, Amin, Dmin, G, C.* See how nicely that flows. Here's what's going on: *E* is the fifth (dominant) of *A*, which is the fifth of *D*, which is the fifth of *G*, which is the fifth and dominant of *C*. We're still in the key of *C*, but we've used the dominants of other chords to lead in chain back to our tonic. This works with both major and minor chords (See Appendix Eight: READING CHORD SYMBOLS.)

5. Using the principle in #4, each one of these chords can also resolve to a related
chord sharing two of the same notes. Therefore, *Emin* can move smoothly to *C* or
F as well as *Ami*.

But before we get too bogged down in theory, remember it is what sounds good to you that is right.

Another important element of ear playing is to learn to identify the chords when they are played. Again, start listening to simple music. Get a friend to play some children's songs and see if you can identify which is the tonic, dominant or sub-dominant. More complicated chords can be found in more complicated music, but that will come later. The more you work with the various chords, the more you will know how they sound.

Dinah LeHoven and her beautiful hand-carved high-headed wire harp. She plays in the traditional Celtic style with her harp on her left shoulder. Photo by Jon Lackey.

SINGING OR ACCOMPANYING WITH YOUR HARP

One of the goals of this book is to help the singer/harper find the best way to combine the two. Appendix Five is an article by voice coach Veronica Diamond about how to produce the best vocal sounds. Here we will take a look at what you should be doing to most effectively set off the voice (or any other instrument you might find yourself accompanying).

If you are doing the singing yourself, you will find it is best to keep the harp part simple. With the exception of two songs in this book, *What Child is This?* and *In the Glade*, the arrangements given here are designed for harp solo and need to be adapted.

The easiest way to accompany yourself is to play simple chords with one or both hands. They can be triads in a block, or you can break them up in interesting patterns. *What Child is This?* is done almost entirely in broken chords.

If you want to base your accompaniment on an arrangement in this book, you can try playing the left hand pretty much as written and playing chords in the right hand. However, this is much more difficult than simply playing chords. Never let the harp part be so complicated that you cannot put your full attention on your singing. If the accompaniment is easy, you can look up from the strings and sing to your audience. That's important both in the projection of the voice and the contact you make with your listeners. Hint: Practice playing in the dark.

If you are playing for someone else, your job is to follow him or her. Listen. Pay attention to the singer's phrasing, the rubato—if any—and the style. You want to complement, not engage in musical combat.

Like everything else, accompaniment is a skill picked up by practice—by doing. And it has its rewards. Janna enjoys improvising under Mallory's vocals so much that she prefers it to solo work.

Singer/harper Michele Woodward with a small lap harp.
Photo by Jon Lackey.

PLAYING DUETS AND IN ENSEMBLES

The first rule of ensemble playing is to *listen to each other*. That sounds hard when you are struggling with your part, but once you learn to listen you will be well on your way. Strive to become a unit, not a group of musical strangers each on his or her own.

Here's a deep, dark secret: When you are playing with others you don't have to play nearly as much as when you are playing solo. We have gathered together some friends who do not play harp and given each person a simple two or three note phrase. Combined with other, complementary, simple parts the whole thing makes quite presentable music, even though those people thought they could never "play in a band."

The two of us began playing together seriously very shortly after we got our first harps. Mallory, who didn't at that time read music, found that he could pick up tunes by ear. Janna was comfortable with chords. Together we made the equivalent of one well-rounded harper. Neither of us could have performed alone in those first months, but as a duo it worked. Try this with a friend. You may have an instant act!

You have everything you need to make harp duets from the material in this book: melodies, chords and written parts which can be divided up. Start simply, perhaps with a round like *Oh, How Lovely is the Evening*.

If you want to join a band, especially an established one, you have a few obstacles to overcome. It is difficult to change keys quickly, and there are some keys in which you simply cannot play. But the other instruments can often play the notes you don't have, filling out the harmonies. You can play what you do have, play fill-ins, lay out or play drum rhythms on your soundboard when the others are off in musical lands uncharted for folk harp. It is a good idea to get another instrument, a small drum or the like, to play as a double. If you already play something else, or sing, you are way ahead. Derek Bell of the Chieftains plays harp, piano, hammered dulcimer and who knows what else. Doubling adds to the musical possibilities in a group. Ask what is wanted, and do some serious listening. Then start out simply and find your niche.

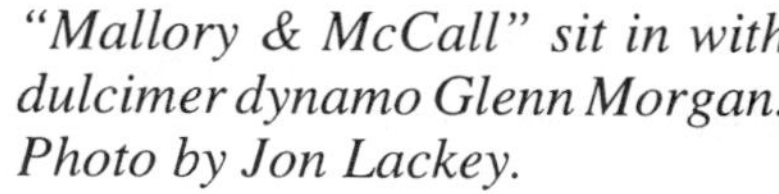

"Mallory & McCall" sit in with dulcimer dynamo Glenn Morgan. Photo by Jon Lackey.

ADAPTING NON-HARP MUSIC

KEYBOARD MUSIC

An especially fertile source of easy to intermediate harp pieces are books for the beginning study of piano. Included in these pages are three exercises from Béla Bartók's *Mikrokosmos*, an unusual approach to graded piano for beginners. Many of these short pieces, often modal, are excellent as they are simple but offer a challenge. Another primer for piano was written by Cécile Couperin and contains useful music and theory. Mozart, Haydn, Bach, and many other great composers wrote elementary music for teaching purposes. Igor Stravinsky composed *Three Easy Pieces on Five Notes,* the first being entirely diatonic.

Many of these pieces are written in "easy" keys and are of simple construction. Some are playable practically as written on the page. The fingering will be different—we only use four fingers on each hand and the right hand is "backwards"—but that part is easily reworked by trial and error. And, if you ever studied piano, you probably have a pile of piano primers already, gathering dust.

If you decide to buy piano books for the purpose of playing the harp, read this part carefully so that you will select books with the highest percentage of usable material.

Our diatonic instrument presents certain problems; what may be considered easy (for example, to flat a *B* in the key of *C* major) can be awkward or sometimes impossible on a harp. Accidentals are our major challenge; we either have to figure out a way to play the note with a lever, leave it out or change it to another note. Some songs, sadly, are simply not do-able.

In selecting a piece to play, check out the following elements:

1. Is it playable as it stands, with no modification? If it is, you're in business. Read it through, noting any obvious piano techniques inappropriate to the harp (pedaling, for example). Much music up to the mid 18th Century has been "edited" with expression, phrasing, pedaling and dynamics that were either conjectures by the editors or blatantly out of period. Early keyboard music was usually written for harpsichord and its cousins. The later pianoforte was revolutionary because it could play with expression (the translation of its name is "soft and loud"). Baroque and Classical keyboard musicians added volume and tonal interest by coupling in extra strings (or pipes on their organs). So you can safely assume that these markings are not original and proceed accordingly.

2. Is the key a good one for your harp? If everything else is do-able, transpose it! Don't let the idea scare you off. Transposing is not really that difficult once you get the hang of it. Establish what key you want to move to, write in the time and key signatures at the beginning of the staff (ie, one sharp for *G*, no sharps or flats for *C*) and decide how many lines and spaces you have to move up or down. Pay attention

to the intervals (skips) in the music and be sure they match the original. Play what you have done from time to time to check your work. And don't get discouraged. If you keep at it, you'll have learned an important skill for musicians—especially harpers.

If you have a full set of levers, consider "transposing" a song that is currently in a flat key to a sharp key that bears the same name. A piece in *D♭* can be played as written in *D* if there are no accidentals. *E♭* can become *E*; *F♯*, *F*; *G♭*, *G*; *A♭*, *A*. If there are a few accidentals, they may have to be altered. Naturals often become sharps or flats. Listening to how it sounds solves most problems.

3. Will it fit on the range of your harp? Most floor harps will accommodate easy keyboard music. If you have a small harp, you may need to transpose. Sometimes this will involve the entire piece (proceed as above); sometimes only a few notes need to be moved up or down an octave. Often all you need to do is to move the entire piece up an octave. Keep music manuscript paper to hand for your use in adapting songs, even ones in this book.

4. Are there any accidentals? This is easy to check in any key. Ignore the key signature and scan the melody for added sharps, flats or naturals. If there aren't any, you will be able to play the tune, although you may have to adapt the accompaniment. Now check the rest of the music. If there are no written accidentals the piece is diatonic and can be played, although you may have to transpose it (see above). If there are only one or two accidentals you may be able to leave them out or play alternate notes. If there are a lot of accidentals, look elsewhere.

5. Is the piece suitable for the style of the harp? As this has a lot to do with your personal concept of what a harp should sound like, it is your judgement call.

6. Do you know the piece already? (If you know how it goes, it is easier to learn.)

7. Is it something you would like to play? That's important!

OTHER SOURCES FOR MUSIC

There are many excellent books of arrangements especially for non-pedal harp. When you join the Folk Harp Society you will not only find music in the *Journal*, but all kinds of ads and reviews about music that is available. Get as much music from as many different harpers as you can. Everyone has a different style and you will find many things that you can incorporate into your own. Listen to tapes (again, many are listed in the *Journal*) and go to concerts. See and hear what others are playing and you'll get some ideas of your own.

Folk music is a fertile source of playable music. Most of it uses simple harmonies which are easily adapted for your harp. Irish, Scottish and English ballads are rich in the modal tradition, but you can find interesting music from all over the world.

Take a look at some of the folk music of the 1960s. We play Bob Dylan and Simon and Garfunkel and there are lots of others.   You'll find country music that works and some popular show tunes as well. We do a duet with the *Music of the Night* theme from *Phantom of the Opera* (omitting the bridge, which goes into a whole different key), as well as songs from *The Fantastiks, Cats* and *The Sound of Music*. It takes some searching, but good music is out there, whatever your tastes.

If you have children, or work with them, the harp is perfect. Most children's music is harpable and the kids love it. Let them run their fingers over the strings and they'll be enthralled.

Explore. Listen. Be creative. Experiment. And, by all means, keep playing! No matter what you do with your harp, you'll grow with it and discover new, enchanting avenues to follow.

A child discovers the harp.
Photo by Mallory.

Part Four: Exercises, Songs and Harping

EXERCISES

We have to say it—it's part of a teacher's job, and is true: if you want to master your instrument, you have to practice. The more you work on technique, the more easily and accurately you'll play. Most of our practice is playing songs, period. So this may be one of those "do as we say, not as we do" situations. That means spending extra time on your weak hand (for most of us the left), playing over and over things that give you difficulty until they are part of you and, yes, doing exercises. Exercises are part of learning an instrument.

We have given you some sample exercises of varying difficulty. There are many books available with harp exercises for the harper interested in developing technique (Deborah Friou's *Harp Exercises for Agility and Speed* is excellent). We strongly urge the motivated student to seek these books out.

If you really can't stand doing exercises to the point that this obstacle will keep you from playing anything, at least commit to try everything in this part at some point. This will give you hands on understanding of fingering, placing, hand position and dealing with chords.

PLACING

In classical harp technique, students are taught to place their fingers on the strings in groups. This increases power and accuracy. Raise your thumb high (but not too stiffly) and place it against the string before playing it. The other three fingers (remember, we don't use the little finger) also rest in place, cupped inward. You should be contacting the strings on the pads of your fingers. As you play a note, pull your fingers inward so that your hand is almost closed after a grouping of notes.

Keep your arms relaxed with your elbows high enough to allow you to move freely around the harp. Don't rest your arms on the soundboard. Use the strength of your hand, not just the tips of your fingers. Your wrists should be straight or bent outward. Bending the wrist inward can cause inflammation of the carpal tunnels.

Here's an exercise to demonstrate placing:

Now let's try a real song. Be sure to place your fingers at the start of each line.

Oh, How Lovely Is the Evening

An Exercise in Placing
Place hand before playing each line

Here's another exercise stressing placing, but it also demonstrates broken chords, which are very useful in accompanying. Play smoothly, placing your fingers on each triad before you play it, but don't lose the beat. Start slowly and then work up speed. This, as well as all the single staff exercises, should be played alternatively with each hand and then with both hands together.

Although this exercise could be played with the same fingering throughout, the alterations make the transitions smoother. As you play the chords, name them in your head and listen to their characteristic sounds.

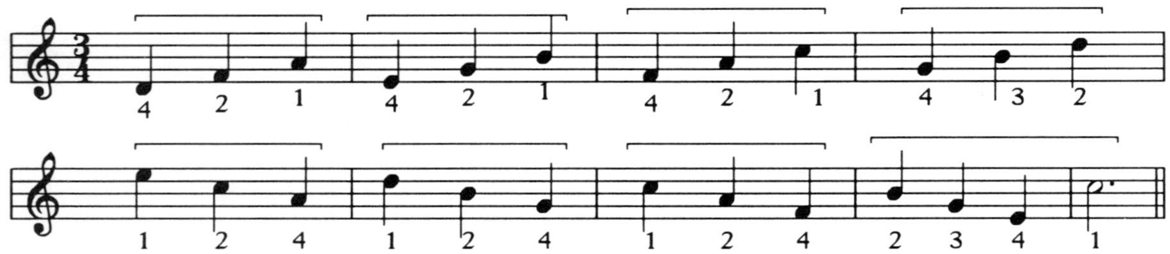

You can try this technique on any number of melodies; in fact, many of the songs in this book use this technique in a more advanced form, but the theory is the same.

SCALES

Playing scales is simpler on the harp than on most other musical instruments. As there are no sharps or flats, they can be fingered the same way in any key. There are several ways of playing scales; the most orthodox is #1 in our examples. The fourth finger is crossed under the thumb on the way up and the thumb crosses over on the way down. This works smoothly when the thumb is held high.

Example #2 is less fluid. Going up, the 2nd finger continually moves under the thumb. The thumb goes over the index finger going down. It doubles as an exercise in proper thumb position.

Example #3 is really a controlled glissando. It may seem a bit squirrelly at first, but when done smoothly it can be quite effective. You can do the entire scale with one finger, but we have found that with glissandi of any length, ending on a different finger assures that one will stop on the right note.

Try these fingerings on all the modes in both the *C* and *G* tunings.

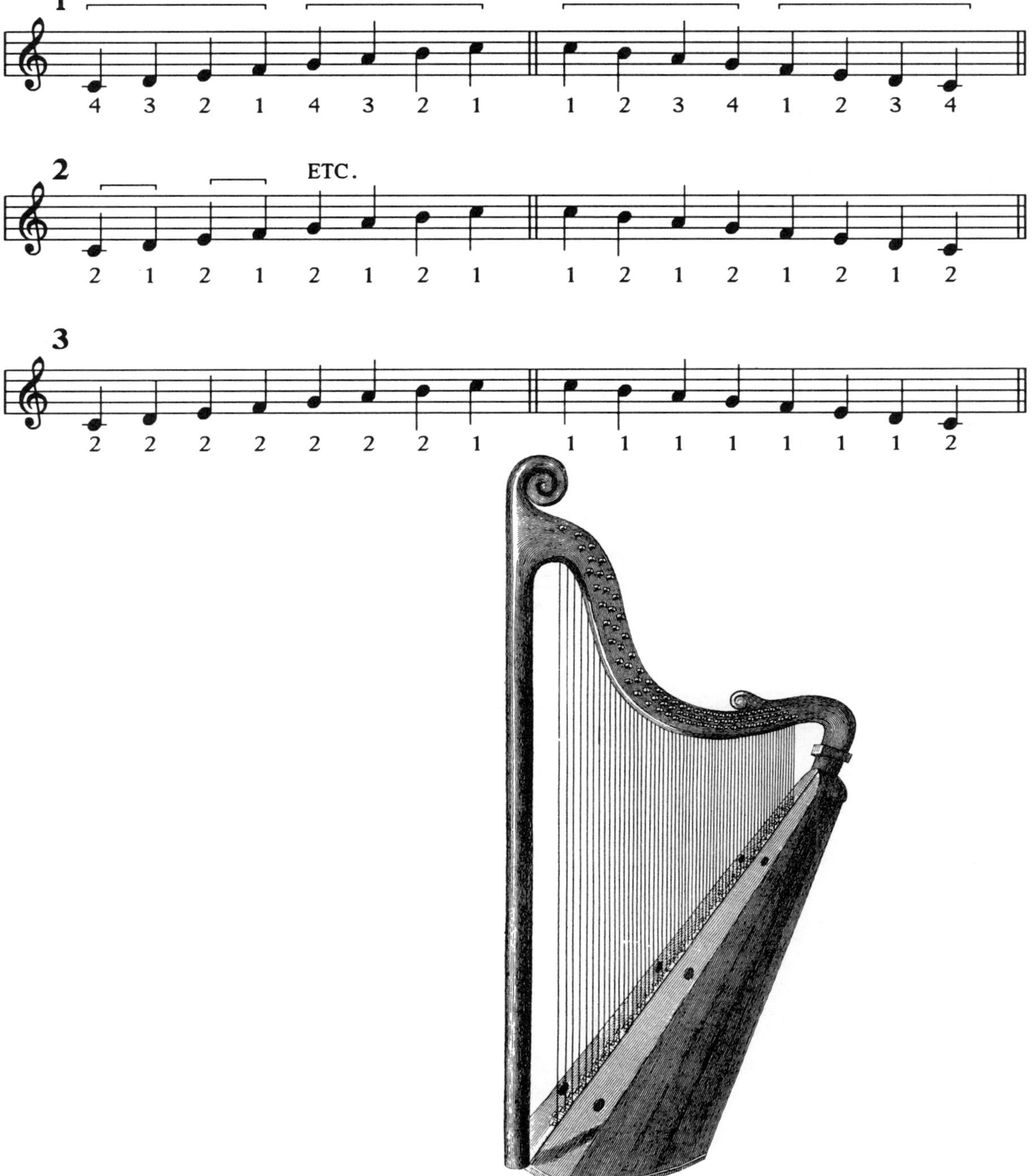

BEING CREATIVE WITH CHORDS

Here are a few of the many ways chords may be arranged for different effects.

The first example is uniform in its pattern, using the broken triads in the same way until the *G7* chord is introduced toward the end to add variety. See this pattern in use in *Wayfaring Stranger*. The second is a demonstration of how passing tones (those notes between the thirds in the chords) may be inserted on the unstressed beats to add interest. Example #3 uses eighth notes that are part of the chord, but some of the chords (the *F* in the second measure is one) are inverted to make the transitions from chord to chord smoother. Remember to place your fingers on each chord pattern before you play it. #4 goes into 4/4 time and the key of *G*. Note how the pattern resembles #2.

All these patterns, and many more, can be used on just about every chord in every key. #5 shows some examples of extended four note chords which give a more contemporary sound. #6 is an old workhorse, the Alberti bass, named after an 18th Century composer who used it extensively. It works well in a left hand accompaniment (you are trying these with each hand, remember!).

Chord patterns—broken chords and arpeggios—can be carried from one hand to the other. See *What Child is This?* for a simple example. Study the left hand parts in the arrangements in this book for suggestions on how to stretch out a chord, which makes a lovely effect on the harp.

ARPEGGIOS

The dictionary tells us that the word comes from the Italian *arpeggiare*, to play the harp (*arpa*). Although many other instruments play arpeggios, the musical effect is so associated with the harp that it bears its name. In an arpeggio, the notes of a chord are played in succession, not simultaneously. An arpeggio can be only three notes or range into several octaves. It is common practice to rapidly arpeggiate (roll) chords of three or more notes in harp music, although not requisite.

In these exercises we demonstrate a few extended arpeggios. This classic harp arpeggio can range from a couple of octaves to up and down the entire harp. They are played with alternating hands. The length of the arpeggio and the speed depends on the music, the size of your harp and your taste.

Arpeggiating three note triads is the easiest: start by spelling out the chord low on the harp and then playing it up each octave in succession, hand over hand (see Exercise). Four note chords are lusher. If your chord does not consist of four notes (as with the dominant seventh) you may add an extra one. Try the second, fourth or sixth. This is useful in duple meters where a three note chord does not fit well within the beat. Notes close together at the bass end of a large harp sound muddy, so if you want a sweeping arpeggio, play only the root and fifth of the chord at the bottom of the harp.

Practice for smoothness and even tone. Try each arpeggio with different chords until you can arpeggiate each available chord on the harp effortlessly. Practice going both up and down and varying the length of the arpeggios from two octaves to the entire range of your particular instrument. An arpeggio often ends with the root note of the chord.

THREE NOTE CHORD ARPEGGIOS (ROLLED)

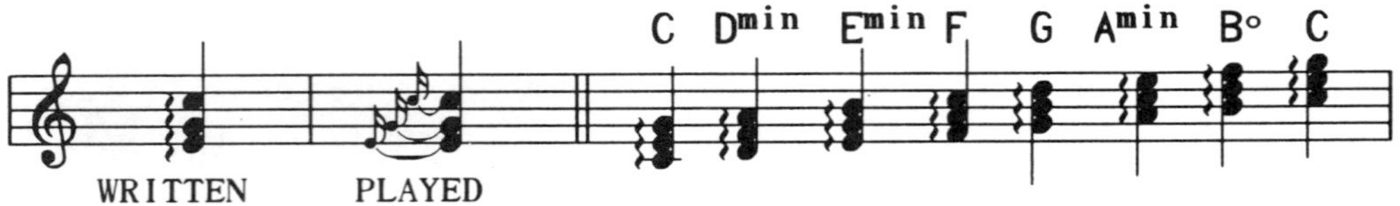

EXTENDED ARPEGGIOS - PRACTICE ON ALL AVAILABLE CHORDS

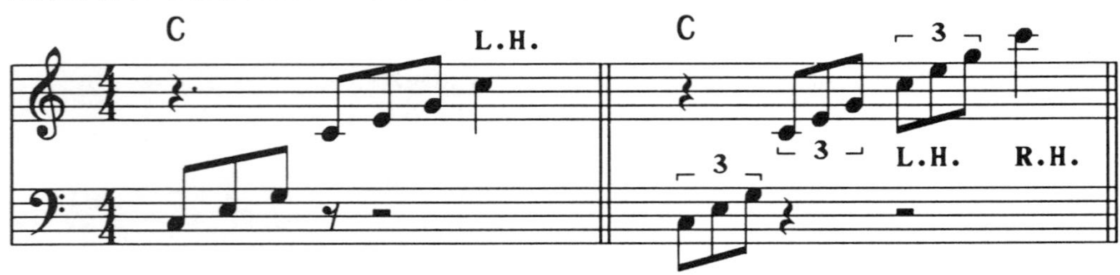

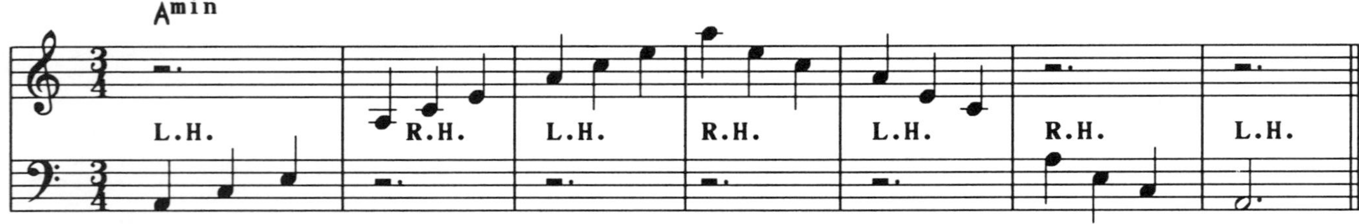

ADDED NOTES

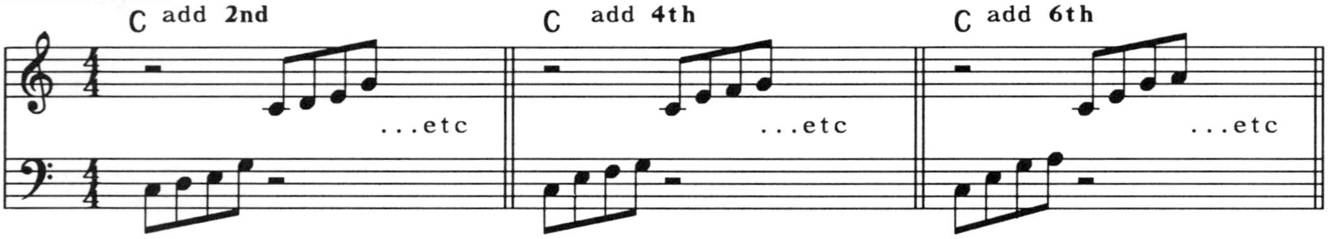

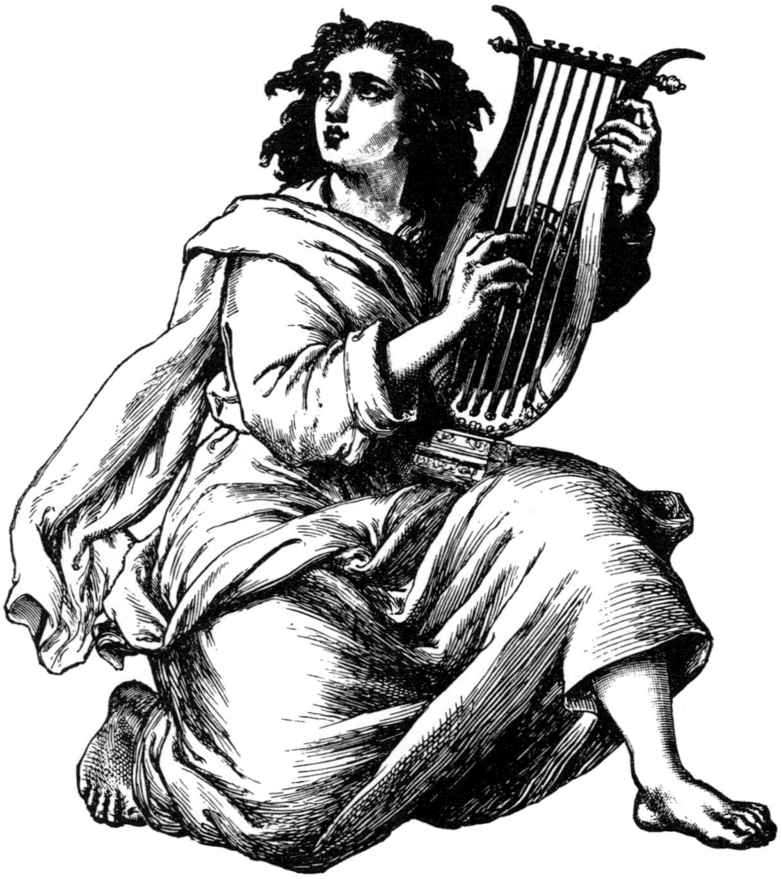

ABOUT THE SONGS AND MUSIC IN
EXPLORING THE FOLK HARP

SOME WORDS ABOUT THE SELECTIONS

The songs in this book have been selected to get you started and range in difficulty from beginning level to intermediate. Some are very familiar; we have tried to include examples of the most requested music. You will also find some pieces that are new to you. There are many more not covered here, including pop songs, show tunes, jazz, experimental electronic music, and on and on.

Many of the songs are folk, traditional or Renaissance tunes that have gone through many changes. It is not unusual to find a number of very different versions of the same song. We have chosen from what we like—often combining lyrics and/or music from several different sources. And by doing so we have continued the tradition, adding and changing a bit to the evolution of the songs.

If you find that our interpretation differs from one you know, by all means adapt the material. If we make no other point in this book, we hope that you come away from it feeling willing and able to make each song, each performance your own, not ours.

As so many harpers are also singers—or play for singers—we have included rather extensive lyrics. Many harp books leave them out altogether, or print them somewhere else in the book. That has frustrated us and so we have come to a compromise that will hopefully work for everyone: we have written the music as instrumental music with the words stuck between the staves instead of providing a special vocal staff (with two exceptions which are designed to show accompanying techniques). Singers will have to pick out their part from the top notes of the treble clef, but we think that is manageable.

We have divided the music into three sections: BALLADS AND FOLK SONGS, RENAISSANCE MUSIC, and SOME FAMOUS COMPOSERS. Within these sections, the music is in rough order of difficulty if the arrangements are played as written. You can start with whichever section interests you most.

HINTS ON STUDYING AND PLAYING THE MUSIC

Beginners don't have to start with the easier arrangements (like *Barbara Allen* or *Wayfaring Stranger*). You can take most any song in the book and pick out the melody by playing only the top notes in the top staffs. *Red River Valley* as written here is challenging, but if you read the melody and add some simple chords you can play it your own way. Practice going through the book and playing the melodies to songs you know. Try playing melodies with your left hand; this will help strengthen it for when you begin to play an accompaniment. Learn the chords and sing the melody while you play them (see WORKING WITH CHORD SYMBOLS). Chords open many doors musically. Do not neglect them.

Many of the arrangements can be simplified by playing only the top note of the top staff and the bottom note of the bottom staff. If it doesn't sound full enough, add some of the inner notes. And you can always use the chords to help you improvise.

Work with a friend or a group. You will motivate each other. One musician can play the treble part and the other the bass, or one can play the melody while the other chords. (See PLAYING DUETS AND IN ENSEMBLE, above)

A harpers circle.
Mallory, Janna, Ann Finnin, Colleen Vierra, Leslie Ann Snow, and True Thomas
(aka Robert Seutter).
Photo by Dave Finnin.

Encourage people to sing with your harp. It is usually not effective to double the melody with a singer, so you can either make up an accompaniment from the chords or play the bass part as written in the left hand and chord with the right. It is always OK to simplify. (See ACCOMPANYING WITH YOUR HARP above for further ideas.)

Do take at least a few pieces and learn them as they are written. This discipline is important. Analyze the pieces, work out the fingering, check out the chords, the rhythms and the structure until you not only know the notes but you can describe just how the whole thing is put together. More and more music teachers encourage this, and we support it wholeheartedly. This intensive study not only helps in learning the piece but it can get you out of a problem if you make a mistake when playing in public. If you know how the piece works you can often improvise around your mistake and get back on track. Most in the audience will never notice the error if you keep your composure and continue on, without pause. Never stop in the middle and start over when playing for an audience (except in the rare case where your goof is such a disaster that you can only laugh, throw up your hands with a shrug and start again from the top). Some musicians candidly admit that when they make a mistake they often play it that way again on the repeat so that the audience will think that was what was meant all along.

Make a point in your formal practice sessions to include a bit of improvisation, free-form music and other unstructured playing, even if—or especially if—this comes hard for you. This will add greatly to your musicality.

Don't get discouraged. You will find that your learning will come in spurts. If you don't seem to be making the progress you want with a certain piece, or improvising or chord reading, switch to something else. By all means, *keep playing*.   The more you play—play anything—the more you are practicing. And the more you practice anything, the better harper you will become. Keep your harp in tune, and make some kind of music with it regularly, even if only for five minutes at a time.

You may find that some of the arrangements will not fit on your harp. Most in the book assume that the harp has a low *G* and a compass of about four octaves. If your harp is smaller you will need to adapt. First, see if you can play the whole thing up an octave; you may want to do that anyway on some of the songs. If you run out of notes on the top then you will have to alter the left hand part. In many cases, notes which are too low can be individually moved up an octave. Or, using the chord symbols, you can invent your own arrangement. If your harp is *C* to *C*, you can often transpose the whole piece (see *Russian Folk Song* for an example).

If your harp is big and you have lots of extra unused strings, by all means go down the octave for some of those thrilling low notes! You can also play some sections up an octave for variety and add arpeggios for effect.

But enough reading about making music. Pick a song and get started.

Ballads and Folk Songs

Barbara Allen

English, Scottish, American

This is a very old song that has many versions. The famous 17th Century diarist Samuel Pepys mentions the actress Mrs Knipp singing it and, according to The Fireside Book of Folk Songs, *there have been collected something in the neighborhood of ninety-eight different variations in Virginia alone. And that was in 1947! The name of the hero is variously given as John Graeme, Johnny Armstrong, Jemmy Grove, William Green or omitted altogether. There is even a version where the plot is reversed and Barbara becomes "Barbry," a man. As we have combined several versions here, we have added one more link to the chain. Singers should consider pronouncing her second name "Ellen." There is a precedent and the rhymes seem to confirm it.*

This simple arrangement demonstrates the use of a root/fifth pattern in the left hand. It would work to continue it all the way to the end of the song, but some variations were added to make things a bit more interesting. This is a good song to experiment with. For instance, try playing full chords in the left hand, rolled if you wish (read them from the chord names above the treble staff). Singers should chord in accompaniment and not play the melody.

It is our opinion that fingering is best learned and most effective when it is worked out by the individual harper. It is not unusual for teachers to change the given fingerings in harp pieces to suit the student. For these reasons, we have omitted fingering for most of the songs in this book. Barbara Allen *has been fingered to give you a start; feel free to change it to suit your style.*

Review some of the exercises for hints on developing your personal fingering on these pieces. Remember to work out how you will be placing as well.

Barbara Allen

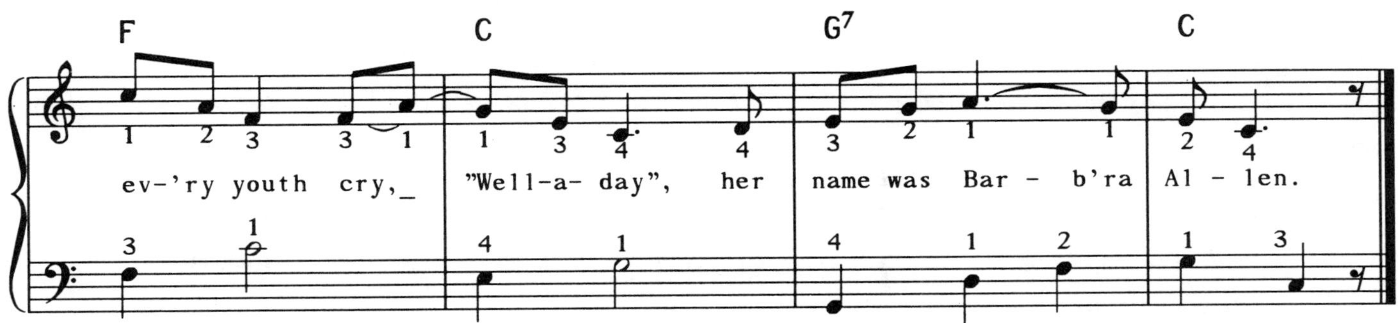

In Scarlet Town where I was born
There lived a fair maid dwellin',
Made ev'ry youth cry, "Well-a-day,"
Her name was Barb'ra Allen.

'Twas in the merry month of May,
When green buds they were swellin',
Young Jemmy Grove on his death-bed lay,
For the love of Barb'ra Allen.

He sent his men down through the town,
To the place where she was dwellin';
"O haste and come to my master dear,
If your name be Barb'ra Allen."

So slowly, slowly she came up
And slowly she came nigh him,
And all she said when there she came,
"Young man, I think you're dying!"

He turned his face unto the wall,
For death was with him dwellin',
"Adieu, adieu, my dear friends all,
Be kind to Barb'ra Allen."

And slowly, slowly raise she up,
And slowly, slowly left him,
And sighing said, she could not stay,
Since death of life had reft him.

As she was walking o'er the fields,
She heard the death bell knellin'
And ev'ry stroke did seem to say,
"Unworthy Barb'ra Allen."

When he was dead and laid in grave,
Her heart was struck with sorrow,
"O Mother, Mother, make my bed
For I shall die tomorrow."

"Farewell," she said, "ye virgins all,
And shun the fault I fell in,
Henceforth take warning by the fall
Of cruel Barb'ra Allen."

Wayfaring Stranger

American

This American lament was sung by the tired, the poor, the disenfranchised, the illiterate: folks who had come to this fresh new world in search of something—some dream of freedom, of a place where they could prosper spiritually as well as find a better life. The Revolution, which ushered in our new nation, gave added hope. These "religious radicals" cast aside the hymns of the old world and brought the folk song into the church meetings— brought the worship closer to the lives of the people. Out of this came the Shape Note and the Sacred Harp singing movements that continue to this day.

In Wayfaring Stranger *one hears some of the elements of the blues. It, like the American adaptations of* Amazing Grace, *echoes the roots and hearts of the people. This song has traveled by oral tradition down through the years, all over the country; again, we have combined several versions. It is pitched in a low key for the sake of those contralto/baritones who rarely find anything printed in a singable key.*

The left hand in Wayfaring Stranger *takes the root/fifth bass pattern to the logical continuation of adding the third note of the chord, spelling it out. In the second-to-last measure the intervals of parallel sixths (inverted thirds) suggests the underlying chords with only two notes.*

The large **C**s *on the bass and treble staves after the clefs at the beginning of the song stand for Common, or 4/4 time. The arch with the dot inside over the last note in the bass is called a **fermata** and means that the note should be held longer than is indicated by the note's value.*

Wayfaring Stranger

Wayfaring Stranger

I'm just a poor wayfaring stranger
A-traveling through this world of woe;
But there's no sickness, toil or danger
In that bright world to which I go.
I'm going home to see my father,
I'm going there no more to roam;
I'm just a-going over Jordan,
I'm just a-going over home.

I know dark clouds will gather 'round me.
I know my way is rough and steep,
But beauteous fields lie just beyond me
Where souls redeemed their vigil keep.
I'm going there to meet my mother,
She said she'd meet me when I come;
I'm only going over Jordan,
I'm only going over home.

I want to wear a crown of glory
When I get home to that bright land;
I want to shout salvation's story,
In concert with that bloodwashed band.
I'm going there to meet my Savior,
To sing his praise forever more;
I'm only going over Jordan,
I'm only going over home.

Shalom Chaverim

Israeli

This traditional melody is in Hebrew and is sometimes played as a round.

Shalom Chaverim *is in one sharp—what we have been calling the G tuning, although it is actually in the key of E minor, the relative minor of G. If you have sharping levers on your harp, sharp the F levers. If you do not have levers, tune your Fs to F♯. You may have discovered that if you are playing the song as it is written, you only have to tune the notes that you will be playing. It is, however, a good idea to get used to changing all the notes in a new key because as you start to improvise (even if only by repeating the song up an octave) you will find you will be playing those notes.*

The first melody note of this song is easier to play with the left hand. This allows you to place the fingers of both hands on the strings before you begin. Note that we are still spelling out chords in the accompaniment but that they are sometimes in open (spread) and inverted positions.

Tune your F's to F♯ or
flip your F sharping
levers.

The Great Silkie of Sule Skerry

Traditional Scottish

This otherworldly Scottish ballad tells of a woman who is seduced by the Great Silkie of Sule Skerry. Sule Skerry is a small island off the northern coast of Scotland. A Silkie is an enchanted creature who, though a seal in the sea, comes as a man to land. She bears him a baby and suckles it for seven years until the Silkie comes for it, offering only a nursing fee. He vows to raise the child in the sea although he predicts that she will find a human husband who will try to slay both the Silkie and his son—and in many versions this does, indeed, come to pass. We have given enough lyrics to suggest the story, but if you search you will discover more. This song is especially effective when sung hauntingly.

The Great Silkie is in the Mixolydian mode which, when tuned in C, starts on G. The difference between this mode and the G major scale is that the F is not sharped.

The Great Silkie

GLOSSARY:

APO: upon

AUGHT A BAINRN: had a child

BAIRNY: baby

FAEM: foam

FRAE: from

GIE: give

GOUD: gold

GRUMLEY: sullen, savage

HET: hot

KEN: know

LAN: land

LILLY WEAN: lovely child

MITHER: mother

NOURRIS: nurse

PAT: put

SALL: shall

SCHOT, SCHOOTS: shot, shoots

SIMMER: summer

SIN: sun

STANE: stone

STAPS: lives

TAEN: taken

The Great Silkie

An earthly mither sits and sings
And, aye, she sings, "Ba lilly wean.
Little ken I my bairny's father,
Far less the land that he staps in."

Then in steps he to her bed feet,
And a grumley guest I'm sure was he;
Saying, "Here I am, thy bairny's father,
Although I be na' comely.

"I am a man apo the lan,
And I am a Silkie in the sea,
And when I'm far and far frae lan,
Ma dwelling is in Sule Skerry."

"It was na' weel," quo' the maiden fair,
"It was na' weel," indeed quo' she,
"That the Great Silkie of Sule Skerry,
Suld hae come and aught a bairn ta me."

Then he has taen a purse of goud,
And he has pat it on her knee,
Saying, "Gie to me my little young son,
An' tak thee up thy nourris fee.

"An' it sall come to pass on a simmer's day
When the sin shines het on evera stane
That I will tak my little young son
An' teach him how to swim the faem.

"And ye sall marry a proud gunner
An' aye a gunner good is he
An' the very first schot that ere he schoots
Will be at thy young son an' me."

"Alas, alas," the mither cried,
"This weary fate's been laid for me."
And then she said, and then she said,
"I'll bury me in Sule Skerry."

Believe Me, If All Those Endearing Young Charms

Irish

by Thomas Moore, 1779-1852

This beautiful song was written by Irish poet Thomas Moore to affirm his love for his wife. When she contracted a disfiguring skin disease, she feared he would no longer care for her. This is his eloquent answer.

The songs of Thomas Moore were widely sung in the Victorian Age, and they are still beloved today. Charles Dickens enjoyed entertaining his friends and family by singing Moore's songs.

Play it freely and smoothly in the romantic tradition of the time. Put special emphasis on the descending 10ths (that is 3rds plus an octave) under the words "charms which I gaze," "arms like- fair-(y)," etc. This accentuates the romantic style.

Believe Me, If All Those Endearing Young Charms

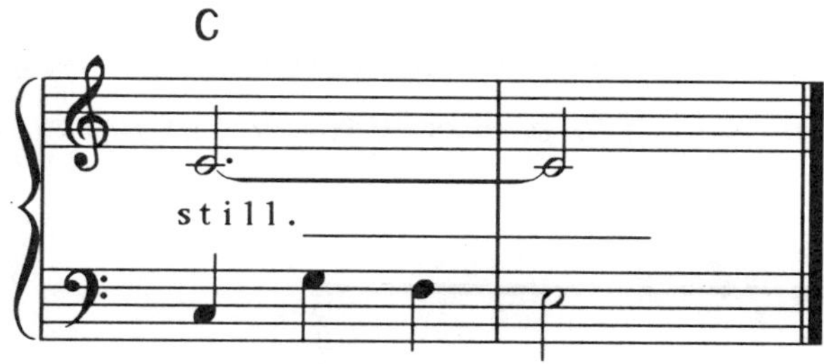

Believe me, if all those endearing young charms
Which I gaze on so fondly today,
Were to change by tomorrow, and fleet in my arms
Like fairy gifts fading away;
Thou wouldst still be adored
As this moment thou art,
Let thy loveliness fade as it will.
And around the dear ruin each wish of my heart
Would entwine itself verdantly still.

It is not while beauty and youth are thine own,
And thy cheeks unprofaned by a tear,
That the fervour and faith of a soul can be known,
To which time will but make thee more dear.
No, the heart that has truly loved never forgets,
But as truly loves on to the close,
As the sun-flower turns on her god, when he sets,
The same look which she turned when he rose.

Raggle-Taggle Gypsies-O

An Irish version

This ballad is popular in Ireland, England and America but may well be of Scottish origin. It is claimed that the tale is a true one, perhaps dating back before 1624 when the Gypsies were banished from Scotland. It tells of a new bride who is bewitched by the mystery of the Gypsies. These are the lyrics we sing, but many other variations in words and melody may be found.

Raggle-Taggle (or Wraggle-Taggle) Gypsies-O can be played ethereally, but one also hears it in a lively up-tempo. If you want to play it fast, simplify the left hand, perhaps with a root/fifth pattern. If you, like us, are more taken with the tale it tells, sing and play it flowingly.

Ian Abramovitch, Jon Lackey and Janna.
Photo by Mallory.

Raggle-Taggle Gypsies-O

Raise your F's
to F♯.

Irish

Arr. J. McCall Geller

Raggle-Taggle Gypsies-O

A fair lady sat in a chamber alone
And under the moon sang three Gypsies-O.
One sang high and the other sang low,
And the other sang, "Bonny, bonny Biscayo."
   (or: "Bonny Bay of Biscay-O.")

They sang so sweet, they sang so shrill
That fast her tears began to flow,
And she laid down her silken gown,
Her golden combs and all her show.

It was late that night when her lord came home
Enquiring for his lady-O.
The servants said on every hand,
"She's gone with the raggle-taggle Gypsies-O."

"O, saddle for me my milk white steed,
Go fetch me my pony-O,
That I may ride to seek my bride,
Who is gone with the raggle-taggle Gypsies-O."

O, he rode high and he rode low,
He rode through the woods and copses-O,
Until he came to a wide open field,
And there he spied his lady-O.

"O, what made you leave your house and land?
What made you leave your treasure-O?
What made you leave your new-wedded lord,
To be off with the raggle-taggle Gypsies-O?"

"O, what care I for my house and land?
What care I for treasure-O?
What care I for my new-wedded lord?
I'm off with the raggle-taggle Gypsies-O!"

"Last night I slept in a goosefeather bed
With the sheet turned down so bravely-O,
But tonight I shall sleep in a cold open field,
Along with the raggle-taggle Gypsies-O!"
   (or: In the arms of a raggle-taggle Gypsy-O!")

Ash Grove

Welsh

This popular ballad is sung all over the English-speaking world. There are several versions of the lyrics; these are the words Mallory sings.

Like Raggle-Taggle, *there is a temptation to play this air as a fairly fast instrumental. There are varying opinions as to how appropriate that might be. Mallory argues that it is a poignant poem; Janna agrees, but likes the contagiously toe-tapping tune. We've been known to do it both ways—but not in the same set!*

At the end of the middle section ("joy of my *heart") you'll find a C$\sharp$ in parenthesis. This is the more usual melody note. You have the option of reaching up and flipping the lever for the accidental or taking the higher note, thus slightly altering the melody. Either way is fine and will not conflict with anyone singing or playing along.*

Ash Grove *is given here in the key of G major which has one sharp.*

Ash Grove

Raise F's to F#

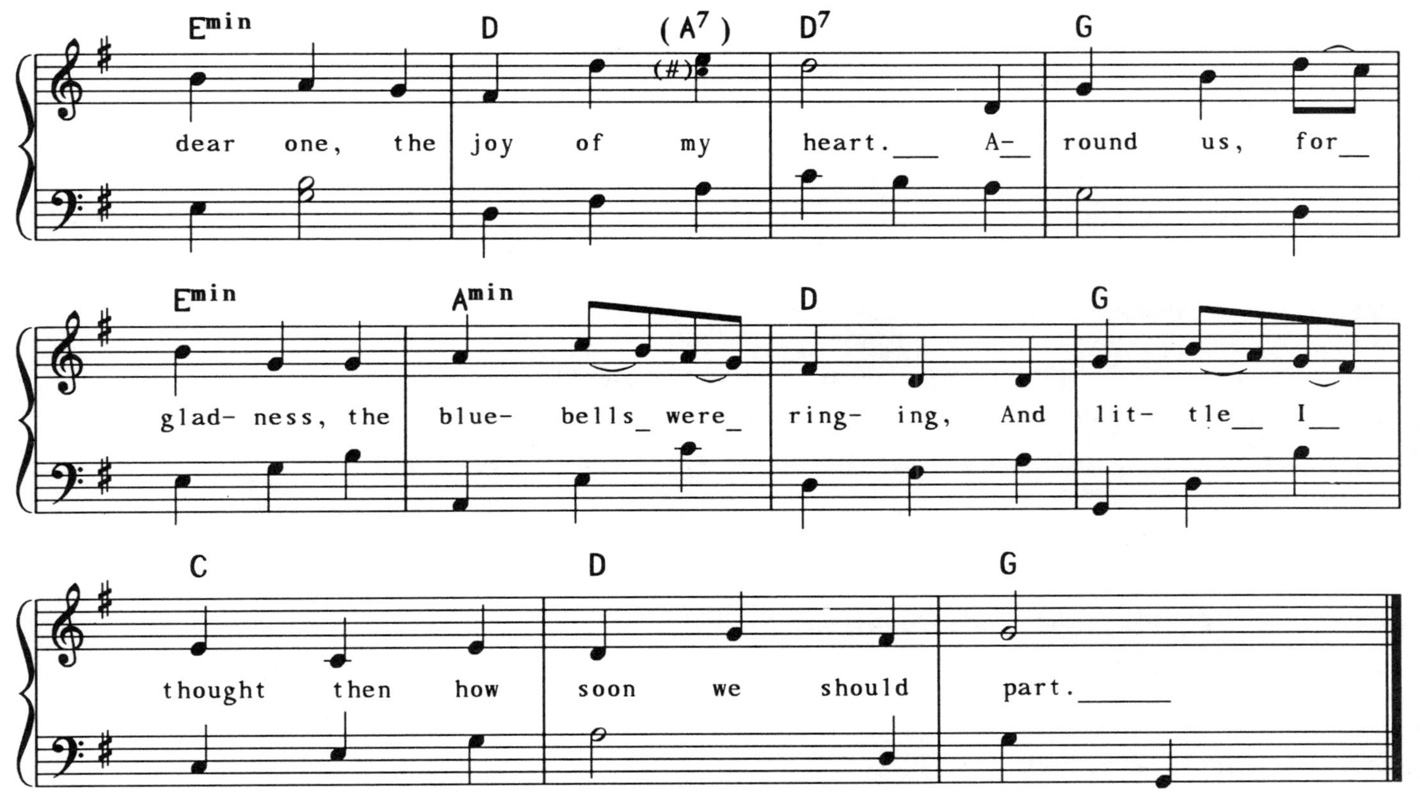

Third verse adapted by Mallory Geller

Down yonder green valley, where streamlets meander,
When twilight is fading I pensively rove.
Or at the bright noontide, in solitude wander
Amid the dark shades of the lonely Ash Grove.
'Twas there, while the blackbird was joyfully singing,
I first met my dear one, the joy of my heart.
Around us, for gladness, the bluebells were ringing,
And little I thought then how soon we should part.

Still glows the bright sunshine o'er valley and mountain;
Still warbles the blackbird his note from the tree;
Still trembles the moonbeam on streamlet and fountain—
But what are the beauties of nature to me?
With sorrow, deep sorrow, my bosom is laden;
All day I go mourning in search of my love.
Ye echoes—Oh, tell me: Where is my sweet loved one?
She sleeps 'neath the green grass down by the Ash Grove.

The Ash Grove, how graceful, how plainly 'tis speaking,
The harp through it playing steals soft on my ear.
I yearn to rekindle the past and its brightness,
The dear one I mourn for again greets me here.
Toward every dark shadow, replete with her presence,
Each step wakes a mem'ry, as slowly I roam.
With soft whispers laden, its leaves rustle o'er me;
The Ash Grove forever and always my home.

Amazing Grace

English/American, 18th Century

John Newton was a clergyman in 18th Century England when he wrote these famous words. Newton had been a slave trader but, when he found God, he turned his energies to the Church. Amazing Grace has become more than a hymn. It is a folk anthem, sung in may styles and heard from rural congregations to bagpipe bands to the concert stage. It has even been the subject of a PBS documentary.

The arrangement here gives the bare bones of the melody and harmony in full size notes. Since coming to America, however, both are frequently expanded and ornamented. The small notes give a suggestion of some of the folk ornaments that are often used, but there are many others. Try playing the melody alone and then adding variations of your own (sing it first if you are having a problem finding the notes). Now add the chords and the bass accompaniment.

Three note chords for the right hand are introduced with this hymn (the melody is the top note). Chords of three notes or more are usually rolled, a fast arpeggio from the bottom note up. Practice moving up and down the scale playing rolled triads in both root position and in inversions. Placing the fingers properly makes this much easier. (See ARPEGGIOS in Part Four)

Amazing Grace

Amazing grace, how sweet the sound
That saved a wretch like me.
I once was lost, but now am found,
Was blind, but now I see.

'Twas grace that taught my heart to fear,
And grace my fears relieved;
How precious did that grace appear
The hour I first believed.

Thro' many dangers, toils and snares,
I have already come;
'Tis grace hath Bro't me safe thus far,
And grace will lead me home.

Cielito Lindo

Mexican
Music by C. Fernandez
Lyrics to Version One by Quirino Mendoza

Cielito Lindo means "Pretty Sky." We discovered two sets of lyrics from two different sources which, we are told by a Spanish-speaking friend, tell quite different stories. The first one, given on the music, suggests that the bird who leaves his first nest should not cry if he returns and finds it occupied. He should, instead, sing, because singing hearts are happy.

The second version hints of romance from a pair of black eyes secretively coming down from the "brown mountain." Sounds tantalizing! Both have a chorus of "Ay, ay, ay, ay, sing and don't cry because singing hearts— pretty sky—are happy." We have given you both versions—you can sing them both or take your pick.

Play the music lightly and liltingly. You may find it easier at first to play the right hand by itself. When you are sure you know the melody, you can hum it while you play the left hand. If you are singing, or playing for someone who is singing, try playing the bass in the left hand as written and chords from the symbols in the right hand. More advanced players can experiment with filling in the chords or playing parts of it in thirds (see La Paloma).

Cielito Lindo

"Pretty Sky"

Music by C. Fernandez

Words of Version One by Quirino Mendoza

Pájaro que abandona su primer nido, su primer nido

Si lo encuentra ocupado, cielito lindo muy merecido.

Ay, Ay, Ay, Ay! canta y no llores,

Por que cantando se alegran, cielito lindo, los corazones.

Version Two:

De la sierra morena, cielito lindo, vienen bajando

Un par de ojitos negros, cielito lindo, de contrabando.

Ay, Ay, Ay, Ay! canta y no llores,

Por que cantando se alegran, cielito lindo, los corazones.

Scarborough Fair

Traditional English

Just how old this song is has not been determined to our knowledge, but it has been popular in many incarnations for a long time. It seems to us that the singer has a lot to ask of his true love, let alone the messenger who is actually going to the fair! But it is a lovely song and one we enjoy performing.

Notice how the three note chords continue to ring even though they are notated as quarter notes. That is intentional here, as it makes the music more readable. The ringing sound is part of the unique "harp" quality. As you experiment with your playing, you will want to try damping the strings (that is, stopping their vibration) for special effects, but here you should let them sound.

Notice, also, that the thumb slides downward from the B to the A going from the fifth to the sixth bar in the bass. It is very common to use the thumb in this manner. You will find that as you begin to play more chords in the right hand, the thumb will play more and more of the melody. Use it this way in the third measure from the end ("was__").

This version is a variant, older, we understand, than the melody that Simon and Garfunkel made so popular. If you want to play that other version, try picking it out on your harp. Some hints: It is in the Dorian mode (in the C tuning, the scale starts on D). You can play it with three chords: Dmin, C and F. The first three notes are D, D, A, and the first chord is a Dmin. Now you're on your own.

Scarborough Fair

English

Arr. J. Mc Call Geller

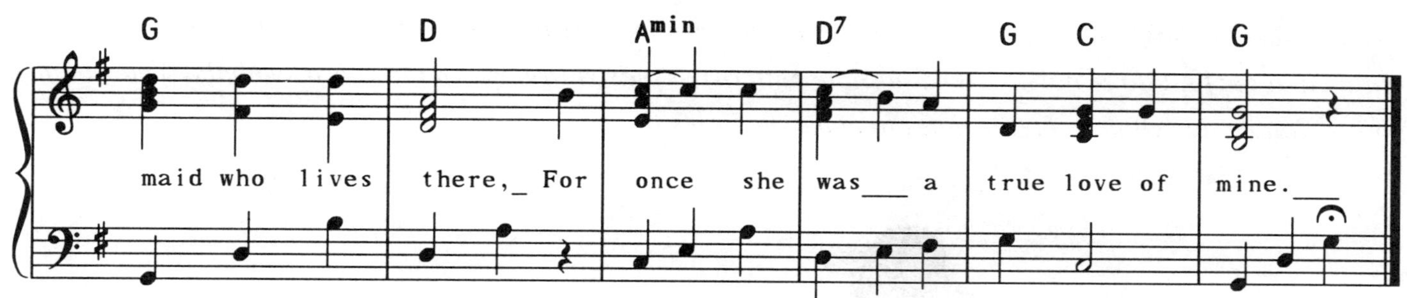

Oh, are you going to Scarb'ro Fair?
Savory, sage, rosemary and thyme.
Remember me to a maid who lives there,
For once she was a true love of mine.

And tell her to make me a cambric shirt,
Savory, sage, rosemary and thyme,
Without any seam or needle work,
And then she shall be a true love of mine.

And tell her to wash it in yonder well,
Savory, sage, rosemary and thyme,
Where no water sprung, nor a drop of rain fell,
And then she shall be a true love of mine.

Tell her to dry it on yonder thorn,
Savory, sage, rosemary and thyme,
Which never bore blossom since Adam was born,
And then she shall be a true love of mine.

Oh, will you find me an acre of land,
Savory, sage, rosemary and thyme,
Between the sea foam and the white sea sand?
Or never be a true love of mine.

(Optional: Repeat Verse One)

I Know Where I'm Going

Irish

The Lichtbob's Lassie

Scottish

The song I Know Where I'm Going, *is well known as a sweet and haunting Irish ballad. Less well known is the lusty Scottish version,* The Lichtbob's Lassie, *which is the tale of a lassie who fancied Lichtbobs, soldiers of the Light Brigade.*

The arrangement given here is designed to demonstrate an arpeggiated (broken) chord pattern that works especially well on the harp. Place your fingers on the entire chord before playing and you'll find you'll play more easily and with more accuracy. Practice this pattern with other chord progressions and with both hands; you'll find many uses for it. Do not be daunted by the 16th notes; they are only as fast as you choose to play them. This is a slow song (at least in version one) and the tempo is moderate. Although 2/4 is indicated (two beats a measure, each a quarter note) it may feel better to you to give each measure four beats an eighth note long.

The squiggles beside the chord at the end indicates that it is to be arpeggiated. The fermata tells you to hold it out and let it ring.

If you choose to sing the Scots version, the florid pattern may be inappropriate; you can play block chords (outlined in the first three notes of the four note pattern) or play entirely from the chord symbols. You will also have to double up syllables on the notes to make the lyrics fit.

I Know Where I'm Going

Raise your F's to F♯s.

(The Lichtbob's Lassie)

Irish and Scottish

Arr. J. McCall Geller

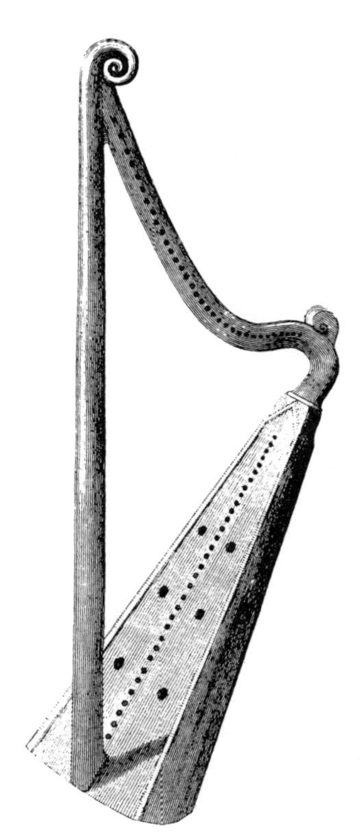

I Know Where I'm Going

I know where I'm going
And I know who's going with me.
I know who I love,
But the Dear knows who I'll marry.

Some say he's dark,
Some say he's bonny,
But the fairest of them all
Is my handsome, winsome Johnny.

I have stockings of silk,
Shoes of fine green leather,
Combs to bind my hair,
And a ring for every finger.

Feather beds are soft,
And painted rooms are bonny,
But I would leave them all
To go with my love Johnny.

I know where I'm going
And I know who's going with me.
I know who I love,
But the Dear knows who I'll marry.

The Lichtbob's Lassie

Air: *I Know Where I'm Going*

First fin I cam' tae the toon,
They ca'd me young and bonnie;
Noo they've changed my name,
Ca'd me the Lichtbob's honey.

First fin I cam' tae the toon,
They ca'd me proud an' saucy;
Noo they've changed my name,
Ca'd me the Lichtbob's lassie.

I'll dye my petticoats red,
And face them wi' the yellow;
I'll tell the dyster lad
That the Lichtbobs I'm tae follow.

Feather beds are saft,
Painted rooms are bonnie;
I will leave them a',
An' jog awa' wi' Johnnie.

Oh, my back's been sair,
Shearin' Craigie's corn;
I winna see him the nicht,
But I'll see him the morn.

Oh for Saterday nicht,
Syne I'll see my dearie,
He'll come whistlin' in,
Fan I am tired an' weary.

Danny Boy

Londonderry Air
Irish

This is the most requested song since we started playing harps (with the possible exception of Green Sleeves*). The tune is much older than the* Danny Boy *lyrics.* Would I Were Erin's Apple Blossom O'er You *by Alfred Perceval Graves is said to be the first known set of words.* My Gentle Harp *by Thomas Moore is sometimes sung to this tune, but the fit is awkward.*

This arrangement goes down to a low F, a note not found on some folk harps. If you do not have it, play the note in parentheses or play the whole thing up an octave.

If you are singing, you should simply chord in accompaniment. You can even leave out some of the less important ones (your ear will tell you what they are). It is difficult enough to sing well without having to worry about the arrangement! With this song, simple is better—it is easy to overdo the pathos.

Rit. *is short for ritard, a gradual slowing of the tempo.*

Danny Boy

Londonderry Air

Arr. J. McCall Geller

Note: Do not play notes in parentheses ( ) unless your harp does not have a low F.

Danny Boy

Oh Danny Boy, the pipes, the pipes are callin'
From glen to glen, and down the mountainside.
The summer's gone, and all the roses fallin';
'Tis you, 'tis you must go and I must bide.
But come ye back when summer's in the meadow,
Or when the valley's hushed and white with snow,
'Tis I'll be here in sunshine or in shadow,
Oh Danny Boy, oh Danny boy I love you so.

And when ye come and all the flowers are dying,
If I am dead, as dead I well may be.
You'll come and find the place where I am lying,
And kneel and say an Ave there for me.
And I shall hear tho' soft you tread above me,
And all my grave will warmer, sweeter be
If you will bend and tell me that you love me,
Then I shall sleep in peace until you come to me.

Jock o'Hazeldean

Traditional Scottish

This is one of many ballads where the heroine shuns a life of leisure for the sake of love. It is a variant of Johnny of Hazelgreen *and is of interest because Sir Walter Scott, not knowing the rest of the original, wrote his own version of the tale. We have discovered two more verses which we have added. Scott's version consisted of the first (old) verse and the three he wrote.*

Have you ever noticed how the rhythm and melody of the old Scots ballads seem to catch the lilt of their speech? The sixteenth notes in this song seem to lean into the note they precede and should be played as if they are attached to the note like a grace note. If you are having problems with the rhythms, play it evenly as eighth notes until you get the feel of the tune. Then add the dotted notes for that wonderful Scottish lilt.

If the rhythm of this, or any song, eludes you, try tapping it out. In this case, tap with your toe a steady beat four beats per measure (1 and 2 and, etc) to get the rhythm. The sixteenth notes fall between those beats. Tap out the melody with your right hand.

Jock O'Hazeldean

Jock O'Hazeldean

Verses marked with * are by Sir Walter Scott

"Why weepè by the tide, lassie, why weepè by the tide?
I'll wed ye tae my youngest son and ye sall be his bryde.
And ye sall be his bryde, lassie,
Sae comely tae be seen."
But aye she loot the tears doon fa' for Jock o'Hazeldean.

"O, what na man is Hazeldean? I pray ye tell tae me."
Said she, "There's na a finer man in a' the soothe countree;
His step is first in peaceful ha',
His sword in battle keen."
And aye she loot the tears doon fa' for Jock o'Hazeldean.

*"Now let this wilfu' grief be done, and dry that cheek so pale,
Young Frank is Chief of Errington, and Lord of Langley-Dale.
His step is first in peaceful ha',
His sword in battle keen:"
But aye she loot the tears doon fa' for Jock o'Hazeldean.

*"A chain of gold ye shall not lack, nor braid to bind your hair;
Nor mettl'd hound, nor manag'd hawk, nor palfrey fresh and fair;
And you, the foremost o' them a',
Shall ride our forest Queen:"
But aye she loot the tears doon fa' for Jock o'Hazeldean.

The kirk was decked at Morning-tide, an' Dame an' knight were there;
Wi' armour bright an' managed hawk
An' palfrey fresh an' fair;
They sought her baith by bower an' ha',
The ladye wasna seen—
She's o'er the borders an' awa' wi' Jock o'Hazeldean!

Alternate final verse:

*The kirk was deck'd at Morning-tide, the tapers glimmer'd fair;
The priest and bridegroom wait the bride, and Dame and Knight are there.
They sought her both by bower and ha',
The ladye was na seen!
She's o'er the borders, an' awa' wi' Jock o'Hazeldean.

Red River Valley

American, 19th Century

This famous tune of the Old West originated with a popular song, In the Bright Mohawk Valley, *from New York, yet! But when the folks of the South and the West heard it, they made it theirs, cutting away, as John A. and Alan Lomax said in their book,* Folk Song USA, *"most of the original pretentiousness from both the melody and the lyrics." Indeed, it's hard to imagine a more representative cowboy song: loose, easy and engaging. Those of us who have dismissed it as a song suitable "merely" for school and campfire should do well to take another look (and, in the process, discover that music 'round a campfire with a folk harp can be most enchanting indeed!).*

Our first venture into cowboy music on the harp came with an improvised version of Ghost Riders in the Sky, *played impishly after a not-too-serious request from the audience. Just for fun, try picking out* Home on the Range, On Top of Old Smokey *and other old western favorites.*

The arrangement given here is challenging. The original intention was to do something simple, but as Janna experimented with the tune on her harp, she liked the rich sounds of full chords with the easy-going melody. There are passing chords—not part of the basic structure of the original—inserted to enrich the harmonies. These, when indicated in chord notation, are in parenthesis. You can, of course, choose to play the melody and accompany yourself with a simple left hand based on the chord symbols.

The words and melody given here are, once again, combined from more than one source. If you remember it differently, suit your preference.

Janna playing a floor harp.
Photo by Mallory.

Red River Valley

From this valley they say you are going,
We will miss your bright eyes and sweet smile,
For they say you are taking the sunshine,
That brightens our pathway a while.

CHORUS:
Come and sit by my side if you love me,
Do not hasten to bid me adieu.
But remember the Red River Valley,
 And the cowboy who (girl who has) loved you so true.

I've been thinking a long time, my darling,
Of the sweet words you never would say.
Now, alas, must my fond hopes all vanish?
For they say you are going away.
CHORUS

Do you think of the valley you're leaving?
O how lonely and how dreary it will be.
Do you think of the kind hearts you're breaking?
And the pain you are causing to me?
CHORUS

They will bury me where you have wandered,
Near the hills where the daffodils grow,
When you're gone from the Red River Valley,
For I can't live without you, I know.
CHORUS

Annie Laurie

Scottish

Poem by William Douglas, circa 1685

Back in 1685 William Douglas of Fingland, Scotland proposed to the daughter of the First Baronet of Maxwellton and, as in all good romances, the beautiful Annie Laurie said yes. And they lived happily ever after—at least in song. History does not record if he did have to lay himself "doon and dee" for her. The melody was set later and it became a big hit with the British soldiers in the Crimean War.

Annie Laurie was one of the first songs we picked out on the harp. Bravely we ventured out in public with our duet: Mallory played the melody (two fingered) while Janna chorded an accompaniment. As unadorned as it was, people enjoyed it, which goes to support our feeling that even the simplest music is well received on the harp. We still play it much the same way, as it suits the song which could be over-sentimentalized all too easily.

In this version, note that the thirds of the D7 and E7 chords have been omitted as those notes are sharped and not easily available. Another alternative in arranging this tune would be to substitute chords that are available: Amin works in the third measure instead of the D7. And the words "ne'er forgot will be" can be harmonized in the same way as "me her promise true." Instead of the E7 in the last line, you can try G7. There are many options when adapting harp music.

As with most of the songs in this book, the arrangement can be simplified. You can, if you wish, skip the right hand chords and just play the melody. Or drop the bottom note on the four note chords. They are there because four fingered chords are especially effective on the harp.

Try some four note chord exercises: Practice any chord progression (use the songs in this book for starters), playing four notes for each chord. When the chord has only three notes, duplicate the top note an octave down.

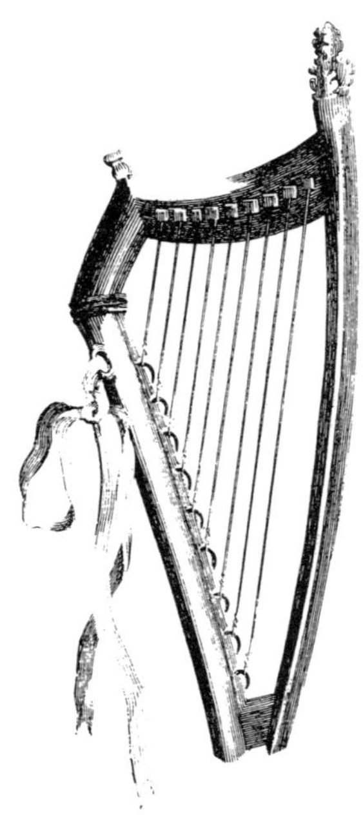

Annie Laurie

Annie Laurie

Poem by William Douglas

Maxwellton's braes are bonnie,
Where early fa's the dew;
And it's there that Annie Laurie
Gave me her promise true.
Gave me her promise true,
Which ne'er forgot will be.
And for bonnie Annie Laurie
I'd lay me doon and dee.

Her brow is like the snawdrift,
Her throat is like the swan.
Her face it is the fairest
That e'er the sun shone on.
That e'er the sun shone on,
And dark blue is her e'e,
And for bonnie Annie Laurie
I'd lay me doon and dee.

Like dew on the gowan lying,
Is the fa' o' her fairy feet,
And like winds in summer sighing
Her voice is low and sweet.
Her voice is low and sweet,
And she's a' the world to me,
And for bonnie Annie Laurie
I'd lay me doon and dee.

La Paloma

"The Dove"
Cuban

In this beautiful Cuban love song a young man sings of how he imagines it will be wed to his pretty sweetheart. He pleads with her and tells her that if a dove comes to her window, she should treat it as himself, tell it of love and bring flowers.

For the harper not used to this graceful latin rhythm, the juxtaposition of three beats with two beats may prove a bit difficult at first. For some reason, most of us can easily manage eighth note triplets but find quarter note triplets more challenging. But they are really the same thing. Although the speed of this piece is not fast, it should be felt in two beats per measure. Tap a slow two beat with your foot and practice playing three beats followed by two beats, back and forth. Then tap the rhythm of the melody of the song. There is no place in this arrangement where you are required to play two beats against three. However, the adventuresome may want to continue the left hand pattern (two beats) from the first measure into other parts of the song. Please don't be daunted by the rhythms! As long as you keep a steady tempo, some "mistakes" in the rhythm will not ruin the song. But do try to get them; it's worth it.

The thirds can be played with the first and second finger "pinching" them, but that is jerky and awkward in some sections. When you have a skip of a third as in the last four notes in the treble part in the third full measure, it will play more smoothly if you place over the whole triad and finger the descending thirds 1,2 then 2,3 (or 4, shown both ways on the music). As always, work out the fingering that suits you best, or, if you wish, you can simplify the arrangement and omit some or all of the thirds until you are up to playing them.

An effect that can be interesting with the bass figure in measure one is to damp the notes rhythmically after you play them. Don't pull your fingers away from the strings in the usual manner but immediately replace them on the strings. This gives a rather percussive sound that fits well with the music.

La Paloma

The Dove

108

Cuando salí de la Havana, valgame Dios!
Nadie me ha visto salir si no fuí yo
Y una linda Gauchinangas alla voy yo
Que se vino tras de mi que sí señor.

    Si a tu ventana llega una paloma
    Tratala con carino que es mi persona.
    Cuéntale tus amores bien de mi vida
    Coronala de flores que es cosa mía.

    Ay! chinita que si. Ay! que dame tu amor
    Ay! que vente conmigo chinita a donde vivo yo.
    Ay! chinita que si. Ay que dame tu amor
    Ay! que vente conmigo chinita a donde vivo yo.

El dia que nos casemos valgame Dios!
En la semana hay que ir me hace reir,
Desde la Iglesia juntitos que sí señor
Nos iremos a dormir alla voy yo.

    Si a tu ventana—etc.

Cuando el curita nos eche la bendición
En la Iglesia Catedral alla voy yo,
Yo te daré la manita con mucho amor
Y el cura dos hisopazos que sí señor.

    Si a tu ventana—etc.

Auld Lang Syne

"The Good Old Times"
Scottish

This old song has become a cliché for a rowdy New Year's Eve. We have taken a second look at the tune and feel it deserves something better than the traditional drunken wail. We play it, like The Parting Glass, *at the close of a warm, special get-together.*

The poet Robert Burns collected old songs, a tradition that continues to this day, thankfully for the survival of folk and regional music. The tune is pentatonic, and was sung to Burns by a very old man. Burns took it to the British Museum, and thus it was preserved. (Burns could not resist writing two verses of his own—verses 2 and 3—to stand beside the much older stanzas.)

This is a good song on which to experiment with your own arrangements. Try it very simple, perhaps with bagpipe drone-like open fifths in the bass (try using only the first chord of a measure, or the most basic chords—the Amin chords often substitute here for a D chord). Or try putting the melody up an octave from the bass and using full four note chords. Try different harmonies.

Another possible way of doing this song is to play up the Scottish lyrics and play it with more gusto.

Auld Lang Syne
"The Good Old Times"

Raise your F's to F#s.

Scottish
Collected by Robert Burns

Arr. J. McCall Geller

Auld Lang Syne

Collected by Robert Burns
Verses 2 and 3 (*) by R. Burns, others older

Should auld acquaintance be forgot and never brought to mind?
Should auld acquaintance be forgot and days of auld lang syne?
   For auld lang syne, my dear, for auld lang syne,
   We'll tak' a cup o' kindness, yet, for auld lang syne.

* We twa ha'e run aboot the braes and pu'd the gowans fine,
We've wander'd mony a weary foot, sin' auld lang syne.
   Sin' auld lang syne, my dear, sin' auld lang syne,
   We've wander'd mony a weary foot, sin' auld lang syne.

* We twa ha'e sported i' the burn, from morning sun till dine,
But seas between us braid ha'e roar'd sin' auld lang syne.
   Sin' auld lang syne, my dear, sin' auld lang syne,
   But seas between us braid ha'e roar'd sin' auld lang syne.

And surely ye'll be your pint-stowp! and surely I'll be mine!
And we'll tak' a cup o' kindness, yet, for auld lang syne.
   For auld lang syne, my dear, for auld lang syne,
   We'll tak' a cup o' kindness, yet, for auld lang syne.

And here's a hand, my trusty frien', and gie's a hand o' thine;
We'll tak' a cup o' kindness, yet, for auld lang syne.
   For auld lang syne, my dear, for auld lang syne,
   We'll tak' a cup o' kindness, yet, for auld lang syne.

And there's a hand, my trusty frien' and gie's a hand o' thine!
And we'll tak' a right gude-willy waught, for auld lang syne.
   For auld lang syne, my dear, for auld lang syne,
   We'll tak' a right gude-willy waught, for auld lang syne.

The Parting Glass
Irish

The Parting Glass is another song for the end of a special evening, when everyone is mellow and warm with good company and good Irish grog. Its strange, compelling beauty echoes on after the last draught is downed and the final note dies away.

If you do not already know this song, you may have some difficulty with the changing meter from 6/8 to 4/8, that is a pattern of three beat rhythmic sections alternating with two beat sections. 6/8 is really counted in two groups of three: 1, 2, 3, 4, 5, 6. 4/8 consists of two groups of two beats: 1, 2, 3, 4. Each 8th note gets one beat. If you count it beat by beat you'll find it easier.

But The Parting Glass is not meant to be played or sung in strict rhythm. The fermatas sprinkled through the music indicate those notes are to be drawn out, extended. Make it sound free and easy—the rhythm of the music almost conversational. Relax with it and the meter will fall in place.

The Parting Glass

The Parting Glass

Oh, all the money that e're I spent,
I spent it in good company,
And all the harm that e're I've done,
Alas it was to none but me.
And all I've done for want of wit
To mem'ry now I can't recall.
So fill to me the parting glass,
Good night, and joy be with you all.

If I had money enough to spend,
And leisure time to sit awhile,
There is a fair maid in this town
That sorely has my heart beguiled.
Her rosy cheeks and ruby lips
I own she has my heart enthralled.
So fill to me the parting glass,
Good night and joy be with you all.

Oh, all the comrades that e're I had,
Are sorry for my going away,
And all the sweethearts that e're I had
Would wish me one more day to stay.
But since it falls unto my lot
That I should rise and you should not,
I'll gently rise and softly call,
"Good night, and joy be with you all."

Songs From the English Renaissance

In recent years an increasing number of us have found happy retreat into a bygone time and place at the many Renaissance fairs held all over the country. In this fantasy world of a might-have-been past, we garb ourselves in laced bodices or doublet and hose and, harp to hand, put some of the hustle of modern day aside, if only for a weekend.

The harp is very much at home at these events. But few harpers know the appropriate music, much less understand the style of the period. Some of us see the Renaissance through nineteenth century eyes: a romantic rendering that, while a charming fantasy, softens the edges on what was a very earthy time.

We have asked Jon Lackey to introduce this section. Jon, an artist by instinct and profession, is a student of the Renaissance and its music, a harper (ancient Celtic wire) and a recorder player who frequently performs with us. Jon offers his personal insights on how the music should be approached, based on his extensive research, enthusiastic listening and spirited playing of early music. Many of the songs presented here are from his collection.

Jon Lackey playing a wire harp.
Photo by Janna.

DEVELOPING HISTORICAL SENSE AND STYLE

by Jon Lackey

Many of us are drawn to the harp because of its ancient associations and "archaic" harmonies. The diatonic tuning and modal scales which may be employed make it possible to re-create a singular aspect of the harp's illustrious past. It was once a courtly instrument, played by musicians who were highly regarded and well rewarded. Theirs was the finest music of their time.

Music is very personal, and it changes and evolves over generations of musicians. It becomes fixed in time only when it is *collected;* that is, it is written down. Fortunately, by late Medieval times notation had been invented; and the Renaissance gave us the printing press and a booming industry of music publishing. There is an amazing variety of early music which has come down to us in manuscript and in print, and current early music artists have a good deal of source material on which to base their interpretations.

Style is harder to convey. It has been only in the past century, since the invention of the early wax-cylinder recordings, that there is finally a method of documenting the essentials of style. Still, a feeling for early music is best acquired by listening to the recordings of the many artists and ensembles who are currently performing on "original instruments" and in an "authentic" style.

The Renaissance was a time of extraordinary energy and enterprise. The flourishing middle class had some leisure time, and a great love of music. Professional musicians could earn a good living composing and arranging for a large market of amateur musicians who needed to entertain themselves on long winter evenings. Popular music became available in towns, often in the form of songs with lyrics so current and topical that if some political cause or controversy suddenly appeared, a song about it would be in print and for sale as a single sheet *broadside* the very next day—with more songs in rebuttal before the week was out.

Popular music was treated very inventively. There were rowdy drinking songs, pious psalm settings, love songs, epic tales set to music, political diatribes, outrageous ribaldries, and every imaginable sort of parody and lampoon. Some are full of philosophy and abstract reflection. Some seem to be intentional gibberish.

At what might be considered a higher level, early music also includes the work of the greatest talents of their age—highly skilled musicians who produced choral and organ music for the church, vocal settings for voices for domestic use, lutesongs and instrumental pieces of a very high order of craftsmanship and originality, and some very impressive ceremonial music for occasions of state. While most of this is beyond the reach of our scope in harp playing, there is much to learn in absorbing its style.

There is little actual harp music available from early sources—but composers tended not to specify an instrument. Indeed, they considered it quite appropriate to adapt to the instruments available. Versatility was considered a great virtue in musicians and their music. These are qualities we identify in our own time with folk and popular music.

And it is this approach which we should apply when we seek to bring what we learn and absorb from the style of early music to the harp. If you want to understand the music of a time and place, learn about that time and place.

Attend concerts and listen to recordings. Search for sheet music—for harp if you're lucky, but also for guitar, keyboard and recorder ensemble. Don't be discouraged by a few chromatic notes and accidentals. The earlier the music the easier it is to adapt for diatonic tuning. (See ADAPTING KEYBOARD MUSIC FOR THE HARP.) Music can be much more than merely playing from a page of someone else's notation. It can be a gradual process of study and the playing of music that is increasingly your own expression. The examples given in this book and others are just a starting point.

SOME TECHNIQUES

Style may be found in the movement of a melody, especially in the endings of phrases, and in the *ornamentations* of certain notes, such as trills and grace-notes, or in small syncopations. Style differs from century to century and country to country; every period and ethnicity uses ornaments in its own unique way. Our focus here is Renaissance-style ornaments. The beginning harper is often discouraged by a lot of ornaments yet should try to do them where they are easy or especially effective. Listen to recordings for examples and use what you hear to embellish the music you play.

Remember, it is the **hand** that plays an ornamental figure, and not the brain. Train your hand to do a few standard ornaments, and you won't have to think so much about them. When you are working up a new piece that has some ornaments indicated, practice it without ornamentation until you are up to full speed, or close to it. Then start using the ornaments, and try using a few where they're not indicated. Try applying a few of the same sort in other pieces where you think they might work. Listen and consider. In truly **making** music, you must learn to develop a musician's instincts about what works rather than pursuing a "correct" decision. That's what makes it **your** music.

Be your own audience. Be patient. Enjoy each infinitesimally small improvement. They add up over time.

A tune may be quite straightforward, and in its **simplest** form you have little control over it, except to use it or not. But in applying **style** to playing it, you can do much—since what you do is **add** whatever you feel it needs. To the melody you can add a progression of changing harmonies. You can do a lot with the six diatonic chords. (See DIATONIC MUSIC AND MODES.) You can produce a very complete feeling for certain tunes with a single chord played in good rhythm. Even a repeated note in the bass, or a very simple two or three-note figure, repeated endlessly, will not necessarily seem monotonous under an animated melody. The earlier Medieval music is full of this style. Listen to it in recordings.

As music evolved and harmonies became more complex so did harp playing. Harmonic devices such as suspensions, passing notes and the like created the tangy dissonances which contribute so well to the dynamics of music and allowed the harp to compete—for a while—with the newly developed chromaticism available on harpsichords, lutes and organs. This was, after all, a period of innovation and the composers of the courts and great households were pushing away at music's frontiers.

One form of these dissonances appeared in harp music with its sweet and simple diatonic harmonies through the introduction of a note within a chord which seemed discordant, followed by another chord in which that note, held throughout, found resolution. It was, in effect, parts of two chords played at once in such a way that one would seem to pull with a directional energy toward a satisfying place of repose. This is called a *suspension*. An example is the 4-3 suspension. A chord is first played with its fourth sounding instead of the third, and in the next beat, the note moves to the third, resolving the dissonance (see READING CHORD SYMBOLS in the Appendix).

In a fuller progression of chords, suspensions can be played in a manner which gives the impression of a voice moving from note to note in contrast to the movement of the melody.

In Renaissance music, the dominant seventh chord is used very sparely and only in passing from one chord to the next.

While other instruments can do more, using chromatic notes, the Renaissance harper playing in the Renaissance style, working with diatonic scales, can utilize many of these same tricks of dissonance-and-resolution. It makes those sweet consonances seem sweeter.

Finally, an important aspect of early music—late Medieval and early Renaissance, especially—is that it tended to favor the effect of several things happening simultaneously, always in contrast with one another. Thus a melody was accompanied by one or several other melodies—even if only a bass line—and often they seemed to have equal importance, though one might predominate over another, and then submerge. Voices would often move against each other in a musical process called **contrary motion**, one going up while another went down. On the harp, the two hands, playing treble and bass, have the effect of separate instruments. This effect is called **polyphony**, meaning many voices. The effect is often like a conversation among equals, and is considered one of the most attractive qualities of Renaissance music.

There was also a different approach which began early and took some time to gain pre-eminence, called **homophony**, which stressed the importance of the melody—and the voice or instrument playing it—and the subservience of the other parts. This featured chords which moved beneath the top voice, accompanying it without competition for our attention. Songs were constructed in such a way as to stress the syllables of the lyrics, with a strong commitment to making them sound much as they might be spoken. Ornaments were used mainly in the melody (the soprano), while the other voices moved together, note-by-note, without much individuality. A boldly separate melody might permit a more complex accompaniment, but the emphasis was clearly homophonic. This style reached its height in the Baroque period during the next century.

There is no ready-made method for becoming your own sort of musician. Style, even based on historical models, must develop organically as you grow in your musicianship. Certainly early music is well-suited to the harp. It constitutes the harp's earliest surviving body of useful music, and makes a solid foundation upon which to produce a good performing repertoire.

So study what is available and get a feel for what you want to do, then jump in, be brave, experiment and have fun exploring the music of a world that, though gone in time, has contributed richly to our culture and is still very much with us.

ABOUT THE RENAISSANCE SONGS IN THIS SECTION:
SOME NOTES FROM THE ARRANGER

The music in this section has been selected with three criteria: adaptability to the harp, playability (that is, not too challenging for the advanced beginner), and appeal. There are ballads, laments and lively dance tunes. There is even a song supposedly written by Henry VIII himself. These selections, however, are by no means a representative cross section of the diverse music of the period. Music was part of everyday life, from the ale house to the manor house to the palace to the cathedral. This was the Renaissance, the time when great artists, writers and composers were beginning to find their eyes, their pens and their voices.

Within these pages are mostly pop songs, the Top Forty of their day. The fact that they have survived (albeit in numerous forms as many were not written down until some time after they first appeared) demonstrates their popularity—at court and in the countryside.

So treat them with the respect they deserve: a lusty, hearty, energetic respect much like many of us give that special Beatles tune well remembered, or a delicious Cole Porter standard. This respect includes keeping the performance as close as possible to the style of the original. Rock and Roll played by a symphony orchestra sounds silly. Renaissance songs sentimentalized in the Victorian tradition are just as inappropriate.

Many of these songs, even *Green Sleeves,* started out as dance tunes. The merry rhythms of percussion, hand-clapping and foot stomping were often part of the whole effect. Too many of us consider music of the past to be veiled in some kind of mystery and attempt to play it with a reverence not always appropriate. If you want to cry into your tankard over the fate of the hero in *Three Ravens,* by all means do so. But when you perform it, do it in the style of a Sixteenth Century minstrel, not like an Irish tenor crooning *Danny Boy.*

This does not mean you can't ham it up. Remember, they didn't have amplification back then. Unless you were in intimate surroundings, if you wanted to be seen and heard, you had to perform in a broad style. Mallory has fun miming the words to *In the Glade* as he sings them, and audiences seem to love it.

Renaissance music should be played in a steady tempo with few, if any, ritards (slowings of tempo), even at the end. A lot of us break this rule as we are used to going for an extended ending that says "this is it, now everyone applaud!" If you want to stay true to period, don't go for that kind of big finish (it is acceptable to hold the final note a bit). It is startling and delightful to listen to a Renaissance band playing along full tilt and suddenly ending the piece resoundingly and solidly on the final beat without slowing one jot. It's a different kind of big finish, but effective, nonetheless. Still, if you want to stretch out the ending a bit, we won't tell on you as long as you realize it's not quite in period.

Keep your playing and singing crisp. On the up-tempo pieces like *Pastime With Good Company* and *In the Glade,* imagine percussion if you don't actually have it. Tap your foot. When singing syllables that extend for more than one note, accent with your voice the pitch changes (for example: "dow-<u>own</u>" when the word "down" covers two notes). Jon Lackey suggests that dotted notes should be rendered in an exaggerated manner ("DUM____ta Dum" in a three beat phrase, "DUM____ta, Dum____ta" in two or four). To do this, hold the first note a bit longer, stealing duration from the second. In 6/8 (see *The Hunt is Up*) the triplets are often dotted this way even if written straight.

Quite a few of the pieces that have surviving words have many, many verses. Ten or more is not uncommon. When we first discovered a version of *Green Sleeves* with eighteen verses, we were delighted. We performed them once, only. Can you imagine the audience's reaction to eighteen verses of *Green Sleeves*? Everyone, including ourselves, was well sick of the song by the time we finished. We suggest you limit your numbers to four minutes or less, unless it is a special circumstance.

We have rather arbitrarily picked out the verses included here based on our personal tastes. When more than one contemporary source was available for a tune, we have selected either one we liked best or one that was most suited for the harp. In the case of *Essex's Last Goodnight,* the treatments were so very different we opted to print two versions.

If you are really motivated to know every verse and/or every tune available for the songs, then you will probably enjoy doing research on them. There is extensive material available if you dig a bit. Start with libraries (college and university music departments are often useful), published collections, recordings, early music societies and the like. If you find any especially harpable goodies, send us a copy for our collection. We are always on the lookout for more music!

A Fyne Faire Day for Musick.
Glenn Morgan, Jon Lackey, and Janna.
Photo by Mallory.

ABOUT THE ADAPTATION OF THESE SONGS

Everything we say in the section about adapting music for the harp applies to these arrangements. We have attempted to retain the feel of the original material (see notes on individual songs) while simplifying and making the music fit on the diatonic harp. Many of the originals come from lute or virginal (a small harpsichord) arrangements printed in the early 1600s, some time after the songs were first popular. Part of the task was to "de-arrange" them, that is, try to approximate how they would have been played before they were adapted for chromatic instruments.

Whenever practical, we have indicated where the major changes were made, especially when a singer or other chromatic musician might want to play the alternate melody with its accidentals. If you are accompanying on the harp, omit the altered notes or you will clash. (See also the section SINGING OR ACCOMPANYING WITH YOUR HARP.)

You may find some of these songs rather difficult as the bass plays in counterpoint to the melody. It is worth the extra effort to play these notes as they give the music the flavor of the period. However, do not give up on a song you like because you have difficulty mastering it (or because, for that matter, you find it too simple and wish it more complex). Renaissance music is not cut and dried; improvisation should be the rule rather than the exception. If you, or others, are singing, playing block chords (or even just the root of the chord in the bass if you're in an ensemble) is perfectly acceptable. We have included the chord symbols (not usual for early music) because we want you to have the freedom to make this music your own.

NOTE: *Scarborough Fair, Barbara Allen, Raggle-Taggle Gypsies-O* and, most probably, some of the other ballads included in the previous section have roots in the Renaissance, but we have not included them in this section as they have become so much a part of our folk tradition.

Green Sleeves

English Renaissance

It is only fitting to begin a section on the English Renaissance with the popular Green Sleeves *(rendered as two words in our historical source). It is the one song from the period almost everyone knows, if only from the much later* What Child is This? Green Sleeves *was first played in England as a rhythmic dance—a galliard. Galliards can be recognized by the characteristic six beat phrase in the rhythm of "my country, 'tis of thee." You can find that beat pattern throughout the song.*

It must have been slowed down a bit for the singer's sake when the eighteen or so verses telling the tale of Lady Green Sleeves were added; Elizabethans did not have sound bites or music videos and a very long song was to be admired, and some of them were very long indeed. Folks in the 16th Century had all night. But Green Sleeves *never dragged into a languid ballad as is often heard.*

We start you with two versions. One is our source, from a lute transcription circa 1600, and not suitable for the diatonic harp. This was a time when musicians with lutes, virginals and recorders were beginning to explore beyond the modes and into chromatic music and the major and minor key structures more familiar to the modern listener. Modal music was still very much played, but it was co-existing with the new, "modern" sounds, which may well have shocked the conservatives as much as new music does today.

Look at the lute transcription. If you play keyboard, try it out. It is an interesting mix of major and minor, with a bit of the modes thrown in. The key signature of two sharps doesn't make too much sense unless they started in E Dorian and then proceeded to change it about. What is clear is that they were experimenting, evolving their music.

The harp adaptation, then, is sort of a devolution to what the song might have sounded like a bit earlier in its history. This diatonic rendering is quite valid, especially for the Renaissance fairs as it is more in the correct period. It is very like the lute arrangement without the accidentals (we did change one chord, the first in the third line, as it is more common to play a G chord than a D).

We made one other change: we limited the verses to a more manageable size for modern audiences. We learned that from experience.

Green Sleeves

For chromatic instruments

From Sir John Hawkins' transcripts,
William Ballet's Lute Book, circa 1600

Galliard
English, 16th Century

Green Sleeves

Raise your Fs to F♯s.

Transcribed from William Ballet's Lute Book, circa 1600

English

Adapted to natural minor (Aeolian) for harp

Arr. J. McCall Geller

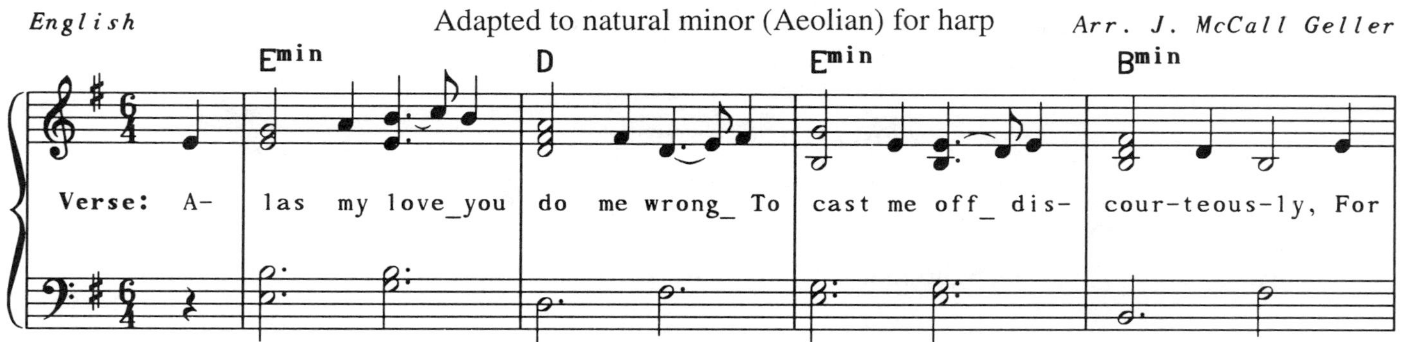

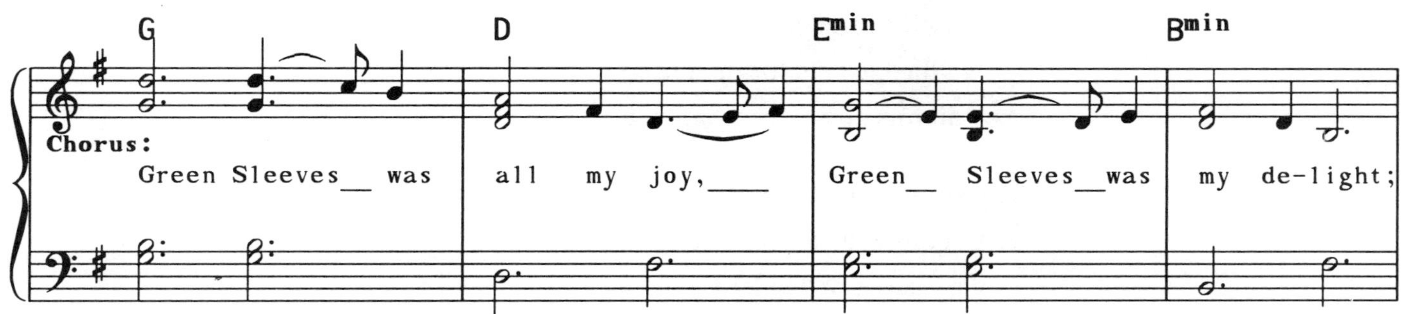

Green Sleeves

(You can sing the chorus after every verse or after every other verse. We perform the latter.)

Alas, my love, you do me wrong
To cast me off discourteously,
For I have lovèd you so long
Delighting in your company.

I have been ready at your hand
To grant whatever you would crave,
I have both wagèd life and land
Your love and good will for to have.

CHORUS: Green Sleeves was all my joy,
Green Sleeves was my delight;
Green sleeves was my heart of gold,
And who but Lady Green Sleeves

I bought thee petticoats of the best,
The cloth so fine as fine might be;
I gave thee jewels for thy chest,
And all this cost I spent on thee.

Thy smock of silk, both fair and white,
With gold embroidered gorgeously;
Thy petticoat of sendal right,
All these I bought thee gladly.   CHORUS

They set thee up, they took thee down,
They served thee with humility;
Thy foot might not once touch the ground,
And yet thou wouldst not love me.

Green Sleeves, now, Farewell! Adieu!
God I pray to prosper thee!
For I am still thy lover true,
Come once again and love me.   CHORUS

The Old Year Now Away is Fled

English, 17th Century

From an old broadside, collected in *New Christmas Carols*, 1642

What Child is This?

English

Lyrics by H. C. Dix, 1837-1898

Air: *Green Sleeves*

Here are two sets of Christmas lyrics to the melody of Green Sleeves. What Child is This? *is fairly modern but we have included it here as part of the* Green Sleeves *saga. Another carol using the same tune,* The Old Year Now Away is Fled, *dates back to the 17th Century. It was not at all unusual to use the same tune for completely different words—or, for that matter, a different melody for a given set of lyrics. If something is good, why not use it again and again? Recycling is a very old concept, indeed!.*

The Old Year Now Away is Fled *should be played and sung in the Renaisance style of Green Sleeves.*

You may have a dilemma, however, when you play and sing What Child is This?: *you can either play it in the Renaissance style or fancy it up a bit, make it more (early music purists, please stop reading here) romantic in style. Many people love it as a flowing, 19th Century Christmas lullaby and may never even have heard of the secular Renaissance dance and ballad that it is based upon. Frankly, we like it both ways.*

The version given here is to accompany a singer or an instrument (flute, violin, recorder, etc.) and leans toward the later interpretation. Instrumentalists may want to play the melody up an octave.

The Old Year Now Away Is Fled

Air: Green Sleeves

The old year now away is fled,
The new year it is enterèd;
Then let us now our sins down-tread,
And joyfully all appear:
Let's merry be this day,
And let us now both sport and play:
Hang grief, cast care away!
God send you a happy New Year!

The name-day now of Christ we keep,
Who for our sins did often weep;
His hands and feet were wounded deep,
And His blessèd side with a spear;
His head they crowned with thorn,
And at Him they did laugh and scorn,
Who for our good was born:
God send us a happy New Year!

And now with New Year's gift each friend
Unto each other they do send:
God grant we may all our lives amend,
And that the truth may appear.
Now, like the snake, your skin
Cast off, of evil thoughts and sin,
And so the year begin:
God send us a happy New Year!

What Child Is This?

Lyrics by H. C. Dix

Air: *Green Sleeves*

What Child is this, who, laid to rest,
On Mary's lap is sleeping?
Whom angels greet with anthems sweet,
While shepherds watch are keeping?
This, this is Christ the King,
Whom shepherds guard and angels sing:
Haste, haste to bring Him laud,
The Babe, the Son of Mary!

Why lies He in such mean estate,
Where ox and ass are feeding?
Good Christian, fear, for sinners here
The silent word is pleading;
Nails, spear, shall pierce Him through,
The cross be borne for me, for you:
Hail, hail, the Word made flesh,
The Babe, the Son of Mary!

So bring Him incense, gold and myrrh,
Come peasant, king to own Him;
The King of Kings salvation brings;
Let loving hearts enthrone Him.
Raise, raise the song on high,
The virgin sings her lullaby:
Joy, joy, for Christ is born,
The Babe, the Son of Mary.

What Child Is This?

130

This, this is Christ the King, Whom shep - herds guard and
an - gels sing: Haste, haste to bring Him laud, The
Babe the Son of Ma - ry.
G
D
Emin
B
G
D
Emin
B
Emin

131

Fortune, My Foe

English Renaissance

Shakespeare mentions this song in The Merry Wives of Windsor. *Our source, a facsimile of an original printing of the lyrics subtitles* Fortune, My Foe *"The lovers' complaint for the loss of his love: A sweet Sonnet wherein the* Lover *doth exclaim against* Fortune, *for the loss of his Ladies favour, almost past hope to get it again, and in the end receives a comfortable Answer, and attains his desire, as may here appear." Eleven mournful verses follow. We give you just a sample as it is too much dismay to take in its entirety.*

Once again the third in the dominant chord (B in our key of E minor) does not need to be played by the harp. The D♯ only appears in the melody at the very end and can be avoided in several ways (see explanation under the music). However, this might be a chance for you to try flipping the single D♯ lever above middle C "on the fly" at the end of the song. Do it in the third measure from the end. But don't forget to put it back down unless you omit the D naturals above middle C in the third line. If you do that and do not transpose octaves, you can sharp the D from the first. That allows you to add the missing D♯ to the B chords. Up or down, if you decide to change it you have to be on your toes. If this all confuses you, read it again, referring to the music until you understand.

*Mallory singing in Renaissance attire.
Photo by Jon Lackey.*

Fortune, My Foe

Raise your F's to F♯s.

*Original melody is the D♯. If solo, harp may play F♯ or D♮. You also have the option of flipping your D♯ lever at that point. Singers can sing either the D♯ or D♮. When playing with chromatic instruments, the harp is safe playing the F♯.

Fortune, My Foe

Fortune, my foe, why dost thou frown on me?
And will thy favours never greater be?
Wilt thou, I say, forever breed me pain?
And wilt thou ne'er restore my joys again?

Fortune hath wrought me grief and great annoy,
Fortune hath falsely stol'n my love away,
My love, and joy, whose sight did make me glad;
Such great misfortunes never young man had.

In vain I sigh, in vain I wail and weep;
In vain mine eyes refrain from quiet sleep;
In vain I shed my tears both night and day,
In vain my love my sorrows do bewray.

No man alive can Fortunes spight withstand,
With wisdom, skill, or mighty strength of hand;
In midst of mirth she bringeth bitter moan,
And woe to me that hath her hatred known.

If wisdoms eyes blind Fortune had but seen,
Then had my love, my love for ever been;
Then, love farewell, though Fortune favour thee,
No Fortune frail shall ever conquer me.

The Hunt is Up

Tudor England

The Hunt is Up, and its numerous variants, were in vogue as early as the 1530s and there are many different lyrics, including one for good queen Bess. "Harry" in this version is Henry VIII. A Hunt's-Up song was any song, even a love song, intended to arouse in the morning. This particular version would certainly get the juices going!

Play this with a swinging rhythm in 2; that is, beats 1 and 4 are accented, the first beats of triplets. If 6/8 is new to you, listen to some Sousa marches (the one used for the Monty Python theme comes to mind) which are often in that time signature. (Other marches are in 2/4, which beat 1 and 2 and) 6/8 is also used in songs that are meant to represent the rhythm of galloping horses (the Light Calvary Overture *for instance).*

If you have trouble with the dotted eighth note, sixteenth note or eighth note triplets, try playing them even until you get the feel of the piece. Then put the dotted rhythm back in. And remember, your job with this one is to wake people up!

The Hunt Is Up

The hunt is up, the hunt is up
And it is well nigh day;
And Harry our kinge is gone hunting
To bring his deere to bay.

The east is bright with morning light,
And darkness it is fled,
And the merie horne wakes up the morne
To leave his idle bed.

Behold the skyes with golden dyes
Are glowing all around;
The grass is greene, and so are the treene,
All laughing with the sound.

The horses snort to be at the sport,
The dogges are running free,
The woddes rejoyce at the mery noise
Of hey tantara tee ree!

The sunne is glad to see us clad
All in our lustie greene,
And smiles in the skye as he riseth nye,
To see and to be seene.

Awake, all men, I say agen,
Be merry as you may,
For Harry our Kinge is gone hunting,
To bring his deere to bay.

(Optional: Repeat Verse One)

Three Ravens

English, 16th Century

The Three Ravens is said to be found in Thomas Ravenscroft's 1611 collection of popular songs, Melismata, *but likely dates from even earlier. In its many forms it has become part of our folk heritage.*

This ballad (a song that tells a story) works best for us in a free, conversational style, but it can also be performed in strict tempo.

Three Ravens

Raise your F's to F♯s.

English

Arr. J. McCall Geller

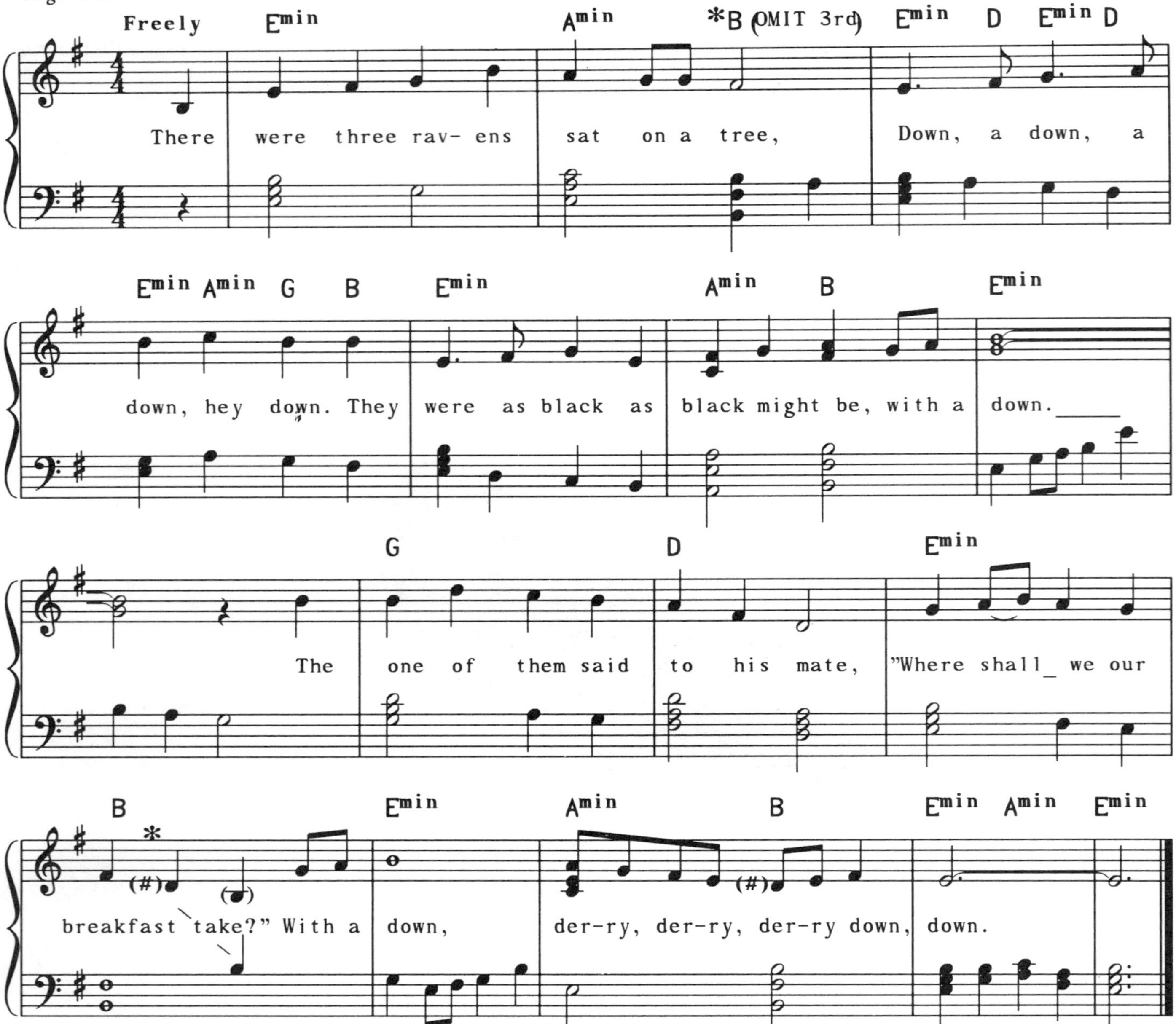

*Note: Play B chords without the 3rd (D♯). Sharps in parenthesis are for optional use of singers and chromatic instruments. When these are played, the harp should omit those notes.

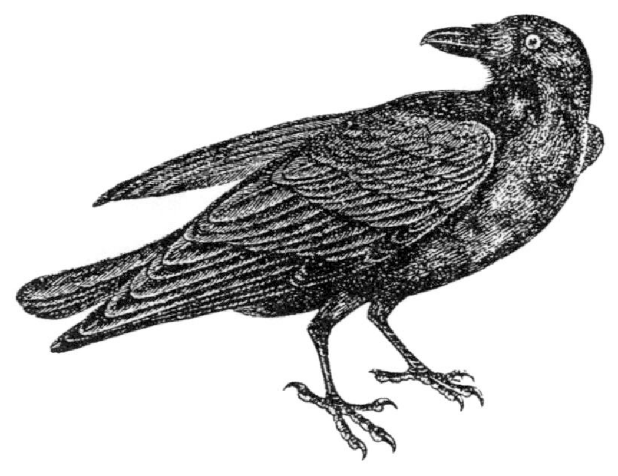

Three Ravens

There were three ravens sat on a tree,
Down, a down, a down, hey down.
They were as black as black might be, with a down.
The one of them said to his mate,
"Where shall we our breakfast take?"
With a down, derry, derry, derry down, down.

Down in yonder green field,
Down, a down, a down, hey down,
There lies a knight slain under his shield, with a down.
His hounds they lie down at his feet;
So well do they their master keep,
With a down, derry, derry, derry down, down.

His hawks they fly so eagerly,
Down, a down, a down, hey down,
No other fowle dare him come nigh, with a down.
Down there comes a fallow doe
As heavy with young as she might go,
With a down, derry, derry, derry down, down.

She lifted up his bloody head,
Down, a down, a down, hey down,
And kissed his wounds that were so red, with a down.
She got him up upon her back
And carried him to an earthen lake,
With a down, derry, derry, derry down, down.

She buried him before the prime;
Down, a down, a down, hey down.
She was dead herself ere Evensong time, with a down.
God send every gentleman
Such hawks, such hounds, and such leman,
With a down, derry, derry, derry down, down.

Lord Willoughby

English Renaissance

This musical account of an Elizabethan battle was one way of spreading the news, no doubt with a few dramatic embellishments.

Our original had several accidentals, however we have heard this tune played without them. If you are singing with your harp, you might sing them but not play them (see the sharps in parentheses in the music).

Raise your F's to F♯s.

Lord Willoughby

English
Adapted from Wm. Byrd

Arr. J. McCall Geller & Jon Lackey

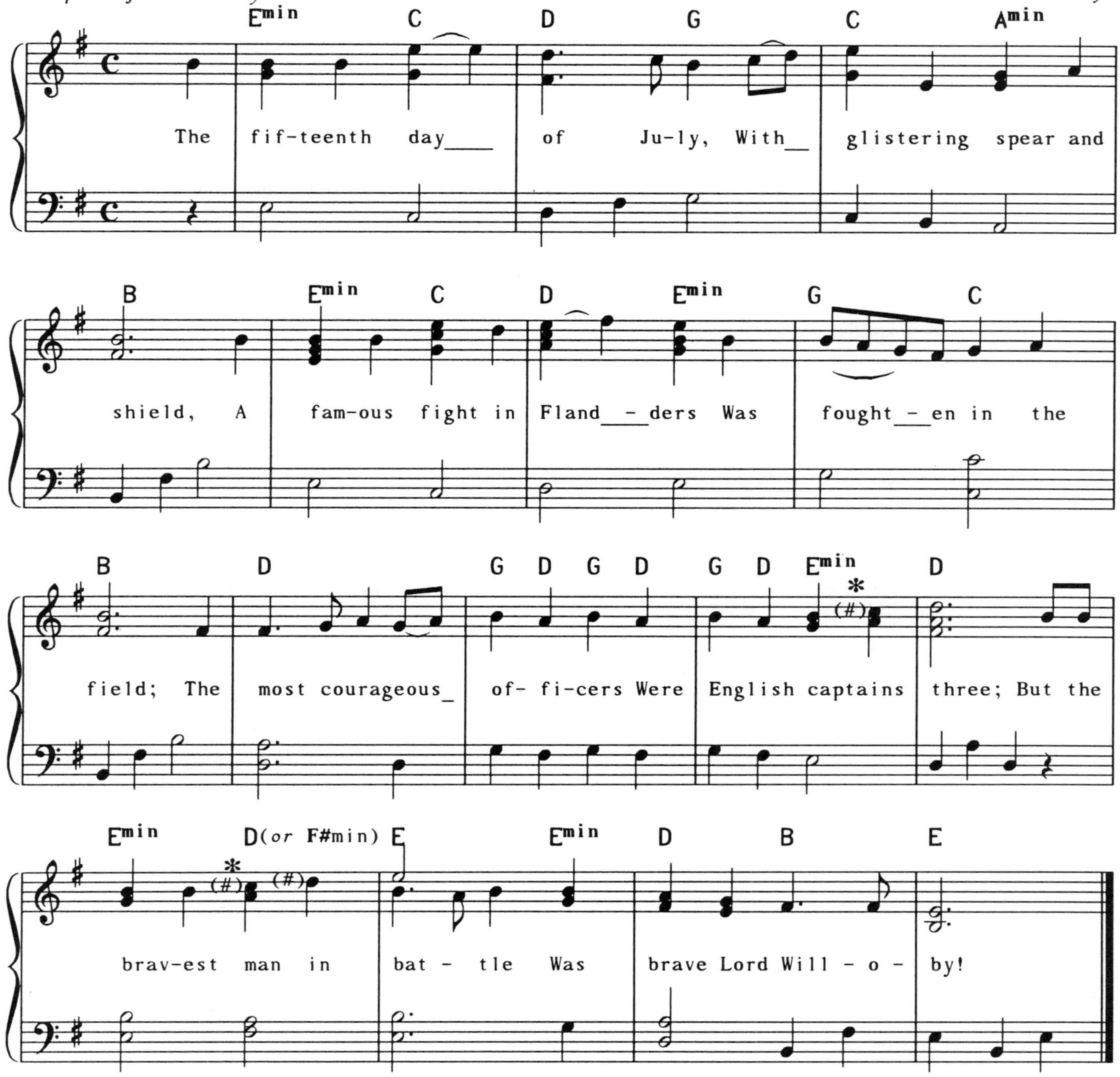

*Note: (♯) marks are optional melodic accidentals for singers, etc. When another performer is playing the sharps, omit these notes on harp. When playing chromatically, replace D chord in last line, first measure, with F♯min.

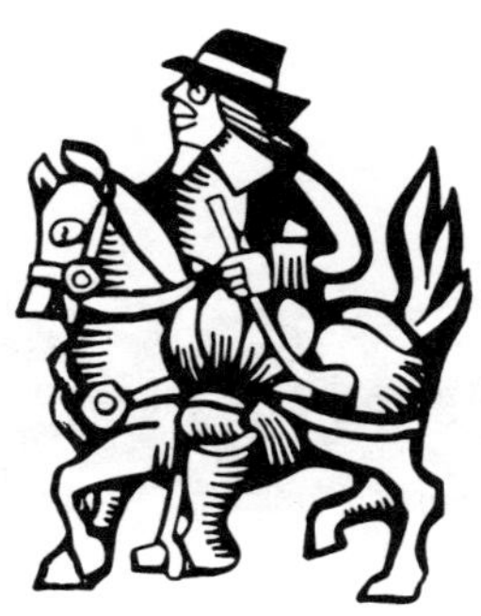

Lord Willoughby

The fifteenth day of July,
With glistering spear and shield,
A famous fight in Flanders
Was foughten in the field;
The most courageous officers
Were English captains three;
But the bravest man in battle
Was brave Lord Willoughby.

The next was Captain Norris,
A valiant man was he;
The other, Captain Turner,
That from field would never flee.
With fifteen hundred fighting men,
Alas, there was no more,
They fought with forty thousand then,
Upon the bloody shore.

"Stand to it, noble pike-men,
And look you 'round about;
And shoot you right, you bow-men,
And we will keep them out;
You musket and caliver men,
Do you prove true to me,
I'll be the foremost man in fight,"
Says brave Lord Willoughby.

And then the bloody enemy
They fiercely did assail,
And fought it out most valiantly,
Not doubting to prevail;
The wounded men on both sides fell,
Most piteous for to see,
Yet nothing could the courage quell
Of brave Lord Willoughby.

For seven hours to all men's view
This fight endurèd sore,
Until our men so feeble grew
That they could fight no more;
And then upon dead horses
Full savorly they eat,
And drank the puddle water,
For no better they could get.

The sharp steel-pointed arrows
And bullets thick did fly;
Then did our valiant soldiers
Charge on most furiously;
Which made the Spaniards waver,
They thought it best to flee,
They feared the stout behaviour
Of brave Lord Willoughby.

And then the fearful enemy
Was quickly put to flight;
Our men pursued courageously,
And rout their forces quite.
At last they gave a shout
Which echoed through the sky,
"God and Saint George for England!"
The conquerors did cry.

Then courage, noble Englishmen,
And never be dismayed,
If that we be but one to ten,
We will not be afraid
To fight with foreign enemies,
And set our country free;
And thus I end this bloody bout
Of brave Lord Willoughby.

Essex's Last Goodnight

Versions One and Two

English, Early 17th Century

These two renderings of the same theme are from Jon Lackey's collection. "O Hone" and "Well-a-day" are laments: moans of distress, or, sometimes, yearning. Lord Essex was charming—a patron of the arts, a poet and (as any fan of old Bette Davis movies knows) a great favorite of Queen Elizabeth. He was, however, no soldier or statesman, nor was he particularly prudent, and for these character flaws he lost his head—literally.

We give two variants here (and there are more) to demonstrate once again how difficult it is to give a definitive version. In a time when there was little in the way of mass communication, an idea, or a bit of a tune was transformed by each new performer until the song is hardly recognizable.

Essex's Last Good-Night

Version One

From *Elizabeth Rogers' Virginal Book*

English

Arr. J. McCall Geller

All you that cry, "O Hone, O Hone,"
Come now and sing O Lord with me;
For why our Jewell is from us gone,
The valiant Knight of Chivalry.

Of rich and poore beloved was he,
In time an honorable Knight:
When by our lawes condemned was he,
And lately tooke his last good-night.

Essex's Last Good-Night

Version Two

English

Arr. J. McCall Geller

Essex's Last Goodnight

Version Two

Sweet England's pride is gone,
Well-a-day, well-a-day;
Which makes her sigh and grone
Ever-more still.
    He did her fame advance
    In Ireland, Spain and France;
    And now by dismall chance
    Is from us tane.

He was a vertuous Peere,
Well-a-day, well-a-day;
And was esteemèd deare,
Ever-more still.
    He allwayes helpt the poore,
    Which makes them sigh full sore;
    His death they do deplore,
    In every place.

Brave honour grac'd him still,
Gallantly, gallantly;
He nere did deed of ill,
Well it is knowne.
    But Envy, that Foule Fiend,
    Whose malice nere did end,
    Hath brought true vertues friend
    Unto his thrall.

Pastime With Good Company

English, 16th Century
Henry VIII, 1491-1547

This Renaissance song is attributed to Henry VIII himself. Given the content of the lyrics and the good monarch's reputation, we tend to believe it.

Some adjustments have been made to the melody to accommodate the diatonic harp. Many students of the music of that period feel that this is the proper way to play the tunes on harp. For those of you who wish to sing the melody and only accompany yourself on the harp we have notated the original melody at the bottom. The $G\sharp$ has been omitted in the E chords to allow us to avoid flipping levers (you may, of course, do so if you like).

Play with rhythm and energy.

Pastime with Good Company

NOTE: See melody alternatives below.

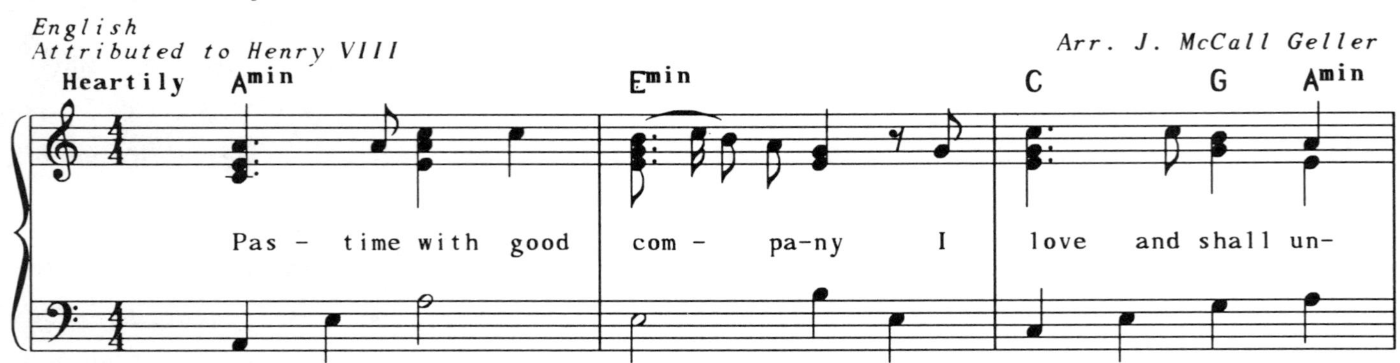

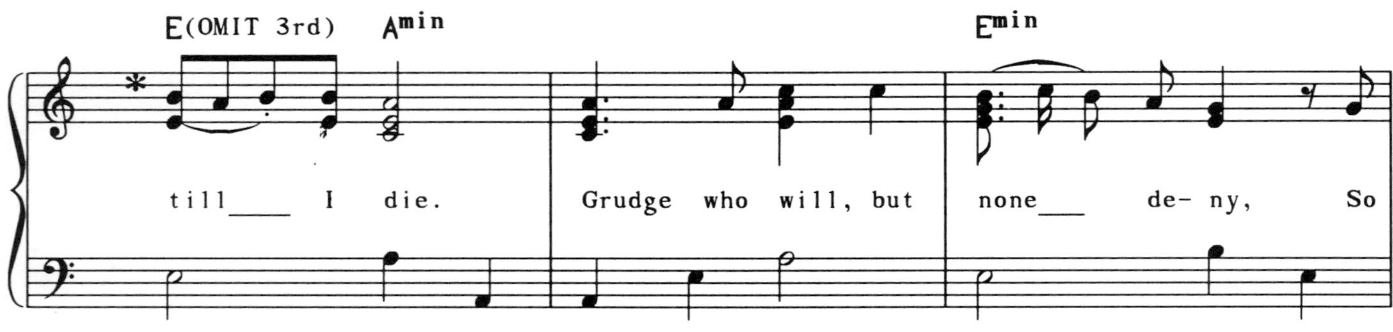

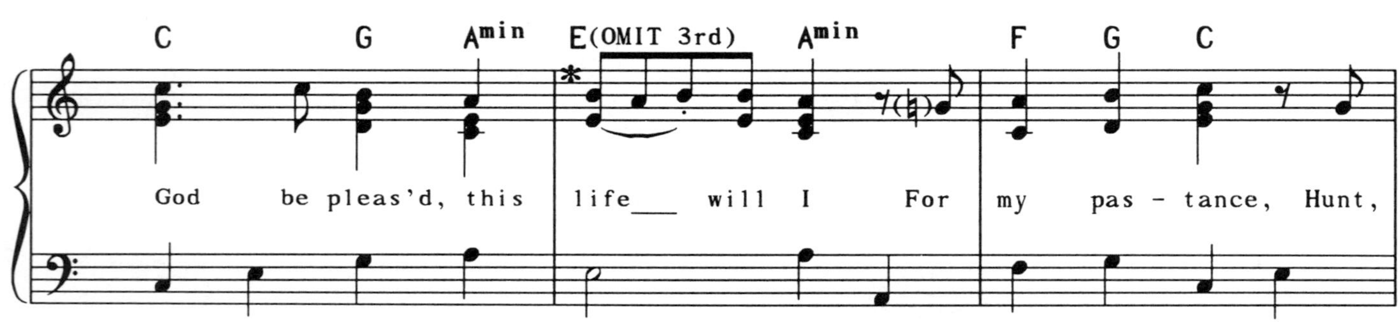

148

*The melody we give above was modified for the harp to avoid flipping the G lever. Singers may prefer the original given below (A). An alternate favored by some is to sing and play the G♮ (see example B).

Pastime with good company
I love and shall until I die.
Grudge who will, but none deny,
So God be pleas'd, this life will I
For my pastance,
Hunt, sing and dance;
My heart is set,
All goodly sport,
To my comfort,
Who shall me let?

Youth will needs have dalliance,
Of good or ill some pastance;
Company me thinketh the best
All thoughts and fantasies to digest.
For idleness
Is chief mistress
Of vices all;
Then who can say
But pass the day
Is best of all?

Company with honesty
Is virtue; and vice to flee.
Company is good or ill,
But every man hath his free will.
The best I sue,
The worst eschew;
My mind shall be
Virtue to use,
Vice to refuse,
I shall use me.

The Spanish Lady

English, 16th Century

This song, dating from the later part of Elizabeth's reign, tells the tale of a captured lady who fell for a gallant but faithful English nobleman (much speculation was made as to the identity of the noble in question, but none is conclusive). England and Spain were enemies during this period and several songs (with similar names) tell the tales of conflict...and love.

The music takes a refreshing turn at the words "Of a comely..." which may take you unaware. Those of us accustomed to more modern popular and folk tunes are often surprised when Renaissance music goes in unexpected directions. That is part of the charm of early music.

The Spanish Lady

Raise your F's to F♯s.

English

Air Notated Circa 1615

Arr. J. McCall Geller

The Spanish Lady

Will you hear a Spanish Lady,
How she woo'd an English man?
Garments rare and rich as may be
Deck'd with jewels she had on.
Of a comely countenance and grace was she,
And by birth and parentage of high degree.

But at last there came commandment
For to set the ladies free
With their jewels still adornèd
None to do them injury.
Then said this lady mild, "Full woe is me,
O, let me sustain this kind captivity."

"Courteous lady, leave this fancy,
Here comes all that breeds thee strife,
I in England have already
A sweet woman to my wife.
I'll not falsify my vow for gold and gain,
Nor for all the fairest dames that live in Spain."

"Then commend me to thy lady,
Bear to her this chain of gold,
And these bracelets for a token,
Grieving that I was so bold.
See, my jewels in like sort take thou with thee,
They are fitting for thy wife, but not for me."

In the Glade

English, 16th Century
Words by Mallory and McCall, 1992

Ding, Dong Merrily on High

English Christmas Song
Words by George R. Woodward

Air: *Bransle Officiale*

This lively tune was a Renaissance dance, the Bransle (pronounced "brawl") Officiale. Later, words were added and thus it became the popular Christmas song, Ding, Dong, Merrily on High. *We had so much fun singing this in the Yule season that we searched for secular lyrics in order to perform it all year long. We could find none and listened in frustration as Renaissance sackbut bands played hearty renditions at the fairs. So we decided to invent some frolicsome words of our own and pass them off as practically the real thing—with a broad wink, of course.*

This arrangement demonstrates one way to handle a fast, rhythmic tune either when someone is singing the melody or you are in a group where another instrument is playing it. Keep a steady rhythm at all costs, even if you have to simplify the accompaniment further.

*Mallory & McCall in the glade.
Photo by Jon Lackey.*

In the Glade

Raise F's to F♯s.
"Ding, Dong Merrily on High"
Air: Bransle Officiale
New Lyrics by Janna McCall Geller & Mallory Geller
Arr. J. McCall Geller
Renaissance Dance Tune
With High Spirits
A young man strol-ling in the glade es-
pied a lass, for-lorn-ing. "What sor-rows ye,_ fair__ maid, on
such a fine sum - mer's morn - ing?" Sing Fa, la, la, la, la,

D
Emin
D
Fa, la, la, la, la,
Fa, la, la, la, la,
Fa, la, la, la, la

C
D
Amin
D
G
Fa, la, la, la, la,
Fa, La, La. "On
such a fine sum-mer's
morn- ing!"

In The Glade

Secular words by Janna McCall Geller and Mallory Geller
Air: *Bransle Officiale*

A young man strolling in the glade espied a lass, forlorning.
"What sorrows ye__, fair maid, on such a fine summer's morning?"

    CHORUS: Sing Fa__, la, la, la, la__, (5 times)

        Fa, la, la,

        "On such a fine summer's morning!"

Said she, "I do__ not__ grieve, 'tis but__ my heart's romancing.
For if I only had the leave, I long__ to go a-dancing!"

    CHORUS: Sing Fa__, etc.

        "I Long__ to go a-dancing!"

"Then cast away__ your__ chores," said he__ in words beguiling.
"Seize the day, for it is yours. Come, let__ me see thee smiling."

    CHORUS: Sing Fa__, etc.

        "Come, let__ me see thee smiling."

"Take care in what__ ye__ say," she cried__ with eyes a-snapping.
"I dare not fly__ a-way, although__ my toes be tapping!"

    CHORUS: Sing Fa__, etc.

        "Yea, how__ my toes be tapping!"

"Come flee with me__ Sweet__ Miss," (upon his knee he stoopèd.)

"For we are guaranteed of bliss; Terpsichore is our Cupid!"

    CHORUS: Sing Fa__, etc.
        "Terpsichore is our Cupid!"

Yea, love, O love was in the day; two hearts__ in rhythm, prancing.
And so they hurried on their way, their feet__ a-gaily dancing.

    CHORUS: Sing Fa__, etc.
        Their feet__ a-gaily dancing!

Ding Dong Merrily On High

Words by George R. Woodword

Air: *Bransle Officiale*

Ding dong! merrily on high
In heav'n the bells are ringing:
Ding dong! verily the sky
Is riv'n with angel singing.
Glo-______________ria!
Hosanna in excelsis!

E'en so here below, below,
Let steeple bells be swungen,
And i-o, i-o, i-o,
By priest and people sungen.
Glo-______________ria!
Hosanna in excelsis!

Pray you, dutifully prime
Your matin chime, ye ringers;
May you beautifully rime
Your evetime song, ye singers.
Glo-______________ria!
Hosanna in excelsis!

157

Yonder Comes a Courteous Knight

English, circa 1609

The title of this song of the English Renaissance seems to announce a tale of gracious chivalry. But our Courteous Knight is "Lustely raking over the lay." Yes, we know, the meaning here is not exactly what the words might seem to the modern reader (he is taking a merry look at the lay of the land), but the slight alteration in the perceived meaning doesn't change the fact that a comely lasse was his primary interest! And this is, indeed, a very lusty tale, in the best traditions of the hearty, robust and often ribald Elizabethans (and therefore, parental discretion is advised). From that zest comes much of their best popular music. Our source takes this song from the Freemen's Songs for Four Voices, Deuteromelia, 1609, but it dates somewhat earlier.

Playing this song may present somewhat of a challenge. Every effort has been made to preserve the essence of the original when adapting and simplifying it. The rapid chord changes would prove awkward and in some places well nigh impossible as written in our source so we have attempted to retain the spirit with an active, full, representative bass line. As the air should be played with elan and energy, you will want to practice both hands until you can manage the music effortlessly. You will notice that there are some E, A and D major chords that are not complete. Once again, we have omitted the third which is not available in the C tuning. The first part of this song is in the Mixolydian mode (with a G major tonic chord), but if you play the above mentioned major chords as written with the sharped thirds, you'll find yourself in the Ionian mode (good ol' __modern__ G major). We prefer the chords left in open, neutral 5ths; it sounds to us more authentically period.

We give you eleven verses—our early music authority, Jon, insists that the story cannot be told without them all— with the original spelling.

Yonder Comes a Courteous Knight

English *Arr. J. McCall Geller*

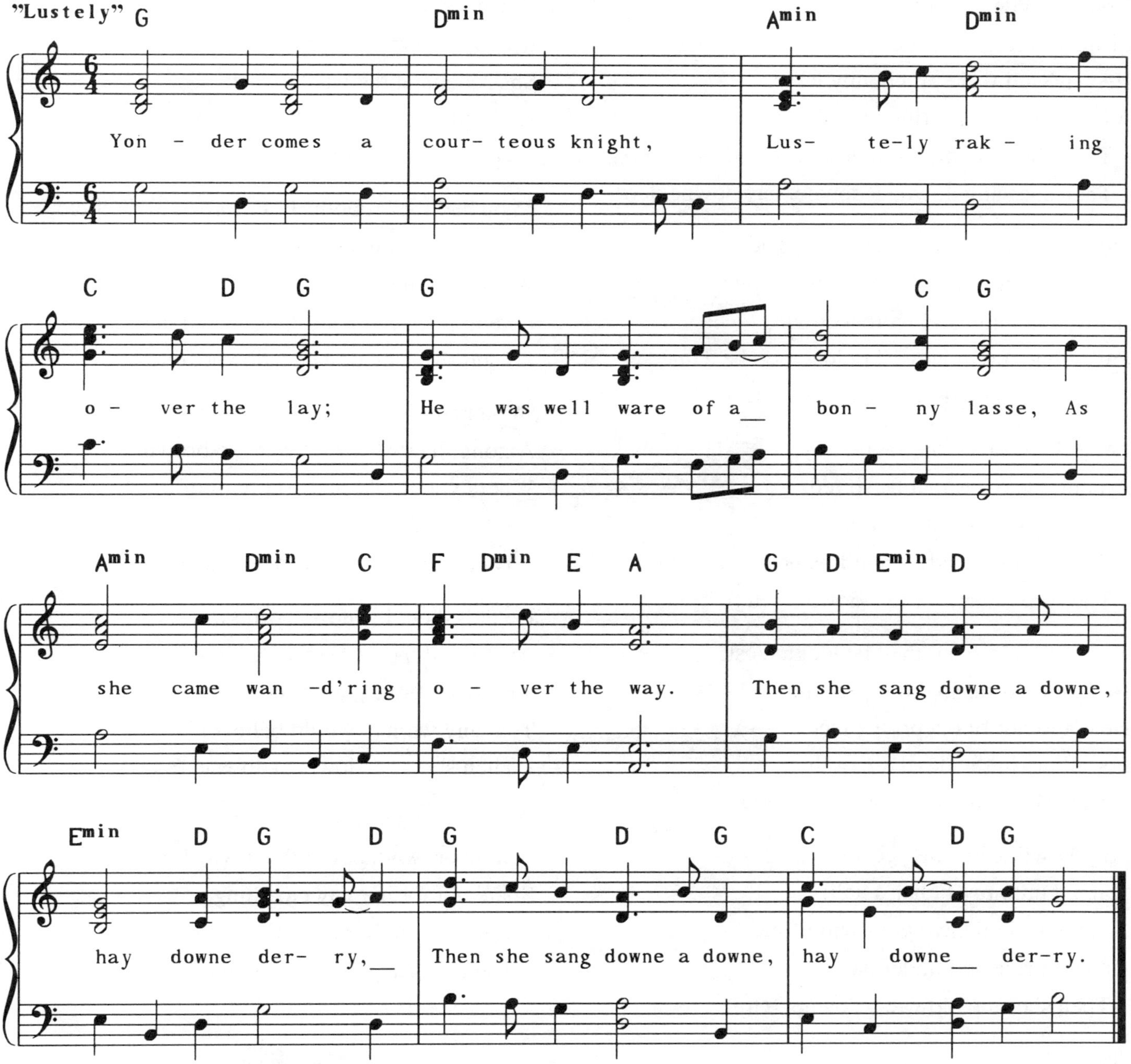

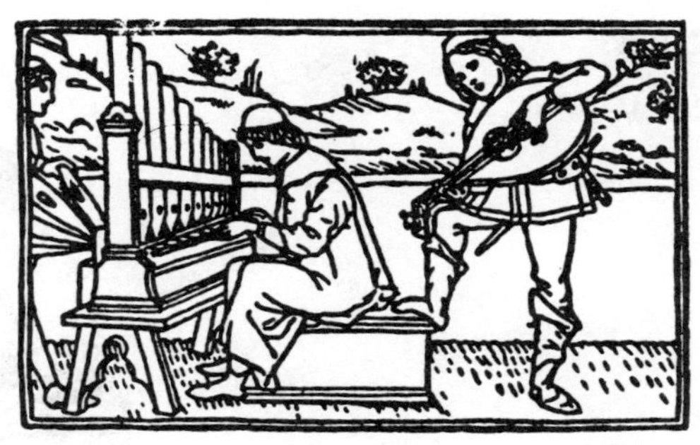

Yonder Comes A Courteous Knight

Yonder comes a courteous knight,
Lustely raking over the lay;
He was well ware of a bonny lasse,
As she came wand'ring over the way.
   Then she sang downe a downe, hay downe derry,
   Then she sang downe a downe, hay downe derry.

"Jove you speed, fayre lady," he said,
"Amongst the leaves that be so greene;
If I were a king, and wore a crown,
Full soone, fayre lady, shouldst thou be a queen."
   Then she sang downe a downe, (etc.)

"Also Jove save you, fayre lady,
Among the roses that be so red;
If I have not my will of you,
Full soon, fayre lady, shall I be dead."
   Then she sang downe a downe, (etc.)

Then he lookt East, then he lookt West,
He lookt North, so did he South;
He could not find a privy place,
For all lay in the devil's mouth.
   Then she sang downe a downe, (etc.)

"If you will carry me, gentle sir,
A maid unto my father's hall;
Then you shall have your will of me
Under purple and under pall."
   Then she sang downe a downe, (etc.)

He set her upon a steed,
And himself upon another;
And all the day he rode her by,
As tho' they had been sister and brother.
   Then she sang downe a downe, (etc.)

When she came to her father's hall,
It was well walled round about;
She rode in at the wicket gate,
And shut the four ear'd fool without.
   Then she sang downe a downe, (etc.)

"You had me" (quoth she) "abroad in the field,
Among the corn, amidst the hay,
Where you might had your will of me,
Fore in good faith, sir, I ne'er said nay."
   Then she sang downe a downe, (etc.)

"You had me also amid the field,
Among the rushes that were so brown;
Where you might had your will of me,
But you had not the face to lay me down."
   Then she sang downe a downe, (etc.)

He pull'd out his nut-brown sword,
And wip'd the rust off with his sleeve;
And said, "Jove's curse come to his heart,
That any woman would believe."
   Then she sang downe a downe, (etc.)

When you have your own true love,
A mile or twain out of the town,
Spare not for her gay cloathing,
But lay her body flat on the ground.
   Then she sang downe a downe, (etc.)

Some Famous Composers

The music in this section was composed or arranged by respected composers of "art music" and is here to give you an idea of some places to look for further pieces to play. We have also included two selections from the Irish harper Carolan, said by some to be Ireland's greatest composer.

Many of the great composers of western music wrote keyboard pieces from which to teach students. The Anna Magdalena Bach book and the workbook of Leopold Mozart (Wolfgang's musician father) are famous examples. Many of these are collected in the numerous piano methods for beginners.

Unlike the music in the previous sections, all but the two Carolan selections are meant to be played as written (although Mozart was a consummate improviser and his father probably encouraged him to do variations on each keyboard study). These are good pieces to use to work on your technique.

All the keyboard music in this sampling is either as written or very lightly adapted (moved into a more harpable key or parts transposed up or down an octave). See the section on adapting music for the harp for some suggestions on how you can select suitable music from the piano repertoire.

Mikrokosmos

Béla Bartók, 1881-1945

Béla Bartók is best known for his complex polytonal works but he also wrote many simple pieces for piano students. These form a wealth of worthwhile material for the harp.

The music here may seem a bit unusual. It doesn't always go where one expects. No matter how far Bartók was led in his explorations of new horizons in contemporary music, he still retained his love for the folk music of his nativeHungary. Bartók used the modes in his own special ways. He made the simple seem new. These pieces were meant to be played at exactly the tempo given (he even indicated how long they should take!). Be sure that both hands play exactly together and that the tempo is steady.

Here, as with all keyboard music, we have to deal with the fact that we use one less finger on each hand. Therefore, what may be a very easy five finger exercise for the pianist becomes more complex with four fingers.When approaching piano music, work through the fingerings, ignoring what indications the composer has given.We have indicated possible harp fingerings here but you may want to explore fingerings of your own.

*Janna in an Edwardian dress at a floor harp.
Photo by Mallory.*

Mikrokosmos #3

(Progressive Piano Pieces)

Unison Melody – Dorian Mode

Mikrokosmos #16

Parallel Motion and Change of Position

Mikrokosmos #22

Imitation and Counterpoint

Russian Folk Song

Ludwig van Beethoven, 1770-1827

This miniature is a simple arrangement of a melody that apparently caught Beethoven's fancy. Many great composers developed music from what they heard around them. Ralph Vaughn Williams was a great collector of English folk songs; Mozart wrote variations on Twinkle, Twinkle Little Star; *Chopin wrote Polish dances— the list is endless.*

There are two versions here to show how you can adapt a piece to fit your harp. The first is the original, as written. The second has been transposed to fit on a lap harp. Develop the skill of writing transpositions; it will hugely expand the music available to you.

The dots above the notes mean that they are played staccato; that is, short and crisp. This does not mean you should try to dampen the sound on the harp. Rather, get the phrasing by emphasis. The first two measures, for example, should be played da dit dit dit *stressing slightly the first note. The wedged shaped mark in the last measure indicates that you should stress that note and play it a bit louder than the rest. Note that each section is repeated twice. In the transposed version you have the option of playing the second section 8va, that is, up an octave.*

Work on this until you can play it with a light, gay lilt.

Russian Folk Song

Raise your F's to F♯s.

Russian Folk Song

Transposed and adapted for small harp

Minuet

Leopold Mozart, 1719-1787

This little Minuet *was used by Leopold Mozart to teach his son, Wolferl (an affectionate Austrian nickname—we might say Wolfie) and Nannerl, his daughter, to play the harpsichord. The children were prodigies and played in the great courts of Europe. His son, of course, was the genius Wolfgang Amadeus Mozart. From little pieces like this the children learned the basics of music and soon young Mozart was composing works of his own. It is possible that this minuet was an early work taken down by his father.*

We have moved Minuet *from the key of F to the key of G so that those who have harps with a lowest note G (rather common) will find it fits within the range of their instruments. In that case, the bottom note of the octave Ds will have to be omitted as indicated by parentheses. Or, the whole thing can be put up an octave.*

Like the Russian Folk Song, *this minuet is in the AABB form. That is, the first theme is repeated twice, then the second, B, theme, the same. Repeats of this kind are common in classical period music.*

Raise your F's to F♯s.

Minuet

from Leopold Mozart's Notebook (circa 1760s)

Original in F – no other changes

Leopold Mozart
Austrian

Andantino Grazioso

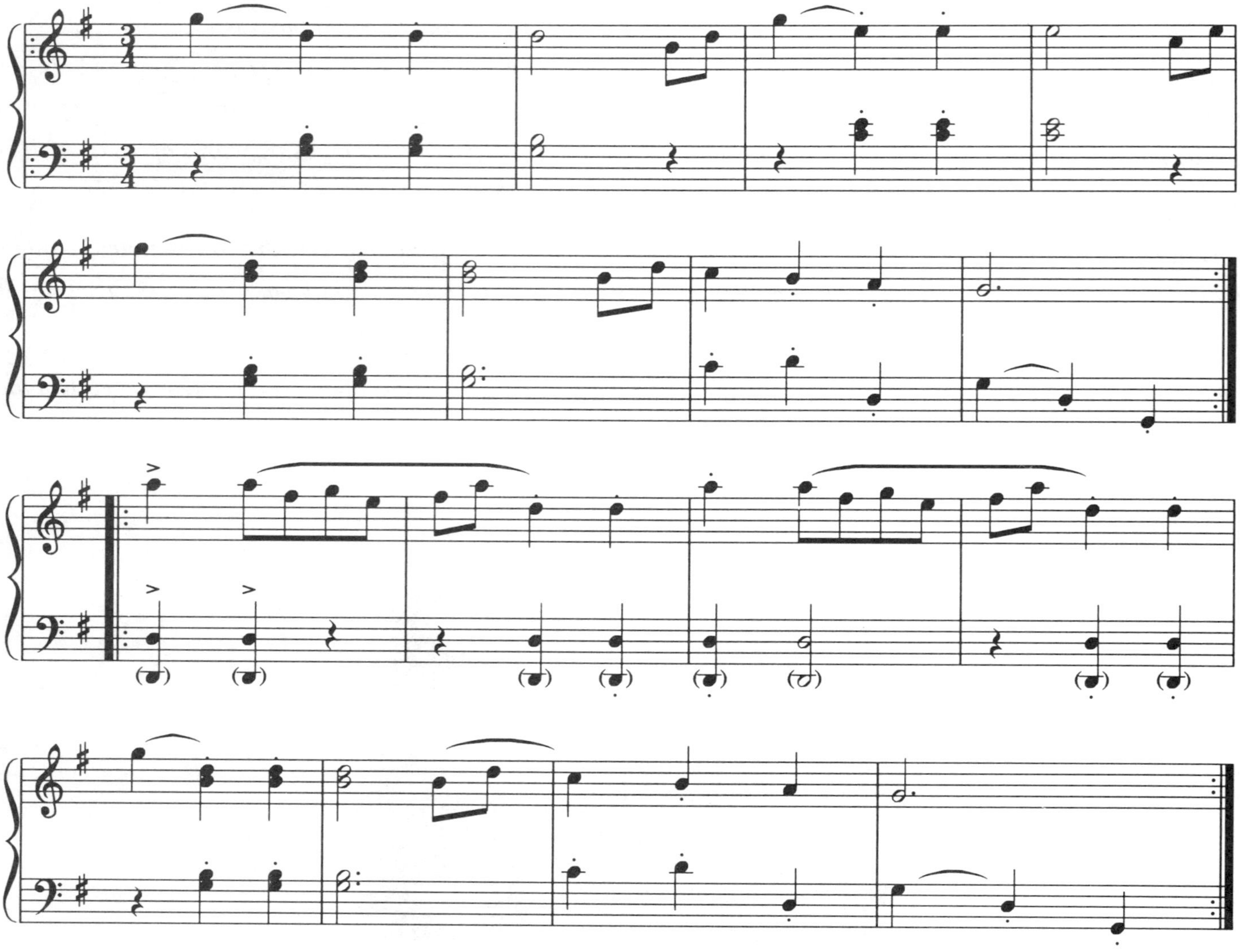

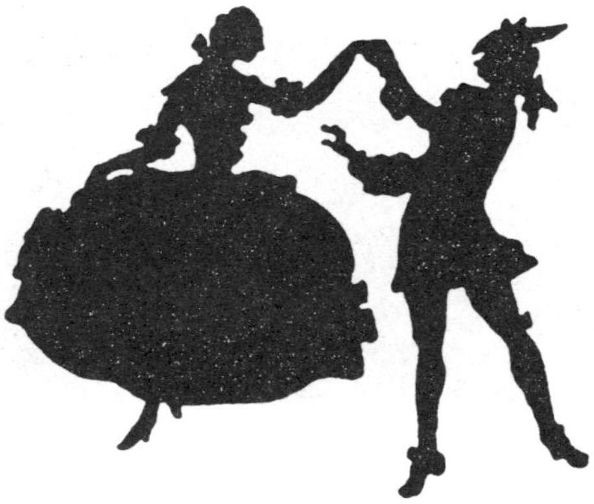

Minuet

Georg Philipp Telemann, 1687-1767

This Minuet *by Telemann has been transposed and adapted to fit a harp with a smaller range. You may need to play it up an octave on a lap harp.*

Once again, note the phrasing. You should analyze all the music you learn—or listen to, for that matter—to determine where the musical phrases (rather like sentences) fall. Try not to think note by note but in lines of musical thought. If you were singing the treble part, where would be the most musical place to breathe? What about the bass?

Note that there are first and second endings in the repeats. The first time, play through to the repeat sign as written. The second time, skip the section marked 1., going right to the second ending, 2.

Go over the fingering carefully and see if it works for you. If not, change it. It is important that you can move smoothly from one note to another.

Minuet

Transposed from G

Gymopédie No. 3

Erik Satie, 1866-1925

Our next offering is a lovely piece that seems made for the harp, although it is usually played on the piano or in an arrangement made by Debussy for orchestra. Its serene and otherworldly mood evokes a multitude of images. After an introduction of tranquil chords, a melody soars high above—floating. A favorite of Mallory's, we have developed it as a duet.

This arrangement is very little changed from the original. Two notes were omitted and some of the bass notes were transposed up an octave to make it easier to play. Practice the left hand until you are comfortable with it. Then add the right hand. It is a challenge, but once you have mastered it, you will have something special.

Gymnopédie No. 3 *makes a lovely duet which is fairly easy to play. The accompaniment should be played on a fairly large harp. Some of the bass notes can go down an octave if you have those notes available on your instrument. The left hand plays the single bass note on the first beat and the right hand plays the chord (except in measures 11 and 13 where the left hand must help fill out the notes). It may be helpful to write the chord names next to the chords on the second beat followed by a slash and the bass note (see READING CHORD SYMBOLS).*

The melody, which comes in on the fifth measure, is notated at the top of the treble clef with the stems always up. It can be played on another harp (nylon or wire) or with a flute, violin, oboe or any other treble instrument. It might even be played by a guitar. Or an electronic keyboard.

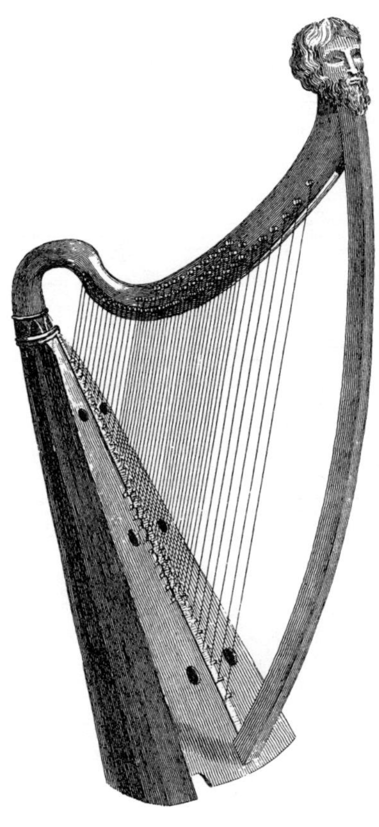

Gymnopédie No. 3

Blind Mary
Separation of Soul and Body

Turlough O'Carolan, 1670-1738

Turlough O'Carolan is included in this section even though he is not usually thought of as a "classical" composer. In much the same manner that ragtime composer Scott Joplin studied the classics and strived to learn from them, Carolan, too, was a serious composer who was influenced by the great Baroque composers of his time. Combining the music of the continent with his native Irish music, he developed a unique style.

Carolan was born in 1670. When he was eighteen he was blinded by smallpox. Fortunately he had a kind mentor who arranged for him to be taught the harp, provided him with an instrument, a horse and a guide and, when deemed ready after three years, sent him to make his way as an itinerant harper (it was not uncommon to teach the blind to make a living playing the harp).

But Turlough was far from a great harper. Fortunately, one of his early patrons suggested he try his hand at composing; his tunes have lived on ever since. Many were written for special people and were well received by great and common folk alike. There are many tales—some tall—about Carolan. He must have been quite a character and most fond of good drink and companionship. But he made music that touched people both then and now.

Unfortunately, we only have the melodies (and, in Gaelic, some of the poetry). The harmonies did not survive. Some of his songs were played at the last gathering of the old harpers at Belfast in 1792 and taken down in keyboard arrangements by nineteen-year-old Edward Bunting, but by then harpers were literally a dying breed and it is not clear if the harmonies for these few tunes reflect how Carolan played them.

So it has become tradition for players of Carolan to make their own arrangements. Some approach with scholarly study of the Irish and Baroque music of the times. Others take the melody as a thing out of time and arrange it as they feel it. Janna has done the latter in the two songs offered here.

Blind Mary *is well known. Sweet, lyrical, it pleases with its simple melody.* Separation of Soul and Body *was an unusual title that caught our attention among the lively tunes and the planxtyes. When we played it, we felt it was something we wanted to include in our repertoire. Perhaps it was an elegy for a lost friend, a poignant farewell.*

Carolan's music is so much of the current Celtic harp movement that it is unusual to hear a concert or an album without him somewhere. Songs are written in his honor, or to evoke the feel of his music. So don't stop here with the two offerings in Janna's style. Search out more. Listen to what others have done to bring the music to life.

When you come across a written arrangement of a Carolan tune consider taking the melody by itself before you play someone's interpretation. What does it say to you? Do you hear harmonies that differ from the version before you? If so, work with it until you make it your own. Does it call for ornamentation? That is quite consistent with the music. Close your eyes and sing or play it. What does it seem to want? Can you make that happen?

Blind Mary

Turlough O'Carolan
Irish
Arr. J. McCall Geller
Freely
C
F
C
Amin
Emin
Dmin
G
C
G
F
Emi
C
Dmin
G
C
L.H.
R.H.
C
Amin
G
Amin
C
Dmin
G
C
Dmin7
Emin
F
C
G
C

Separation of Soul and Body

Appendix One: THE WIRE STRUNG HARP

by Dinah LeHoven

Dinah LeHoven has been playing wire harp since the late 1970s, when she saw her first one at a Renaissance fair. She is the editor of "Ringing Strings," a column in the quarterly Folk Harp Journal *devoted to promoting and encouraging the wire harp. Currently, she works in film and TV production in Los Angeles.*

Dinah LeHoven with her Caswell Gwydion high-headed wire harp. Photo by Jon Lackey.

Although places as disparate as Siberia and South America have developed harps with wire strings, the instrument commonly meant when referring to the wire strung harp comes from the Celtic countries, particularly Ireland and Highland Scotland. There, a centuries-old aristocratic tradition of subtle and sophisticated music had nearly entirely died out by 1792, when a major harp festival in Belfast attracted only ten Irish harpers.

Fortunately, a young church organist named Edward Bunting was hired to note down some of the old tunes. Fascinated by what he heard, he made it his life's work, publishing three volumes of music, lore and technique, between 1796 and 1840. These were greeted with a notable lack of public enthusiasm as chromatic music was then in vogue, along with instruments, like the piano, which could manage it. The wire harp languished, generally ignored, for over a century.

In the 1960s and '70s, a wire harp revival began in Brittany with players like Alan Stivell, whose "Renaissance of the Celtic Harp" still stands as a classic recording which has inspired countless harpers. Builders began reproducing historic instruments, and it once again became feasible to actually acquire a wire strung harp.

In the late 1970s, a Minneapolis musician named Ann Heymann discovered Edward Bunting's *Ancient Music of Ireland*. Undaunted by the fact that he had "arranged" the music for piano, she began to decipher his notes on technique, damping and ornamentation, re-creating an historically based style for the instrument. Meanwhile other players around the world were developing new styles, extending the capabilities of the instrument and applying techniques from other fields. As it stands today, the wire strung harp is at a particularly exciting point in its history, precisely because of this great variety of approaches.

There are three major differences between wire strung harps and the rest of the folk harp world: the sound, the playing techniques and the construction.

CONSTRUCTION: Most commonly, wire harps are built entirely of hardwood in a style and design heavily influenced by the few historical examples remaining. Some builders have begun producing models with spruce soundboards, similar to nylon harp construction. The resulting instrument is less resonant and provides a good gradient for a player switching over from nylon harp who doesn't want the full ringing tone of a more traditional instrument.

Although some makers use steel on the upper strings, brass or phosphor bronze is more common. Guitar strings are definitely not recommended. Replacement strings and directions for restringing should come with the harp; string sources can be found in publications like the *Folk Harp Journal*. [Ed. Note: See RESOURCES in the Appendix.] Whether to choose brass or phosphor bronze is a matter of personal preference; the difference in tone is audible but hard to describe.

You can clean your strings when they get dark or sticky, either with alcohol or 00 (very fine) grade steel wool (you can get the steel wool shavings off your soundboard with a magnet). To color them red and blue use a magic marker. If your harp has wound strings at the bass end don't clean or color them.

Sharping levers do work on wire harps, although they generally affect the tone more noticeably than on nylon strings. It is not uncommon to find them offered as an extra-cost option.

When choosing a wire harp, be aware that string spacing is frequently more narrow, or at very least, more variable from maker to maker than among nylon harps. Tone and amount of ring and sustain also vary, and the amount of sustain you will find desirable may well depend on your own playing style. So it's particularly important to hear the harp before you buy, or clarify the builder's return policy beforehand in case the harp does not meet your expectations. At the same time, consider that it takes the instrument a while to realize it's now a harp and no longer a tree; a new wire harp will take time to stay in tune and will manifest considerable improvement in tone over the first year or so.

PLAYING TECHNIQUES: More than any other folk harpers, wire strung players are in the enviable position of re-creating, discovering and developing playing techniques that are appropriate to their instrument. Perhaps because there are still not as many wire as nylon harpers, or perhaps because the ancient tradition was so thoroughly extinguished, there are few rigorous absolutes yet about wire harping, although identifiable (and very different) styles are developing around well known performers.

The wire harp was traditionally played on the left shoulder. It really makes no difference in technique, and if you already play nylon, or are heavily grounded in keyboard, it's unnecessarily confusing to switch from the "right hand treble, left hand bass" orientation. If you're coming to it fresh, you can decide which way feels most comfortable.

The two primary techniques most characteristic of wire harp playing are the use of fingernails and of damping.

Although it's not absolutely necessary to play with fingernails, the tone produced is brighter and louder. The nails need not be very long. In order for the nails to reach the strings, the hand position is modified from the classic nylon "thumbs up" position. Basically, the palm points more towards the floor, and the thumb points towards the strings in roughly the same plane as the other fingers. (Any good wire harp tutor, such as Ann Heymann's *Secrets of the Gaelic Harp*, will illustrate the position in more detail.)

Damping (the silencing of a plucked string) is perhaps the most controversial facet of wire harp technique, and the one most frequently used to scare off prospective beginners. Ironically, it may have come to seem more complicated than it is precisely because so many different approaches have been successful.

Damping is necessary because wire strings have much greater sustain than nylon or gut. Viewed as a problem, this means that a note or chord followed by disharmonious notes will clash unless something is done to stop the first notes from continuing to sound. Viewed as an opportunity, it means that "arranging" becomes easier, because allowing a selected string to ring on creates a chord as surely as plucking it again. Particularly in the bass this renders a simple, uncluttered arrangement extremely effective, much more so than would be the case if the identical strings were played on a nylon harp.

This characteristic makes the wire harp particularly satisfying for a beginner, because slow, sonorous pieces with "easy" basses sound good right away. More complex damping, such as the creating of subtle chord changes and harmonies can come later, as the player's skills increase.

The key to effective damping is to listen to your particular instrument. Some harps have so little ring they need hardly any damping in the treble range, and even in the bass damping becomes a rhythmic device used more for effect. Some harps are so vibrant that a beautiful arrangement can be done by simply playing the melody, stopping the objectionable notes and adding an occasional bass note for emphasis. Most fall somewhere in between. The type of tune and the effect you wish to produce will also dictate how much damping is necessary.

The various methods and tricks to damping are outside the scope of this chapter; entire books could—and have—been written on the subject. For starters, it may be enough for you to simply consider the need for damping when you first learn the fingering for a tune. For stability and good technique, most often you will be pre-placing your fingers before you pluck them anyway, and a little thoughtful modification of the fingering indicated for nylon players will allow you to place those fingers where you need them to damp strings.

Lastly, we come to the biggest difference between wire and nylon or gut strung harp: **THE SOUND.** A wire harp has a bright, ringing, sustained tone, most frequently compared to the pealing of bells. If you love the sound of the wire harp and prefer it to nylon or gut, then that's what you should choose to play. It's as simple as that, because your pleasure in the sounds you are producing is what will give you incentive to practice.

ARRANGING FOR WIRE HARP

A more appropriate term might be "dearranging for wire harp," because you will find that most arrangements have far more notes in them than you're going to need. [Ed. Note: Including most of the ones in this book.] Beware, especially, of pieces with a lot of consecutive chords; if played as written, these will require a lot of damping to keep them from blurring into mush. Experiment with which chords you can leave out entirely, which you should damp and which ones sound terrific ringing on through the entire measure.

If you are playing chord patterns, either as the bass part to a tune or as an accompaniment to a vocal, it can be a useful trick to damp the bottom three notes by immediately re-placing your fingers, leaving the top note ringing. This creates a pleasing legato effect as you go on to the next chord, while still removing most of the ringing strings.

Usually, traditional Celtic music sounds best played with ornamentation, those quick little grace notes which create a shimmer of sound around the melody itself. Consider the nature of your instrument when you adapt ornamentation from other sources. If you use a harmonious note, or notes, which you will not have to damp, it can ring on to become part of your arrangement. For example, choose a grace note a third away, rather than adjacent to the melody note. When in doubt, you can always retreat back to the melody, arranging it by choosing which strings you want to leave ringing to blend into chords with the following notes. Add some notes in the bass to blend and contrast with your melody. Fifths and octaves work very well; generally "less is more" is a good motto.

A lot of erroneous information has developed on the subject of wire harps, especially among people who do not ordinarily play them. I have not found them to be intrinsically more temperamental than nylon harps; a good wire harp, treated normally with regard to matters of temperature, humidity and hard knocks, is no more likely to break strings or go out of tune than a nylon one. You may hear claims that they are more difficult to play, that keeping long fingernails is too much trouble. The truth is, any harp/harper combination is going to have its own unique joys and difficulties; the challenges a wire harper faces are simply different from the difficulties a nylon harper has.

If you like the sound of the wire harp, don't let yourself be talked out of it simply because nylon harps are more readily available. If you're in an isolated area and concerned about access to teachers, consider that there are some excellent "teach yourself" book/tape combinations aimed specifically at wire harpers. In addition, other players are generally happy to "network" and share tips on everything from damping techniques to nail care.

In fact, your biggest problem may be where to hear this wonderful instrument so that you <u>can</u> fall in love with it. If you have no access to an actual harp, I suggest you try recordings. Not just obvious ones, by wire harp artists such as Alan Stivell or Patrick Ball, but ones where the two types of harps are played together and you can hear the contrast. Anything by the Scottish duo Sileas (several recordings on Green Linnet) is a good example, as is "The Harper's Land" by Ann Heymann and Alison Kinnaird.

Appendix Two: The Pedal Harp

Occasionally people ask us what is the difference between our folk harps and the big golden harps used in the symphony orchestras. Janna has been known to lean on her 38 string Triplett Premiere (a large harp for a folk harp), grin and say, "somewhat more than twenty thousand dollars." True, but there is more to the concert harp than gold gilt and a hefty price-tag.

Most obvious, of course, are the pedals. They are controlled by the harpist's feet and change the pitch of the strings. Each note in the scale has its own pedal and each pedal has three positions: flat, natural and sharp. This allows the harpist to play in all keys and to access all the notes on the chromatic scale (although not necessarily at the same time).

The pillar is straight to accommodate the mechanism, a series of rods and levers connected to the pedals at the base and to two-pronged (or forked) disks—two for each string—on the neck. When the disks rotate the prongs press against the string on opposite sides, thus raising the pitch a half step for each disk. With a pedal harp, all the strings of a given note are altered, ie, all the *Cs* or all the *Ds* (etc.) are sharped or flatted at the same time. This makes changing keys very easy and enables one to play accidentals without removing the hands from the strings. The pedals also facilitate some special effects using enharmonic tones (notes with different names that sound the same pitch, such as *D♯* and *E♭*).

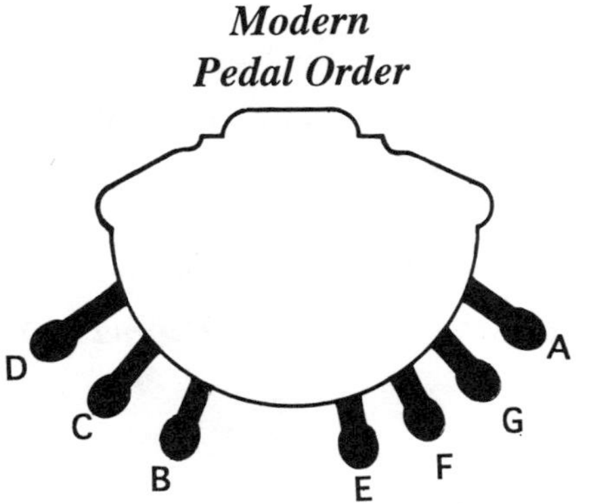

Harp by Salvi

"

The pedals are arranged in a semi-circle at the base of the harp, three on the left and four on the right. Reading from left to right, the pedals are for *D, C, B* on the left and *E, F, G, A* on the right. As most of us are limited to two feet, only two pedals can be operated at a given time. The pedals rest inside stair-step notches. When the pitch is to be lowered, the harpist slides the pedal outward (away) and spring tension moves it upwards to the next highest notch. To sharpen a note, the pedal is pressed straight down and then locked inward (toward you), held by the top of the stepped notch (it is possible to momentarily sharpen a note by pushing down [and away] and not locking it in).

With practice, the harpist knows just where each pedal is located and can quickly shift them around, but arrangements for pedal harp have to allow enough time. Highly chromatic passages, therefore, are difficult or impossible. (The Welsh have a triple strung folk harp with the sharps down the center and the naturals on the two outside rows. There is also a double strung harp where the sharps and the naturals cross in the middle. These are truly chromatic harps and are beginning to attract a new group of performers, much as the wire harp did a couple of decades ago. However, these harps are far more difficult and require dedication.)

If you get a chance to try out a pedal harp, by all means do it! It is a fascinating experience for a folk harper. Your first reaction will probably be that it seems huge, often over six feet tall (although Salvi does make the Daphne, a 40 string pedal harp that is about the same size as a large folk harp and about two thirds the cost of the "inexpensive" low-end giltless concert harps). A full size concert grand has 47 strings, with a low *C* in the bass, although 46 string semi-grand models starting with a *D* are also common. As you pull it to your shoulder you will notice that it seems hefty—sturdy and solid. That is because it has to support the pedal mechanism and the string tension. Most folk harpers find the action (the amount of force needed to pluck a string) to be heavy.

If possible, have the owner give you a tour of his or her instrument. If not, with permission, here are some things you can explore. If the pedals are in a neutral position (that is the harp plays the *C* scale), play something you know that does not require any sharping. Get the feel of the harp before you begin to try the pedals. Do not use your nails—get your pads fully on the strings. Pay attention to the sound. Perceptions differ and harps differ, but our experience is that most pedal harps seem to have a rounder, more mature sound than the average folk harp, but lack the brilliance and presence of the lighter, more nimble instrument. One is not better than the other—only different.

Now, put the harp back up straight and examine the pedals. Be sure they are sticking out, not up (they are hinged for travel). Work one with your hand to get the feel of the action (note they work in mirror image on the two sides). The pedals will most likely be all in the raised (flat) position (which is where you should leave them when you are finished unless instructed to do otherwise) or in the middle position. If they are not in the middle, pull the harp back on your shoulder and carefully move each pedal with your foot into place. Do not release the pedal until you are sure that it has locked under the notch as it has a powerful spring (if it started in the flat position, you will be moving each pedal down and in). Play the *C* scale to be sure that every pedal is in the right place. Put the harp back up and look if necessary.

Now locate the *F* pedal (third from the right) and rest your right foot lightly in place. Play an *F*. Now push down and away from you, keeping your foot on the pedal. The note will sharp. Let it up smoothly and the note will return to its original pitch.

Carefully lock the pedal in the *F♯* position. The harp is now in the *G* tuning. Easy, wasn't it? Want to play in the key of *F*? From the neutral position slide the *B* pedal away, out and up to *B♭*. On a folk harp in *C*, you'd have to retune.

Play something in a minor key where you have been playing an open fifth instead of a full dominant chord on the folk harp. Before you start playing, locate the pedal that controls the third of the dominant (*D♯* for a *B* chord for example). Rest your foot on it when you start and press it when you come to the chord. You can easily now play the entire triad!

At this point you may have a momentary lapse and crave a pedal harp (that is until you again play your folk harp and reexperience its nimble action and bright, singing tone). We have a pedal harp—an old Lyon & Healy—but it gets passed over for the folk harp most of the time. We wouldn't want to give either up; they are different instruments.

There is another thing you should try while you have a pedal harp to hand. You can figure this out yourself, or have the harp's owner position the pedals: a glissando that is not just a scale, but a chord. Common chords used for glissandos are major six/nine chords (that is a major triad with the 6th and the 9th added) and diminished chords. We'll go for a *C 6/9* which is also the pentatonic scale built on *C*.

Moving from left to right, set the pedals in the following positions: *D natural; C natural; B sharped; E natural; F flatted; G natural; A natural.* Now play some glissandos. You'll recognize that pretty sound—it's used all the time. Practiced harpists gliss from chord to chord for a sound unique to the pedal harp.

What exactly happened? The notes left "natural" are the notes of the chord. We sharped *B* which raised it to *B♯* which is enharmonically the same note as *C*. *F* was flatted down to the enharmonic of *E*. These scale notes were effectively cancelled. With three positions possible for each note, there are many permutations. Good composers for harp understand what can be done and make excellent use of the enharmonic notes.

It takes time, but you can get the effect on your folk harp from a *C* tuning if you want to see how it sounds. Sharp all the *B*s, making them *C*s and sharp the *E*s, making them *F*s. This gives you an *F 6/9*, the pentatonic scale starting on *F*. With a pedal harp you can make those changes in seconds.

A loud note of warning if you are looking for a used pedal harp. They are very touchy and can have all sorts of things wrong with them. If a harp doesn't play well and/or all the pedals don't work smoothly, pass it up unless you know a qualified pedal harp repair person who can look it over before you buy (a good idea anyway). We were lucky. Our old harp is far from perfect but it fulfills our needs. But we took a chance buying blind. Don't do it, unless you are willing to have a pretty and expensive prop to decorate your home. Beware especially of antique harps that need restoration. This is not a do-it-yourself task. Many are beyond help. Buy from a reputable harp dealer or have the harp checked out. Contact the American Harp Society for referrals (see RESOURCES in the Appendix).

There is a folk pedal harp that warrants mention. It is Tyrolian and uses a single action. With these harps you can sharp but you cannot flat, just like your lever harp. The pluses are that you don't have to remove your fingers from playing position and the pedals sharp all the strings at the same time. The first pedal harps were single action and were popular in the early part of the 19th Century. The usual tunings for a single action harp are *E♭* or *A♭*.

"Janna's Fantasy"

Janna as Harpo.
Photos by Mallory.

Appendix Three: Should You Build Your Own Harp?

Many people have the dream of making their own harps, either from a kit or from scratch. The idea of creating a harp that is truly personal has much appeal. However, in our dealing with harpmakers we have come to fully appreciate just how much goes into making a fine instrument. Those who have the skills and knowledge to make harps have our highest admiration—they are masters of a fine old tradition.

Whether or not harp building is for you depends on you, your skills, you willingness to research your project and the availability of the necessary tools to complete the task. Let's examine two ways of approaching the project.

Steve Triplett takes time out from harpbuilding and designing.
Photo by Mallory.

BUILDING A HARP FROM A KIT

If you want to save money on your harp by building it from a kit, forget it. It just doesn't work that way. Too many times kits never get built, or get half finished when the maker gives up on it. Kit building at the level of harpmaking requires previous fine woodworking skills, a shop full of tools (the cost of buying all those clamps needed is considerable, just for a start) and a wealth of time and patience. If you really want to make an instrument and have no experience, consider a mountain dulcimer. Harps are simply not for beginners.

Kits come in various types and different ones come and go on the market. If you do decide to consider a kit, do a lot of research on the company selling it and find out exactly what work they do for you on the instrument— and, most important, don't do. For example, Triplett Harps offers kits for some of their models (rather reluctantly because of the misconception that kits are easy and save money) which do some—but far from all—of the most difficult tasks. These kits are designed for someone skilled in woodworking and instrument making who wants to make that one special instrument that is his or hers alone. If that someone is you, by all means investigate the kits; if not, buy your harp fully completed. You'll save time, money and your sanity.

There is another type of kit that is intermittently offered: an unfinished, unstrung but otherwise complete harp. You fine sandpaper it, decorate it, apply a finish and string it. It sounds easy, but we have seen an awful lot of those, too, floating around that are never completed. They are more work than most people think. When they are completed many of them are not exactly artist-quality instruments. The harp is only as good as the design and the materials that go into it. Before any kit maker out there gets his or her hackles up, it must be made clear that kits come in many levels of workmanship. Yours may be wonderful, simple to assemble and sound delightful. If so, we'd like to hear about it so we can recommend it.

Harp makers can not guarantee their kit harps—they did not put them together. Things sometimes happen to even the finest instrument and that extra protection is another good reason to buy your harp ready to play.

If we seem to sound like we are discouraging you from building a kit, you're right. But if you still think that you want to try it, by all means investigate what is available and ask a *lot* of questions before you buy. Get a look at the assembly manual; is it clear and complete? What woods are used? What kind of track record does the maker have? Use your good common sense.

MAKING A HARP FROM SCRATCH

If you are considering going this route we assume you have the basic skills and now need to discover how to use them to make a harp. Once again we suggest you join the Folk Harp Society. There are articles in the *Journal* about others who have made instruments and many of them are more than willing to share what they know.

Do you want to copy an historic harp? Or perhaps create something based on an old painting? Maybe you would like to explore uncharted ground. Tantalizing challenges are waiting for the craftsperson who chooses to become a harpmaker.

You will want to do extensive research to discover just what kind of instrument you want to build. Examine as many harps as you can, old and new. Talk to harpers and builders to find out what works for them. Investigate available plans. Learn about woods, parts availability, string scaling and everything else that goes into making a harp.

Start with a tree!!

Appendix Four: Amplifying Your Harp

If you perform in public, sooner or later you will come up against the question of whether or not to amplify. Sometimes it is essential if you want to be heard. At other times it is a judgement call. Usually the aim is to keep the basic acoustic quality of the instrument but you do have the option of some wild and wonderful special effects using a number of the state-of-the-art electronics available. Without getting technical—which is beyond both the scope of this book and our expertise—here is some miscellany about using sound systems, effects and the like.

You can amplify your harp in several ways. The most usual is with a microphone or pickup, either placed near the instrument or mounted in or on it. It is easy to make a harp loud by these methods, but somewhat more difficult to make it sound good. The sound of a harp is quite complex (and thus difficult to realistically synthesize). Unless you damp them, the strings continue to ring long after they are plucked. Additionally, all the other strings sound sympathetically, a subtle but important part of what makes up the characteristic harp sound. Microphones and PA systems are rarely capable of doing justice.

We have found that with amplification, less is better. Unless you are trying for an effect (see below), don't overdo it. Your harp will sound best when it does not sound artificially enhanced. Setting the optimum volume and tonal levels are next to impossible to do by yourself. Try to have someone whose musical taste you trust perform a sound check before a performance, especially if you are controlling the amp from your harp on stage. Work out a signaling system during the performance in case adjustments are needed; a room full of people is acoustically different from an empty one.

If you plan to do a lot of performing in different places, you should consider getting your own sound system. This gives you more control and allows you to be self-contained.

The least expensive system—usually adequate for casual gigs—starts with a small, all purpose soundboard pick-up (Dean Markley Artist Model, Barcus-Berry Outer, etc). They are available with a gummy back or double sided tape that sticks where you want it. Couple it with a speaker/amp unit and you are in business. Be sure to try out an amp before you buy it, even if you have to take your harp into the store. At this writing, nobody is marketing an amp package specifically for harps. So you will need to get a keyboard, bass or guitar amp—whatever sounds best for your particular instrument.

Be sure that all of your equipment works well together. If you don't know about the intricacies of matching impedances and other such esoterica, find someone who does to help you with your selections. Your aim is to produce a clean, clear sound, free from annoying hum or distortion.

Some experimentation will reveal the ideal place to put the pick-up on the soundboard; try about two-thirds up from the bottom. Play each of the notes, one by one, and you'll probably discover that some are louder than others; you may have to make some compromises. Adding an equalizer will significantly improve the sound on most systems. A second pick-up may be desirable for a larger harp. Convenient and unobtrusive pick-ups can be custom installed inside the instrument with a jack in the lower back or underside of the soundbox.

What is acceptable in a sound system is very much a matter of your taste, your ear and how you plan to use it. Systems for a harp can range from a small piezo pick-up and a battery-run Pignose amp to a sophisticated harp-specific state-of-the-art Planar Wave system as marketed by Barcus-Berry mated with an amp and speakers designed to make even the most jaded audiophile drool. Try not to spend more on your sound system than you have on your harp!

Once you are wired, you may want to experiment with effects. Harp sounds can be processed just like those of a guitar or any other instrument. If you know a musician with guitar effect boxes or pedals try plugging in. It is an experience to play Green Sleeves with a Jimmy Hendrix wail! Or, in another bend of the cosmos, consider harpist Andreas Vollenweider who has sold a lot of records with his highly processed new-age sound. If neither is to your taste, you may still like a touch of subtle electronic sweetening.

Two workable effects are chorus and delay. Both "fatten" the sound, but in different ways. Delay, as the name implies, replays the sound slightly (or not so slightly, depending on the setting) later: the classic echo. Chorus duplicates the sound at a slightly different pitch, giving the effect of more than one instrument playing. "Slightly" is the key word here; don't overdo it unless you have something startling in mind. If wild is for you, blast off to the worlds of flangers, fuzz, phasers and their friends: second star to the right and straight on 'til morning.

Appendix Five: How to Sing Properly

by Veronica Diamond

Veronica Diamond is a voice coach who has worked with just about every style of singer from rock to opera; she was Mallory's teacher. Her dramatic coloratura soprano has won her countless leading roles in opera houses throughout Europe and the United States.

Veronica Diamond, voice coach.

Learning to sing is simple once you understand how your voice works. When you sing you should be able to produce a sound that is clear and free throughout your full range. The purpose of this chapter is to help you identify, understand and reliably recreate some of the correct physical sensations of singing.

Both the harp and the voice are stringed instruments and therefore function in a strikingly similar fashion. When you pluck a string on the harp you make a vibration. This creates a tone—it sings! The same thing happens when you vibrate your vocal cords. Your vibration creates a tone—you sing! When you combine the vibrations of both harp and voice, you are able to produce a sound that is very exciting to the human ear.

When you sing, your head, chest and mouth cavities amplify and resonate your tone just as the soundbox of a harp amplifies the sound of its strings. When you pluck a harp string, the harder you pluck the louder the tone becomes. Likewise, the more breath and voice pressure you exert on your voice box, or larynx, the louder your singing tone becomes. To make a higher pitch on the harp you must tighten a string. When you sing the voice box works in much the same way. The tension in it must be adjusted to make the correct pitch. To sing, you take a breath, allow

189

that breath to vibrate the vocal cords and adjust the voice box tension to create the desired pitch. To sing a high note, you must allow the cords to thin and tighten their tension as their edges vibrate, much like a harp string.

Now let's talk about producing your voice. You will find that singing is simply correct breathing, openings, strong muscle resistance and the ability to throw your voice with an open throat.

Never stress your voice or vocal cords beyond their immediate ability. Don't push or oversing. As your strength and endurance increase your vocal cords will carry a heavier load for you, but you need to become sensitive to when you are overloading your voice. How? You'll feel it. If it doesn't feel good, you are doing something wrong. Stop and analyze what you are doing. Beautiful singing feels good! Protect your cords from strain by learning to put the load of singing onto your breathing muscles, opening muscles and resisting muscles. Try to leave your throat and voice box alone—they have enough to do. The exercises are designed to help you learn to do this, but they will do you no good (and probably won't even make sense) unless you actually do them.

Begin with Exercise One—**BREATHING MUSCLES**. This exercise is designed to help you to become aware of your breathing muscles and to strengthen them. Lie on your back on the floor and take two large phone books and place them on your belly button. Now take a slow, deep, open breath through your mouth and let the air drop all the way down to your navel and fill your lungs. Inhale for a count of six and hold for a count of six. Now sigh this breath out in a noisy exhale, also for a count of six. Repeat twenty times.

Observe how the books rise up as you breathe in and go down as you sigh out. Why? As you inhale, the air fills your lungs, which expand and move the books upward. As you exhale, the air is pushed out of the lungs by the diaphragm muscles. The books move down as you exhale and the lungs empty. They work like weights, strengthening the diaphragm muscles as you do this exercise while teaching you to breathe properly.

Next, feel your opening muscles, which include your throat, tongue and jaw. You have heard that to sing well you must sing with an open throat. What is the physical feeling? How do you repeat it?

Exercise Two—**TONGUE AND JAW**—will help you focus on these muscles and what they are supposed to do. Sit in front of a mirror and yawn deeply. Observe your tongue and jaw as you begin to yawn, before the tongue contracts. As you inhale, feel your throat muscles pressing open with air. This is your correct "open throat" feeling. See that your tongue lies quietly on the floor of your mouth and your jaw slides down and out of the way. Repeat twelve times.

Remind your throat muscles to pull open, not closed. As you yawn, focus on the jaw sliding open, then down and out of the way; focus on the tongue slipping loosely down to the floor of the mouth, lightly lying against the bottom teeth, out of the way. These physical movements help your throat cavities to relax and open, so that your sound comes out of your mouth and is not trapped inside.

Now let's talk about your vocal cords. Exercise Three—**VOCAL CORDS**—will allow you to feel the cords vibrate and become familiar with this feeling. Stand up and yawn. As you yawn, inhale for a count of six, close your mouth and hum for a count of six. Place your fingers on your adam's apple/voice box and notice the vibration of your cords. Exhale for a count of six. Relax and repeat six times.

When you sing, the vocal cords need to vibrate, about six oscillations per second. Anything you do to prevent this natural vibration from happening puts a strain on your cords. Any pressure or strain can eventually cause damage or nodes and distort your natural sound. Generally speaking, the faster the cords vibrate, the healthier the voice.

Next, we want to resist the breath and voice pressure so that the throat stays open and you sing beautiful sound. When you sing, you need to resist the air from rising up and out of your lungs prematurely. Have you ever experienced taking a big breath and still running out of air before a phrase is finished? What happened? Remember the diaphragm? Its job is to push the air out of your body and then invert, like an upside down plate, just under your ribcage. Well, the diaphragm worked very well. It pushed all the air out—before you were finished singing! You need to resist the air from rising and the diaphragm from inverting too soon. The last two exercises are designed to help you solve this problem.

In Exercise Four, **DIAPHRAGM RESISTING,** return to the floor position with books on your navel. Inhale for a count of six, hold for a count of six and exhale for a count of six. As you exhale, push out at your belly button, resisting against the books. This is your resistance point. Feel it. Now take another open mouth breath for a count of six, hold for a count of six, slide the teeth closed and "hiss" the air out slowly. Check your resistance point. "Hiss" the air out as slowly as possible. Now resist more as you "hiss" loud and soft. Feel the diaphragm working for you. Do twenty in a group and then rest and do twenty more. Repeat five sets of twenty or do one hundred per day.

Remember to resist out at the navel and not below it. The lower muscles will move out some, on their own, but your point of resistance is at the navel. As you do Exercise Four, hold the resistance until you are out of breath. You are not forcing anything, simply resisting the diaphragm from pushing the air out and inverting on you, until you are ready. The challenge is to see how long you can go before you need another breath.

Notice the movement of your muscles as you "hiss" loud and soft. This same movement happens when you sing a song. Your resistance steadies your voice and breath. This steady, simultaneous movement is called breath control. Now you have a strong cushion of air that you can float your voice on. This is what it should feel like when you are singing.

Now incorporate Exercise Five—**DIAPHRAGM MOVEMENT**. Stand at the piano or a kitchen counter and press your navel out as you inhale a slow, noisy, open breath through your mouth. Hold this breath and then laugh a big belly laugh, like Santa Claus, "Ho, Ho, Ho." Feel the movement of your diaphragm each time. Now, still standing up, try "hissing." Remember to press out and resist against the piano. Feel the diaphragm move out and in, like a big inner tube placed around your waist. Feel your breath or sound bounce against the inner tube. Now you have the feelings for breath support, breath resistance and making sound using this resistance and movement. These feelings happen when you are singing correctly. Repeat the belly laugh and "hissing" ten times each. Once these feelings become comfortable, you are ready to begin singing songs.

Take a correct breath, resist and sing the first line of *Green Sleeves*. Sing only this one line and remember to resist out until the line is finished. Then sigh the excess breath out, rest a moment, breathe again as you did for line one and sing line two. As you sing, observe where you need to loosen, relax and open more. Sing on the vowels and add the consonants only at the end of the words.

Now that you have an open throat and breath resistance, you are coordinated enough to throw your voice without harm. Pretend you are in a large hall. As you take the correct breath, be sure to slide the tongue and jaw down and out of the way. Check to see if you are pressing your throat open. Resist out, and yell your name as loudly as you can. Go slow. When the throat is open it feels great to yell like this. If you yell on a closed throat, it feels awful. You know if it is correct because it feels good. Trust yourself and repeat only what feels good. If it doesn't feel free and open, stop and correct yourself.

Why have we spent so much time on correct breath? Because correct breath is the foundation for good singing. Let me list the mistakes that happen when you breathe incorrectly:

Mistake One: When you take a high breath, a breath that expands only your chest, you don't get enough air in your lungs to work with.

Mistake Two: When you don't push out and resist, the diaphragm pushes the air out for you and you lose control.

Mistake Three: As air rushes back up your throat, it hits the cords with too much force, and blows them apart, and you sound weak.

Mistake Four: This escaping air hits the bottom of your larynx and pushes the larynx up into your throat. This reduces your volume.

Mistake Five: As your larynx rises up, it activates the base of your tongue. The tongue resists all this pressure by tightening down into your opening. This closes more of your throat opening. All these problems are avoided when the breath and resistance are correct.

This article should be considered only an introduction, but it has given me great pleasure to share this information with you. Remember that your voice is a most precious gift. No singer has the option of going out shopping for a new one. Take care of the one you have been given.

Mallory in full song.
Photo by Janna.

Appendix Six: Tuning by Ear

Before going any further, it would be a good idea to review the mechanics of tuning as described in TUNING YOUR HARP, in Part Two. As we mentioned, the easiest way to tune your harp, especially in a noisy environment, is with the aid of an electronic tuner with lights and/or a meter. If you have a desire to tune by ear, learning to do so will require a certain dedication, and you may need to seek out a quiet place no matter how adept at ear tuning you become.

In order to tune by ear you must possess the basic ability to tell if one tone is higher or lower than another. For some folks this is not as easy as it sounds, but it is the prerequisite to developing the essential skill of ear tuning, which is the matching of tones. If you cannot tell if one tone is sharp or flat of another tone, your needs will be better served by buying an electronic tuner.

At the other end of the spectrum, if you are one of those few people blessed, or, perhaps, cursed, with unfailing absolute pitch—the ability to recognize or sing a given isolated musical tone—you can match one octave of your harp strings to your internal standards, tune by octaves from there, and off you go.

Chances are you are one of the majority and fall somewhere between these extremes. You will need to match a pitch source to tune your harp. This matching is accomplished by listening to two tones sounded together and moving from dissonance to consonance. The dissonance is heard as a beat, wave or fluctuation, which is caused by harmonic interference between the sound waves of one tone and those of the other. Consonance is obtained when the harmonic of the note being tuned is brought into agreement with the same harmonic of the reference note, eliminating this beating to achieve a pure tone.

As the combined sound approaches purity and the waves are brought into congruence, the beating will be heard to slow down and disappear. A good way to visualize this is to imagine two roads running side by side that slowly come together. This effect is the same whether one is matching the sound of two notes of the same pitch, or two notes at some interval—fourth, fifth or octave, for example—apart.

Many people use another musical instrument, such as a piano, as a pitch source. This is fine as long as you happen to have a piano handy, that piano is in tune and you can manage to sound the tone on the piano while matching it on your harp. Having only two hands, this is not an easy thing to do.

There are devices, however, specifically designed to help you. There are three types in general use, all of which are small enough to fit in your pocket or harp case. The easiest to use, but most costly to buy, is electronic, and generates a pure tone at the various pitches you need. The real advantage here is that the device can sound the pitch for as long as required while you put your full attention on plucking the appropriate string with one hand and turning the appropriate tuning pin with the other.

Next lowest in cost and ease of use, but a good compromise, is a pitch pipe. If you hold the pipe in your mouth and blow into the appropriate hole for each of the selected tones, both your hands will be free to pluck and turn until the tones are matched on your harp.

Least costly but most difficult to use is a single tuning fork. The fork is struck against a firm, but not hard, surface—a rubber heel, for example—so that the tines vibrate and sound the selected tone, usually the *A* or *C* above middle *C*. Again, as with the piano example, a third hand would be really useful. One way around this is to hold the fork between your teeth after striking it. This frees your hands and makes the fork a lot easier to hear.

Obviously, using a tuning fork gives you only that one tone and you will need a system to find the other tones in the octave. This is called **setting the temperament**. For more than a century, virtually all music has been written in equal temperament, and that is the kind of temperament we'll deal with here. There are older temperaments, such as meantone, Werkmeister, well-tempered and others, and if you are interested in these earlier forms we encourage you to research them.

There are several good systems in use for setting temperaments but the one given here is probably the quickest and simplest to master. Assuming you have used a *C* fork, after matching your basic *C*, tune the *C* below it to sound a pure octave. This defines the borders of your temperament. Next, move to the *G* a fifth above it and tune that string until any beats are eliminated. Now go down a fourth to the *D* below the *G* just tuned and tune it beatless with the *G*. Again go up a fifth, from the *D* to the *A*, and tune it beatless. Now down a fourth to the *E*, again tuning beatless. Continue up a fifth to the *B* and tune another pure interval.

You have now tuned all the strings in the temperament octave except the *F*. This last note is tuned as a pure fourth by matching it to the *C* below it. It is the only time you tune the top note of a fourth.

This sequence will give a rough temperament that can be refined by slightly narrowing the fifths so that instead of there being a pure interval there is a single beat every two seconds, and slightly widening the fourths so that there is a single beat each second (see below). There are other interval relationships as well. The seconds, thirds and sixths beat quite quickly. But, if the fourths and fifths are correct, the temperament will be correct.

So, go through your temperament tuning again in the same order. The basic *C*s stay the same, but the *G* is tuned just a hair flat, so that there is one beat each two seconds. The next note, *D,* is also tuned flat, so that there is one beat per second. Likewise, the rest of the strings in the octave are tuned slightly flat until you come to the final *F*. This last note is tuned slightly sharp, a beat every second, relative to the lower *C*.

Once these relationships have been achieved, play the scale and listen to the progression of the notes. If there is anything that sounds wrong, fix it by finding the improper beat rates and correcting them. Sometimes, you may have to make the best compromise you can. The rest of the harp can be tuned in pure octaves from the temperament notes, and you're in business.

Mallory tuning his harp.
Photo by Janna.

Appendix Seven: Music Reading Basics

In the world today there are more than 160 nations and literally thousands of languages and dialects. But only music approaches being a universal language, read and understood by diverse peoples everywhere on earth.

As with any language, reading music is a skill that takes some study, formally or informally. Not every musician reads music; every person who speaks words may not be capable of reading those words in print. But just as being able to read and write the printed word greatly aids in coping with the complexities of life, the ability to read music is a big plus for the musician. Written music is a form of communication; a way for one musician to pass a piece of music on to another.

"Reading music" can mean many things. Recently a record producer liked the sound of Janna playing on one of her wire harps and asked her if she could "read." Both knew that he was asking if she could play at first sight music put in front of her in a recording session. She replied that while she could sight-read a lead sheet, what he was asking was probably beyond her current abilities. And yet she is most certainly musically literate—it was, in this case, a matter of degree.

If you can find the notes on the staff and name them, you are reading music. For the purposes of this book, that is half the battle. Don't be discouraged if you can't pick up a tune and play it right off. If you want to work at reading until you can play anything put in front of you cold, your dedication and practice will put you at a high level of music literacy. Symphony orchestra musicians develop this skill as part of their art, but many of the rest of us are content with a more modest accomplishment. So let's take a look at the basics: the "See Dick. See Dick run" of music reading.

There are two fundamental elements (and some auxiliary refinements we'll touch on in a bit) of music notation. The first is the **pitch** of the note. The second is its **duration**—how long it is held.

Musical notes are written as spots—usually with stems and sometimes with flags or barred together—on five-line grids called **staves**. Pitch is indicated by the location of these spots in the same manner that the music sounds. That is, the higher up on the staff the note is located, the higher the pitch. The staves are set up like the harp (conveniently for us) in that they are diatonic: each line or space indicates one named note.

A **clef** is a character placed at the beginning of a staff which indicates which notes are located on that staff. With harp music we are dealing with two clefs (the same used in piano music): the treble (upper) clef and the bass clef. We have an instrument with a wide range, so we need a system that covers the compass from the bottom to the top. Some other instruments read only one of those clefs (or, rarely, an entirely different one).

Take a look at any piece in this book. The two clefs are separated by a wide space. This gives the impression that the clefs are not particularly connected. This is misleading. If you were to draw a line in the center of that space (for middle *C*), the grid of lines would become continuous. But a staff of eleven lines would be confusing and impractical, which is one reason they are spread.

THE EXTENDED STAFF ·

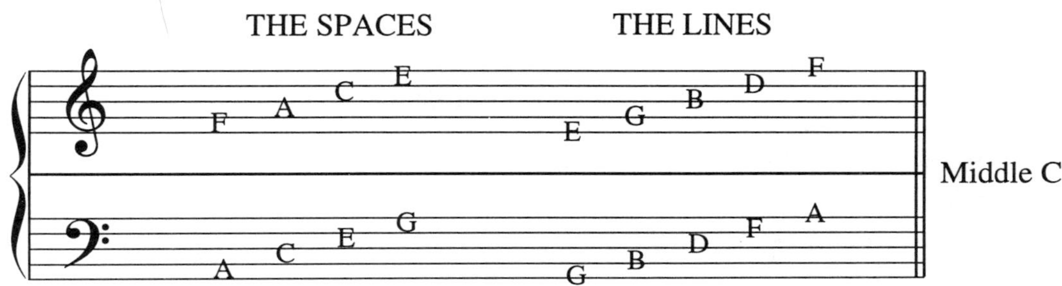

Usually the bass clef indicates music played by the left hand and the treble clef indicates the right. If we were to use a solid eleven line staff and the right hand part went below middle *C*, it would be difficult to tell that it was supposed to be played by that hand. So, with the two staves spread, our middle *C* is indicated by drawing a little line, just big enough for one note, representing that middle line we talked about before. If middle *C* is to be played in the right hand, the line with the note attached to it is placed just below the treble clef. Likewise, middle *C* played in the left hand is indicated by the same notation just above the bass clef. *Believe Me, If All Those Endearing Young Charms* uses middle *Cs* played at different times by different hands.

SOME MIDDLE Cs

These small lines above or below the staves on which notes are written are called ledger lines. They extend the staff to accommodate notes that do not fall within the scope of that staff. So another reason for the big space between the staves is to allow, through the use of ledger lines, one staff (ie, the part for one hand) to indicate notes that would normally be written in the other staff.

So far we have located middle *C*, a very useful note but not enough to play much of a tune. All the lines and all the spaces of the staves have corresponding note names. If the first ledger line below the treble clef is *C*, then the next higher note (the space below the lowest line) is *D*. The first actual staff note at the bottom of the treble clef is, therefore, *E,* and it goes up step by step from there.

The lines, reading from bottom up, are *E, G, B, D* and *F*. The spaces are, from the bottom up, *F, A, C* and *E*. Remembering the spaces is easy: they spell a word, FACE. It is a long standing tradition to give the letters of the note names of the lines a mnemonic tag. The most usual, and rather boring, *Every Good Boy Does Fine* is taught to children. You can do better than that! Figure out something that will stick with you. *Eerie Ghouls Bring Dangerous Forces? Eccentric Geniuses Brilliantly Dance Fandangos?* The sillier it is, the easier it is to recall.

Now let's tackle the bass clef. The lines, from the bottom up, are *G, B, D, F, A* and the spaces are *A, C, E, G.* No easy words here, although you may notice a pattern. In the bass clef everything has moved down a third, so with the spaces of the bass clef you'll notice the *A, C, E* of the FACE (the *F* is on the first space below the staff) with an added *G* on top. You need to find a memory key using either the word ACE and topping it with something that starts with G (*ACE G*rump) or making up another silly sentence. (*Always Catch Elves Grinning?* Naw.) The lines are also shifted down one with the *E* resting on the first ledger line below the bass staff. You can do better than *Great Ballet Dancers' Feet Ache,* can't you... please? Write and tell us your music staff mnemonics.

Sometimes accidentals are added to the music, usually a sharp, flat or natural. Sharp, written ♯, means raise the note one half step. Flat, written ♭, means lower the note one half step. Naturals (♮) cancel out key or accidental sharps or flats. Once a note is altered it remains so for any repeated notes in the same measure.

SOME ACCIDENTALS

Now that we have some idea of what line or what space represents a given pitch we have to add the elements of duration, beat, tempo and meter—all related to **time.**

If music is new to you, so may also be the idea of beating time (as opposed to the Dormouse in *Alice's Adventures in Wonderland* "murdering" time). There are two basic beat patterns that are usual to our music: duple (divisions of 2 beats) and triple (3 beats). These are the units of **time signatures** (those numbers you see at the start of, and, occasionally, in the middle of, pieces [see *Parting Glass*]). Most time signatures are multiples of two or three: 2/4 and 4/4 are accented in two, 3/4 is accented, waltz-like, in three. The first (top) number gives the number of beats in a bar. The lower number indicates what note (in this case, a quarter note) gets a beat. The first note is accented in beating time. If there are more than two or three beats, a secondary beat will be accented as well. In 4/4, or "Common" time, the first and third beat are accented. There's more to it, but this will do for now.

Once you start beating up poor old Time, you have a reference to help you know how long to hold a given note (or how long to rest, ie, not play for a bit). This part gets mathematical, but nothing you can't handle. For our purposes, the whole note is the longest duration within a measure with which we will deal. Two half notes equal a whole note in duration; two quarter notes a half note; two eighth notes a quarter note and so on to sixty-fourth notes, each 1/64th of a whole note.

NOTE TREE

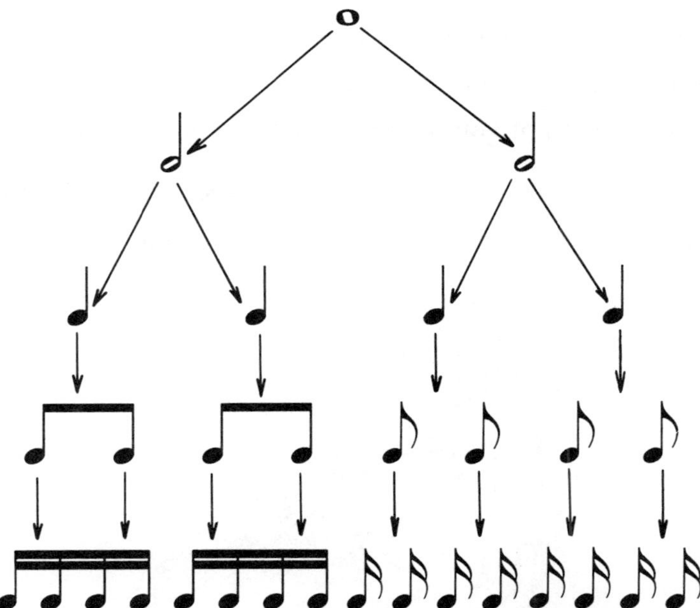

With the majority of music in this book, the quarter note gets one beat. As referred to above, 4/4 indicates four quarter notes per measure, each getting a beat. 3/4 is three quarter notes a measure. 6/4 is six quarter notes per measure (see *Green Sleeves*) and 6/8 means six eighth notes per measure (6/8 is traditionally beat two beats per measure, each beat containing three eighth notes, but the signature technically indicates that each eighth note should have a beat—yet another musical idiosyncracy.)

If there is a dot after a note, that note is held one and a half times its usual value. It is common to see a dotted quarter note followed by an eighth note, adding up to two beats (again see *Believe Me...*).

If a note is held beyond a **bar line** (those are the vertical lines that indicate a new measure has started, and the beat pattern is repeated) or a natural grouping of beats within a bar, it is indicated by a **tie**, a long arc connecting the two notes. Do not replay the second note of a tie.

Slurs look like ties, only they connect two or more notes of different pitch, or a phrase of notes, indicating that those notes are a musical unit. Slurs are often found in vocal music when one word or syllable is sung on more than one pitch.

Many songs do not start on the first beat of a measure. The notes before the first measure are called **pick-up** notes. When there are pick-up notes at the beginning of a song, the duration of those notes is subtracted from the last measure.

There are many, many signs, symbols, word indications and the like that aid in the interpretation of a song. Often at the beginning you will find instructions as to the speed or feeling required. Indications of loudness or softness are frequently given, but we have avoided them in this book, allowing you to use your own good judgment. Other markings are explained when they are first introduced.

Finally, a very important part of written music is the **key signature**. That is always found at the beginning of music, but it can sometimes change within a piece. All the harp songs in this book are limited to two key signatures: no sharps or flats, or one sharp. If there are any sharps or flats in a key, they are indicated right after the clef signs. One sharp means that every time you play the note *F* you must sharp it unless the music tells you otherwise. Always check the key signature and the position of your levers before you play a piece.

As you work with music—especially with songs you know—you will find your reading skills developing naturally. If you want to pursue reading vigorously, get yourself a reading primer and a music dictionary and go for it.

Appendix Eight: Reading Chord Symbols

Chord symbols are used to indicate the harmony without writing out all the notes. They give the name of the chord and indicate any alterations that may be desired. Reading chord symbols allows a musician to create (or "fake") an accompaniment to a melody. Thus collections of songs with only the melody and chords (and sometimes the lyrics) are called **fake books**. A single song written with chords, melody and lyrics is called a **lead sheet** and is often used by songwriters to distribute their songs. Singers sometimes carry lead sheets of songs in their key for the use of accompanists at auditions, rehearsals and gigs.

Many musicians like to ignore the arrangements on sheet music and play from the guitar chords instead. This is a useful technique for singers who play for themselves. Folk music is often presented with only the words, melody and chords as it is designed to be sung and played with chording instruments (guitar, banjo, mandolin, etc.) in a free, improvisational manner. We have provided chord symbols for most of the songs in this book to encourage the fullest possible use of the material.

As a harper, reading chord symbols is a useful skill. This ability helps you to improvise and is a big plus if you want to play with a group. There is quite a bit of material earlier in this book, in the section THE HARMONY OF HARP MUSIC, to help you use the symbols in relation to the harp. This section is an overview on reading chords in general, without special attention to the harp's needs.

Various systems of harmonic shorthand have been in use just about as far back as harmony has been notated. Harpsichord players learn to play a "figured bass" under vocals and instrumental pieces which is a bass line with chord inversions, but not the chord name, notated (it seems a rather complex skill, but those trained in it are able to create remarkable music). Harmony students use a system that indicates chords with Roman numerals (capital for major and lower case for minor). The chords are easily transposable as they are written I (tonic), ii, iii, IV, V, etc. and apply to any key. The I chord of the key of *C* major is *C*; of *G* major is *G*, etc.

The most efficient system for sight reading, at least in our opinion, is the chord symbol which gives the actual chord name (of course whatever system one learns first is the easiest—we may be biased). We like using these chord symbols because no mental conversion is needed—the chord symbol tells you exactly the name of the chord to play. It is also an easy, straightforward (well, there are a *few* kinks) system to learn. Do not be put off by the seeming complexity of some of the material given below; most songs you will be playing use very basic major, minor and seventh chords. We have included many of the less usual chord notations for reference purposes.

All these chord symbols give you the letter name of the chord, usually in the largest type and in capital letters (although some rare variants use lower case letters for minor). Thus, you have one note you can play instantly (presuming it is available on your harp); as that is the root of the chord it usually makes an acceptable (although not always the ideal) bass note.

MAJOR CHORDS. If the letter name of the chord is in capital letters and all by itself, it is a major chord. A major chord is made up of the first, third and fifth notes of its own scale (independent of the key in which you are playing). **Chord symbols are based on the scale of the key of the indicated chord.** Therefore, a *D* chord always has $F\sharp$ as its third, no matter what the key signature says.

Another way to figure out a chord uses intervals: a major chord consists of a major third above the named root with a minor third above that. Or, to put it another way: a major third above the root and a perfect fifth above the root. It all comes out the same no matter how your compute it. So pick a way to figure out the chords that makes sense to you and stick with it. **If all else fails:** the chords used in most harp music are limited, so it would not be difficult to learn them—at least at first—by rote (see THE HARMONY OF HARP MUSIC).

MINOR CHORDS. Minors are written in several similar ways. Usually the capital letter of the chord name is followed by *min, mi* or *m* as in *Dmin, Ami, Bm*. The minor chord is the root, third and fifth notes of the named (natural) minor scale. (Or, in intervals, a minor third on the bottom and a major third on top; or a minor third and a perfect fifth—your pick.)

CHORDS WITH ADDED NOTES. It is rather common to see a chord with a number, or sometimes a series of numbers, after it. These are added notes. Locate them by counting up the scale of the named chord. If an added sixth is indicated, count up six scale notes from the root and add that tone. If a number higher than eight is indicated it just means keep counting from the root. Sometimes the added notes will be raised or lowered. These are indicated by a plus or minus sign or a flat or sharp. Some examples: *C6, G 6-9, G 13, Dmi7*. Practically, especially with the harp, it is not always possible to pick up the added notes when sight reading, but it is important to know what those extra numbers mean.

DOMINANT SEVENTH CHORDS. The dominant seventh chord is so common that it breaks the rules (we said there were a few kinks). It is notated with the named (major) chord followed by a number seven: *G7, D7, B7*, etc. Following the rules you have just, hopefully, hard wired into your brain, that should mean that the seventh note of the named chord's scale is added, right? Wrong. In common usage, it means that the flatted, or minor, seventh is added. The dominant seventh chord is often the chord built on the fifth note of the key you are in (or, following the circle of fifths, the chord that is the fifth of the next chord in the progression—*D7* resolves to *G*; *G7* resolves to *C*. If we lost you, don't worry, just learn what the notes in the chord are. (See also WORKING WITH CHORD SYMBOLS in Part Three.)

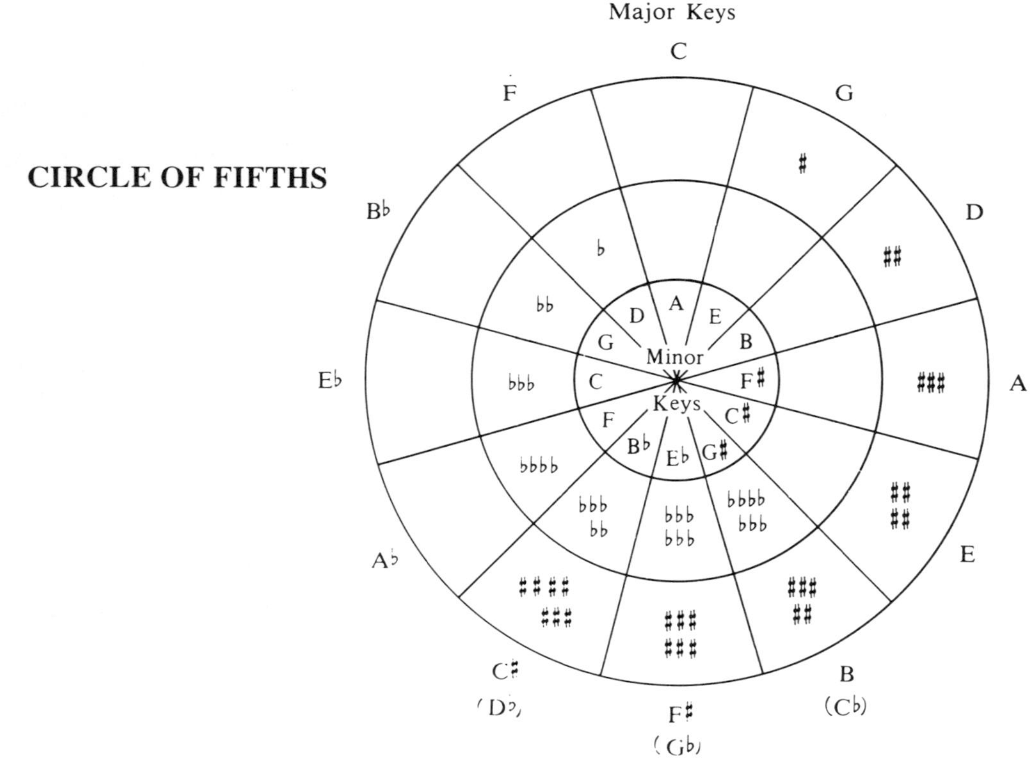

To further add to the kinks, major chords with numbers above seven usually imply that they include the flatted seventh and act like dominant chords. So a *C9* adds a *D*, but it also includes the *B♭*. This was probably designed to reduce the long string of numbers after the chord names common with jazz (although some of them can get a bit hairy, jazz players read them as easily as the rest of us read a major triad). The exception (and back to normalcy) is when another added note (usually *6*) lower than a seventh is added or when the major seventh is indicated (see below).

THE MAJOR SEVENTH CHORD. This is just what it says, a chord with the seventh note of the major scale added. *Cmaj7* adds a *B*. The word "major" here refers to the interval, not the basic chord. Thus one occasionally sees something like *Dmin^{maj7}*, which is a *D* minor chord with a major seventh (*C♯*) added. A *Dmi7* follows the usual rules and adds the seventh note of the minor scale (*C*). Since that is a minor seventh interval, it suggests the dominant seventh and is usually also included in minor chords with numbers indicated above seven. Hang in there.

DIMINISHED AND AUGMENTED CHORDS. A **diminished** chord is written with the chord name followed by *dim* or a little circle: *Bdim, F♯°*. It is made up of a pile of two or three minor thirds. When three are indicated, the chord is usually followed by a *7* as in *Cdim7*. With the unfailing logic of this system, this adds to the diminished triad a diminished seventh, in this case *A* (technically *B♭♭*—B double flat). A pile of minor thirds is easier to remember.

A principal use for a string of diminished seventh chords is to rumble them in menace when the nasty old villain approaches. You have a diminished triad on your harp: *Bdim* in the *C* tuning. It is most useful as a passing chord, or as a substitute for a dominant chord.

Augmented chords are triads made up of two major thirds up from the root. Thus a *C aug* or *C+* is played *C-E-G♯*. There are no augmented chords naturally on the folk harp; you would have to flip a lever. An augmented chord works much like a dominant seventh chord, pulling to the next chord on the minus side of the circle of fifths, in this case *F*.

ALTERED CHORDS. Occasionally you will see something like *C -5*. This tells you to play the chord but flat the fifth giving us *C-E-G♭*. That's fairly straightforward, even if a string of extra numbers follows for added tones.

Less immediately obvious, but very important to early music, is the **suspension.** The most commonly suspended note is the third, but other notes can be suspended as well. A suspended note is often, but not always, a chord note held over from the previous chord which takes the place of a regular note in the current chord. This is resolved to its proper chord note in a beat or so. The most usual way of writing a suspension is *C sus4* which is followed either by a *3* by itself, indicating that the fourth note of the scale resolves to the third, or by simply writing *C* indicating the normal major chord. Some early composers like Corelli refined suspensions to a delicious art form.

EXAMPLES OF SUSPENSIONS

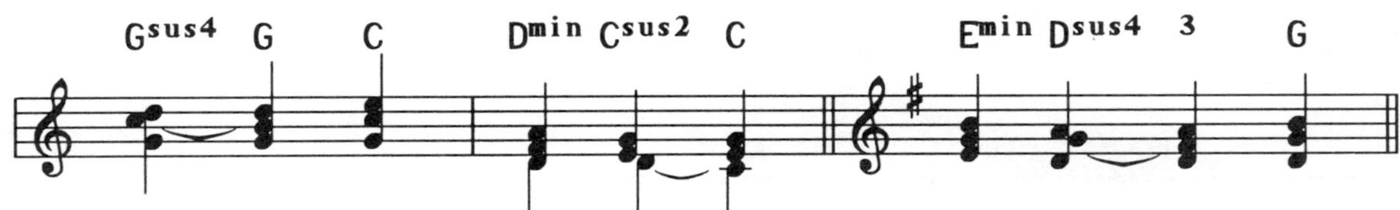

SPECIFIED BASS NOTES. A fairly new addition to the system of chord symbols is the indication of the preferred bass note. That bass note can be a chord note or any note at all that the composer/arranger wants in the bass. The chord is notated fully followed by a slash and the note name of the bass note: *Dm7/G, C/E, Gdim/B♭*. The down side of this, and the reason we don't use it in this book, is that it is easy to confuse the bass note with a chord, ie., in the first example to read it as a *Dm7* followed by a *G* chord, which is not correct. One way around this is to write *Dmi7/G*$_{BASS}$ but that is cumbersome.

If you are having difficultly learning Satie's *Gymnopédie No. 3*, the last selection in *Exploring the Folk Harp*, you might want to notate the chords with the bass notes indicated. The first chord would read *Amin/A*, the second *Emin/ D* and so on.

Like anything else, the way to become comfortable with chord symbols is to play them. A lot. Stick with the basic triads at first, ignoring the added numbers. These can come later. With a very few exceptions, the basic chord will sound all right without the added tones.

By way of summary, here are a variety of different chords all built on the same root note:

DIFFERENT CHORDS BUILT ON THE SAME ROOT NOTE

Knowing chords—and eventually from that, harmony—can also aid you in memorizing a piece. If the chords are not given, figure them out from the notes on the page or by experimentation. If you have learned the chord progression as well as the notes you will find it easier to remember the piece (and easier to rescue yourself if you make a mistake in performance!).

There are many tools to help you in music. Reading music notation and chord symbols are a good start. Understanding harmony, improvisation, composition and technique; listening to recordings and concerts; taking music lessons and attending seminars; playing with others; reading music books; learning the history of the music you play—all are worthwhile and add to the experience. Use as many as you can, but more than anything else, be open and have fun with it. Pass the legacy on to others; it is very precious, indeed.

On the road.
Photo by Mallory.

Bibliography

This is only a partial list of sources. There are many more excellent books on the folk harp which deserve your attention.

American Harp Society, Inc, *The American Harp Journal.* The American Harp Society, Inc.,

Bay Area Folk Harp Society. *Harpbeat of the Bay* (Newsletters)

Bunting, Edward. *The Ancient Music of Ireland.* (3 Volumes) Dublin and London: Hodges and Smith, 1796, 1809, 1840; Reprinted in combined edition Dublin: Cahill Printers Limited, 1981

Calthorpe, Nancy. *Begin the Harp.* Dublin: Walton Mnf. Ltd., 1987

Heymann, Ann. *Secrets of the Gaelic Harp.* Minneapolis: Clairseach Publications, 1988

________, *Legacy of the 1792 Belfast Harp Festival.* Minneapolis: Clairseach Publications, 1992

Friou, Deborah. *Harp Exercises for Ability and Speed.* Glendale: Friou Music, 1990

International Harp Center. *Historisch Harfen/ Historical Harps.* Dornach/ Switzerland: Schola Cantorum Basiliensis, 1991

International Society of Folk Harpers and Craftsmen, Inc. *The Folk Harp Journal.*

Lawrence-King, Andrew. *Der Harpffenschlaeger, An Introduction to "Authentic" Technique for Early Harps.* England: 1988

Lyon & Healy. *Harp Accessory Catalog.* Chicago: Lyon & Healy/Salvi, 1991

O'Carolan, Turlough (1670-1738). *The Complete Works of O'Carolan.* Ireland: Ossian Publications, Second Edition, 1989

Ortiz, Alfredo Rolando. *Latin American Harp Music and Techniques.* Corona: Alfredo Rolando Ortiz, 1979

Rensch, Roslyn. *Harps & Harpists.* Bloomington and Indianapolis, Indiana University Press, 1989

Riley, Laurie. *The Harper's Handbook.* Evanston: Mayapple Publishers, 1991

Riley, Laurie & MacBean, Michael. *Preventing and Correcting Chronic Harp-Related Injury.* Evanston: Mayapple Publishers, 1992

Rimmer, Joan, *The Irish Harp, Clairseach nah Eireann.* Dublin and Cork: Mercier Press, Third Edition, 1984

Robertson, Kim. *Arranging for Folk Harp* (video). Mendocino: Lark in the Morning, 1987

________, *Arranging for Harp, Book 1 & 2.* Santa Barbara: Folk Mote Music, 1984

Sanger, Keith & Kinnaird, Alison. *Tree of Strings, Crann nan Teud.* Midlothian, Scotland: Kinmor Music, 1992

Swanson, Carl. *A Guide for Harpists.* Boston: Boston Editions, 1984

Stivell, Alan. *Alan Stivell in Concert* (video). Pacific: Mel Bay

Woods, Sylvia. *Teach Yourself to Play the Folk Harp.* Los Angeles, Woods Music, 1978

________, *Music Theory and Arranging Techniques for Folk Harps.* Los Angles, Woods Music, 1987

________, *50 Christmas Carols for All Harps.* Los Angeles, Woods Music, 1984, second printing 1986

________, *Summer 1992 Catalog.* Los Angeles, Sylvia Woods Harp Center

Resources

You will be delighted with the wealth of harp related resources available to you. A membership in the Folk Harp Society is the best place to start. In addition, a few sample resources are offered here. Tell them you heard about them in *Exploring the Folk Harp.*

There are scores of harpmakers in the world; the list here is extremely short. As most of the workshops are small, one person operations, they tend to come and go. Some of the most wonderful harps are made by individual craftspeople, but many have a waiting list of years. In a few rare instances, deposits are taken and instruments not delivered. Included here are makers that have long-standing reputations *and* are able to deliver and service their instruments reliably. Absence of any name on this list does not mean that the maker is less worthy.

International Society of Folk Harpers and Craftsmen, Inc. (ISFHC)
4718 Maychelle Dr.
Anaheim, CA 92807-3040   714-998-5717
A must join! Publishes quarterly journal packed with information.

American Harp Society
P.O. Box 38334
Hollywood, CA 90034
The organization of and for pedal harpists.

Bay Area Folk Harp Society
P.O. Box 9666
Berkeley, CA 94709-0666
A chapter of ISFHC, they are active and have an excellent newsletter.

Dragonwhispers Services
P.O. Box 211
Mt. Laguna, CA 91948
619-473-9010 (message), 619-473-0080 (no answering machine)
Accessories, strings, hardware. Catalog.

Dusty Strings Dulcimer Company
3406 Fremont Ave. N
Seattle, WA 98103   206-634-1656
High-end folk harps (3 sizes) with excellent woodworking.

Folk Mote Music
1034 Santa Barbara
Santa Barbara, CA 93101   805-962-0830
Accessories, harps, music and more. Catalog.

Green Willow Music - Laurie Riley.& Michael MacBean
P.O. Box 249
Vashon Island, WA 98070   206-463-6449
Accessories, books, etc. Catalog.

Historical Harp Society
c/o Jean Humphrey
631 North 3rd Ave.
St. Charles, IL 60174

Hummingbird Harps
212 Wayne N.W.
Albuquerque, N.M. 87114   505-897-1725
Popular mid-priced instruments.

Janus Music
P.O. Box 191084
Los Angeles, CA 90019   213-733-7241
That's us! Folk harps and accessories.

Lyon & Healy/Salvi Harps
168 N. Ogden Ave.
Chicago, IL 60607
800-621-3881 (accessories), 312-786-1181 (harps)
Pedal and pre-pedal harps, lever harps and accessories. Catalog.

Robinson's Harp Shop
P.O. Box 161
Mount Laguna, CA 91948   619-473-8556
Strings, harp plans, Latin harps. Catalog.

Triplett Harps
220 Suburban Road, Suite C
San Luis Obispo, CA 93401   805-544-2777
A wide selection of artist-quality instruments, both nylon and wire, beautifully made. Also V.B.C. cases. Catalog.

Sylvia Woods Harp Center
915 North Glendale Ave
Glendale, CA 91206   800-272-HARP
Free catalog of just about everything to do with harps.

Index of Songs